Praise for *Catching Jordan*

"I stayed up all night reading *Catching Jordan*—I couldn't put it down! Jordan Woods is my heroine!" —Simone Elkeles, *New York Times* bestselling author of the Perfect Chemistry series

"Sweetly satisfying." —*VOYA*

"*Catching Jordan* has it all: heart, humor, and a serious set of balls. With a clever, authentic voice, Kenneally proves once and for all that when it comes to making life's toughest calls—on and off the field—girls rule!" —Sarah Ockler, bestselling author of *Twenty Boy Summer* and *The Book of Broken Hearts*

"I fell in love with the hero on page 1. This feel-good romantic comedy about high school football is the novel I've been waiting for. I loved it!" —Jennifer Echols, National Award-Winning author of *Such a Rush* and *Love Story*

"Debut author Kenneally does a solid job of depicting Jordan's conflicted emotions, the pressure she is under, and her testy relationship with her father." —*Publishers Weekly*

"Kenneally makes football accessible—and even enjoyable—for those who might not ordinarily follow the sport. Jordan (or 'Woods,' as her teammates call her) is a fearless captain and the teamwork and camaraderie that's so implicit in the story are great takeaways for readers of any age." —*RT Book Reviews*, 4 Stars

"A beautiful novel with a competitive spirit both on and off the field. With a real and captivating depiction of high school relationships, *Catching Jordan* shows the same reverence for the human heart that it does for the game of football." —Karsten Knight, author of *Wildfire*

Praise for *Stealing Parker*

A Junior Library Guild selection for Fall 2012

"*Stealing Parker* is fresh, fearless, and totally romantic. Kenneally hits another grand slam!" —Sarah Ockler, bestselling author of *Twenty Boy Summer* and *The Book of Broken Hearts*

"Kenneally has hit a home run!" —*RT Book Reviews*, 4 Stars

"Not only will readers want to see Parker find true love, they'll also hope she learns to love herself." —*Publishers Weekly*

"Readers of this teen novel will appreciate its realistic and witty dialogue." —*Kirkus*

"A realistic portrait of a teen who…searches for love in forbidden places. Another engrossing romance from Miranda Kenneally with a hero who will melt your heart." —Jennifer Echols, National Award-Winning author of *Such a Rush* and *Love Story*

Praise for *Things I Can't Forget*

"Kenneally's books have quickly become must–reads." —*VOYA*

"Like Diane Court in *Say Anything*, when sheltered, high-achieving Kate dives into a social life for the first time, she experiences the conflict and messiness of life at the same time she experiences her first love." —*Justine Magazine*

"An up-and-coming young-adult novelist." —*The Washington Post*

"Talented Kenneally is unafraid to tackle challenging topics. Her heroine...[is] incredibly realistic. A worthy read with a dreamy male lead." —*RT Book Reviews*, 4 Stars

"Kate's sheltered worldview is well-drawn, and the hesitant first steps on her spiritual journey are handled sensitively...Kate's growth will keep readers, Christian or otherwise, reading." —*Kirkus*

Racing Savannah

MIRANDA KENNEALLY

sourcebooks
fire

Published by Sourcebooks Fire, an imprint of Sourcebooks, Inc.
P.O. Box 4410, Naperville, Illinois 60567-4410
(630) 961-3900
Fax: (630) 961-2168
teenfire.sourcebooks.com

Library of Congress Cataloging-in-Publication data is on file with the publisher.

Printed and bound in the United States of America.
VP 10 9 8 7 6 5 4 3 2

For my friend, Christy Maier

Roots and Beginnings

Welcome to Cedar Hill Farms of Franklin, Tennessee.

Est. 1854.

John C. Goodwin III, Owner.

Welcome to Hell would be a more appropriate sign, considering Dad just uprooted me from West Virginia and hauled me to Tennessee two days before senior year.

My father couldn't give up this opportunity to work as head groom at a fancy farm that trains horses for the Kentucky Derby and Breeders' Cup, and I didn't want to be the evil daughter who stamped her foot and refused to come.

It doesn't totally matter, because home is where my dad is. But it still sucks that I had to leave my part-time job exercising horses. It would've become a full-time position when I graduated from high school, and now I have to start all over again.

I punch the code into the alarm box, the heavenly white gates swing open, and I steel myself for the half-mile trek to Hillcrest, the staff quarters. My claustrophobic new home. Hillcrest is attached to the gargantuan white manor house, where a smattering of comfy rocking chairs dot the wraparound porch, waiting for someone to sit down.

Back in West Virginia, it was just me and Dad and She Who Must Not Be Named living in our trailer. Now we're sharing quarters with six other staff members and their kids. To escape, I took a walk to downtown Franklin this morning, but I'm cash poor at the moment so there wasn't much to do besides loiter, and the last thing I need before school starts is to gain a reputation as that weird girl who loiters.

So here I am, back in hell, gathering my courage to go talk to the lead trainer about getting some work as an exercise rider so I can cease being cash poor. I used to exercise racehorses at the track and casino in Charles Town. But that was at a totally different level—the horses I rode there were like driving a Ford and here they are like Ferraris. Hell, the Queen of England stables her horses thirty minutes away.

What if the trainer thinks I'm unqualified? Or a hack? I've been riding since I was four, but still. *Just go talk to him, Savannah!* The worst he can say is *no*...and then I can go back to loitering. I inhale then let out the deep breath I've been holding and take in the scent of cornbread, fresh laundry, dirt, cedar trees, and of course, horseshit.

I can do this.

I charge down the driveway and suddenly a wailing, high-pitched alarm goes off. My first thought is: Tornado! But the skies are as blue as a robin's egg. Seconds later I see a brown and white blur streaking across the grass. A racer. Two guys on ponies are chasing it. He must have escaped!

I sprint toward the horse as he zigzags my way. The horse seems curious. But not curious enough to slow down. He zips past me as I yell "Stop!" and take off after him. The horse circles back around. I hold a hand up. "Whoa, there."

The horse slows to a jog, studying me, his expression both wary and nosy. Then he charges me. I reach out and snatch his bridle. With a firm grip, I thrust him away from me, showing him who's boss. That's when I discover he's wearing a saddle.

"Did you throw your rider?" Suddenly he rears up and kicks his feet. When he returns to all fours, I get up in his face again. "Whoa!" He cowers, bowing his head.

One time a horseman told me I have a way with horses. Dad told me not to listen when men say things like that because they're just trying to get into my pants. But I do have a way with horses. Dad, however, does not have a way with words.

I confirm the horse is a boy then gently slap his neck, checking the engraving on his bridle. Tennessee Star is his name.

"You sure are fast," I tell the young horse, petting his nose. He's beautiful—a light brown chestnut with white markings. A Ferrari. I never rode such a well-made colt in Charles Town.

Then, from the fields beyond the manor house, a guy comes riding up on a horse. I don't take my eyes off that rider, even when Tennessee Star tries to yank away.

I haven't met the owner's son yet, but I've seen him riding around like he's king of the place. Which is technically his title, I guess. When we arrived two days ago, Mr. Goodwin's chief of staff told me the Goodwin family is fiercely private and that non-housekeeping staff aren't allowed inside the manor. We were instructed to keep our distance from the Goodwins. Since I don't want Dad to get fired on day three, I haven't spoken to the boy.

Still, he's beautiful. I should start a magazine called *GQ Cowboy*, and he could be the cover model every month. Wavy hair the color of straw curls out from under his cowboy hat. His snowy white button-down shirt is spotless and pressed, tucked into his jeans, the arms rolled up to his elbows. The three coonhounds that always seem to follow him around bound up and sniff my jeans.

Last night a giggling maid told me his name: Jack Goodwin. And he's seventeen, like me. He attends Hundred Oaks High, the school I'm starting on Monday.

"Star!" Jack says, dismounting fluidly. "You're too smart, you know that?" he scolds the horse, then grabs the bridle as I let go. Two farmhands jog up on ponies and Jack wordlessly hands Star off to one of them, slapping the horse's flank before they lead him away.

"If I didn't love that horse so much, I'd send him to drag a tourist carriage in New York City," Jack says in a deep Tennessee drawl. "That'd teach him not to buck his rider and run off."

Once he confirms he has a good grasp on his stallion's reins, Jack turns to me. His blue eyes widen and a bright smile spreads across his face.

"Thanks for catching Star. That was insane how you cornered him with no corner. I've never seen anything like it."

"No problem."

"So what can I do you for?" He tips his cowboy hat in an exaggerated manner and smiles again, revealing perfectly straight white teeth. Behind closed lips, I run my tongue over my slightly crooked front ones. "You're a bit late for the tour. They're at eight a.m. and it's nearly noon now."

He thinks I'm here for the tour?

"No, no," I say, starting to explain, but then he unleashes his megawatt smile. It makes my throat close up and my heart pounds even harder. This guy is hot, but I don't like boys who get whatever they want without trying. I worked damned hard to get my part-time exercise rider job back in Charles Town. Just like I'll work damned hard to get a position here.

"Soo..." Jack says, stroking the stallion's mane. "Do you want a private tour? You know, to say thanks for catching my horse?"

A private tour? Like, me and Jack alone? Dad would kill me for breaking the Goodwins' privacy rules. Besides, hanging around people like Jack is not my thing.

"I'm not here for a tour. I—"

"I didn't know Mom was hosting guests this weekend," Jack says. "I hope she's not having another fashion show for charity, because I barely survived the last one."

"We haven't met."

He thrusts a hand out, grinning. "I know. I'd have remembered you. I'm Jack Goodwin."

I shake his hand quickly. "Savannah." *What a player.* "I gotta get up to the house."

I stalk off and Jack hustles after me. "Wait! I'll escort you."

He'll *escort* me? How primitive.

The horse makes clickety-clack sounds on the pavement. It's a young stallion—probably no older than five—and he's sprinkled with white and black, like Rocky Road. I can't resist touching his nose. "Who's this?"

"This is my bro, Wrigley."

"Your bro?"

"My sister tells me I'm an idiot around girls."

That's the biggest bunch of bull I've ever heard. I can sense the cocky confidence radiating off his tanned skin.

"So why did Star run away?" I ask.

"Two baby raccoons climbed a fence at the track. One of the hands managed to chase them away, but not before a bunch of the colts and fillies started screaming. I think that's why Star took off."

"Makes sense." Anything will scare horses when they're young. Especially if they're Thoroughbreds. Dad says they're crazy because of inbreeding. Thoroughbred bloodlines are worse than the royal families of Europe.

When we reach the top of the hill, the racetracks and barns come into full view.

"Here we are," Jack says, glancing over at me.

Exercise boys are riding around both practice tracks. A field of haystacks sits beyond the tracks, and a garden full of sunflowers and vegetables lies between the tracks and the manor house. The biggest of the six barns is larger than a Walmart. The barn Dad worked at in West Virginia is a shack by comparison.

Wrigley starts sniffing my hair and nuzzles his face against mine.

"Wow," Jack says. "Wrigley doesn't like anybody but me. My father hasn't raced him yet 'cause he's too stubborn and mean."

"Maybe he's just lazy and doesn't want to race." I kiss the horse's muzzle. "And being stubborn is his way of getting out of it."

"Maybe."

"Your dad lets you keep Wrigley even if he can't race?" Caring for a Thoroughbred for one year costs more than a new pickup truck.

Jack pats the horse's neck. "I love him—and I believe we can train him. You're really good with horses. Does your dad own a farm?"

I laugh again. "Me? Own a farm?" Wrigley pushes against me and nickers. He's saying hello. "Hello," I say back.

"Wrigley," Jack says, securing the lead around his hand. "It's not nice to be so forward."

I kiss the horse again. "You're such a pretty boy."

"Thank you," Jack says, grinning.

"I was talking to the horse."

"I don't believe you. My bro Wrigley is nothing compared to me. Right, bro?" He slaps Wrigley's side.

"Is Jack always such an ass?" I ask the horse. I can't believe I said that. I feel my face turning the color of strawberry ice cream, but Jack just laughs and keeps on beaming. I better watch my mouth before the Goodwins boot me right on out of here.

I reach into my back pocket to grab a sucker—an orange one. You know how some people take antianxiety meds? Well, I eat candy. I rip off the crinkly wrapper and stick the sucker in my mouth. Instant relief.

I peek up at Jack's blue eyes. He's nicer than I figured he'd be. And he has a sense of humor too.

"Who are you?" Jack asks with this shit-eating grin on his face. "Did you come with Senator Ralston to meet with my father today? Are you related to him?"

Me? Related to a senator? I look down at my holey jeans, boots, and tight black T-shirt. I'm about to fess up that I've just moved into the Hillcrest dungeons and therefore he and I can never speak because *his family values their privacy* when a man storms out of the house and up the hill to us.

"Jack!" The man is dressed exactly like him—pressed shirt, dark jeans, and cowboy boots. "Abby Winchester has called the house eight times since breakfast looking for you and I'm about to smash the phone against the wall."

Eight times? *Stalk-er*, I sing in my head.

Jack keeps a firm hand on Wrigley's lead and lets out a long breath. "Hi, Dad."

Mr. Goodwin goes on, "Why aren't you answering your cell—" He stops. Takes one look at my red hair, freckled skin, and short, jockey-sized body, and then his eyes grow wide. "Are you Danny Barrow's kid?"

"Yes. Savannah Barrow."

Jack furrows his eyebrows. "You're the new groom's daughter?"

Mr. Goodwin drags a hand through his hair. "Can I see you in my office, son?"

"Yes, sir. Savannah, can I catch up with you later? Maybe we could—"

"Jack. Now," Mr. Goodwin says.

Jack ties Wrigley to a hitching post, his voice changing from casual to super serious. "Nice to meet you, Savannah. If you'll excuse me." Then he disappears inside the house with his father and the three hounds at his ankles.

I gently pat Wrigley's muzzle, as I stare up at the white manor house.

Now that Jack knows who I really am, the groom's daughter, he doesn't even give me a second glance.

Figures.

The Tryout

On my way to Hillcrest to retrieve my riding gear, I skirt the stone wall that doubles as a fence bordering the property. Mom once told me, “They call them slave walls.” It had embarrassed me to hear Mom say something so un-PC, but when I confronted her, she said, “We can ignore history or we can learn from it. I choose to learn from it.”

What I wouldn’t give to hear her voice now.

She died when I was eleven after having been diagnosed with breast cancer the year before. It was stage four by the time the doctors caught it, but Mom fought hard. We didn’t have insurance, so we couldn’t afford the medical bills that skyrocketed to over $200K. Then Mom was suddenly buried…and Dad was buried under a mountain of debt. And without her, my whole world fell apart.

Dad worked as a groom for a wealthy horseman who was more interested in gambling than the racehorses themselves. Mr. Cates didn’t give a crap that his employees didn’t have insurance, and he worked his horses into the ground, racing them when they were injured with stress fractures or worse.

Shortly after my mother died, Dad said he needed my help with a sad mare named Moonshadow, who had been lethargic ever since her first foal had been weaned. Mr. Cates didn't care that the horse was sad, but I did. I told my dad I would help her feel better again.

I rubbed the mare's nose and searched her eyes. "I know how it feels to lose somebody too."

I started riding Moonshadow nearly every day, and she taught me just how great at riding I am. She made me feel proud of myself. As soon as I got to know her, I told her all my secrets.

The first one?

"I love my dad, but I'm never gonna end up working for minimum wage like him. I want more."

• • •

Back in Charles Town, Dad spent 99 percent of his time in the barns, and coming to Tennessee hasn't changed that habit one bit. So I figure he must be in Greenbriar, where the Goodwins' best horses live. It's the fanciest barn I've ever seen; it has a digital contraption that keeps flies and mosquitoes at bay and classical music plays 24/7. I don't even have an iPod, for crying out loud.

After grabbing my riding gear from Hillcrest, I tramp through mud on my way to Greenbriar, passing by two of the smaller barns. The Goodwins own about forty horses, but they have enough barn space to house over 1,200. Apparently they make a lot of their money renting stalls (studio apartments for horses) to Thoroughbred owners who use the Goodwin practice tracks to get ready for the real races on weekends. Mr. Goodwin keeps plenty of people on staff—veterinarians, farriers (blacksmiths) to fix horseshoes, farmers to work the hay, tons of grooms and exercise riders, and stall managers.

I arrive in front of Greenbriar to find Dad and a bunch of guys sitting in lawn chairs.

"What a bunch of lazy asses."

Dad jumps to his feet as the other guys laugh at me. "It's break time." He draws me into his arms for a hug. I bury my nose in his shirt, inhaling his earthy smell of grass and leather and hay. My dad's only thirty-six, and his height makes him look even younger.

When I pull away, I bounce on my tiptoes, scanning the group. "Is Gael around?"

"Gael? What do you need him for?"

"I want to talk to him about riding—"

That's when this douche of a jockey comes strutting out of Greenbriar. Bryant Townsend is 5'1"—an inch taller than me, but I could take him.

"Forget the horse, Barrow. Come ride a cowboy," he says, making rude gestures with his pelvis. What an ass. Dad looks like he might kill Bryant, but I hold him back—I can handle myself.

"Tell me when you see a real cowboy and I will."

"Ooooooh," the guys say, laughing.

"You're all fired," Dad says. He waves an arm at the guys, and they go back to talking horses and trucks, ignoring my father.

"Wow, what a great help you are, Dad." He gives me a noogie, and I duck away. "Not the hair!" It takes forever to bind my red curls in a French braid.

It doesn't surprise me that Dad fits right in here. He's a good head groom—he knows when to be strict, but most of the time he's relaxed, which keeps his staff relaxed, which ultimately keeps the horses calm. And he knows more about horses than anyone I know. I completely understand why Mr. Goodwin snatched him away from Charles Town.

"So how about some lunch?" Dad asks.

"Can you help me find Gael first?"

"We shouldn't waste his time—"

"You don't think I can get a job here, Dad?"

He inclines his head, smiling slightly. "It's worth a try, I guess. But don't get your hopes up. They got some of the best exercise boys I've ever seen."

Exercise riders make $10 per horse per day giving super-fast horses their daily workouts. It's way above minimum wage. If I can make more money by riding horses, I can make a better life for myself than working in a motel or gas station after high school.

So watch out Cedar Hill—here I come.

• • •

We find Gael in the Greenbriar pasture, inspecting a yearling's hoof. Dad told me he's a former jockey from Spain. He's tiny, but he could still beat the crap out of most guys on this farm.

"Can I help you, Barrow?" Gael asks Dad, flashing a glance at me.

"I want to be an exercise rider," I reply, pulling my gloves out of my back pocket. "And I'm trying out today."

"Says who?" Gael asks.

"Says me."

Dad shakes his head at the blue sky. "Generally you ask for a job interview, Shortcake."

"Being an exercise rider is dangerous," Gael says. "Just last month one died in Arizona after being thrown from a horse."

"I'm always careful." I hold up my protective vest and helmet. "And I have plenty of experience from working at the Charles Town Races in West Virginia."

Gael's eyes widen. "Good for you, drama mama."

"Did you just call me drama mama?"

Gael ignores me. "Charles Town is a Grade 2 track. Those horses aren't the fastest, craziest horses in the world. That's what we got here. This is the big show."

"I bet riding a Goodwin horse is safer than the ones I used to ride. It's only truly dangerous to ride injured or weak horses, and you know the Goodwins have the best horses."

Gael gives my dad a grin. "She knows her shit."

"Of course she knows her shit. She's a Barrow." Dad squeezes my shoulder.

"May I try out? Sir?"

Dad gives me a nod, proud I remembered to ask for the job interview this time.

"Well..." Gael says. "I'm afraid it's not my decision."

"Dad, please," I say.

"It's not his call either," Gael says.

"But the lead trainer always makes decisions when it comes to training horses. So whose decision is it?"

"Mine."

I twirl around to find Jack Goodwin. He adjusts his cowboy hat and shoves his hands in his pockets, swaggering toward me with his hounds.

"What's going on?" I ask Dad and Gael.

"You haven't heard?" Jack uses his super serious voice, like when he discovered who I really am. "I'm running the farm this year."

"What do you mean you're running the farm?"

"It's one of his father's tests to get him ready to run the farm one day," Gael mutters to me. "He made Jack learn to drive a truck when he was ten. And he started drawing up stud fee contracts when he was twelve."

Hell, I'm happy I passed algebra II last year. And he has to run a farm?

"And you're going to school too?" I ask Jack. "Senior year isn't gonna be easy."

"I'll get it done."

Talk about a busy schedule. Can he go to school, run the farm, sleep, and be stalked by this Abby Winchester girl all at once?

"So what's the deal with me getting a tryout?" I ask.

"Jack wants me to clear all decisions with him," Gael says, not sounding at all perturbed he has to take orders from a seventeen-year-old. "It's up to him if you get one."

"So can I try out? Sir?"

A tiny smirk appears on Jack's face. "What are your qualifications?"

"Let's see. I've been riding since I was four years old. I was an exercise rider at Charles Town Races. And oh yeah, I caught Star on foot this morning. Remember that?"

Jack's smirk erupts into a full-blown grin.

"You caught Tennessee Star on foot?" Dad exclaims.

Gael looks from me to Jack. "What?"

"Just 'cause she caught Star once doesn't mean she could handle him on the track," Jack says, staring me down. "You want a job as an exercise rider? Then I want to see you ride Star."

"No," Dad says. "He bucks all his riders."

"C'mon, please? I've been riding for thirteen years. You know I can do this!"

Dad throws his head back. "Could she at least ride another horse besides Star?"

Jack thinks for a sec. "Let's see her ride Mystic Minerva. But I reserve the right to see her ride Star before I make a decision."

Why is he so interested in me riding Star?

Dad snaps and points at a tall groom with a mess of floppy brown hair who's been eavesdropping. "Get Minerva saddled up, Whitfield."

"Townsend," Gael barks. "Get on Lucky Strikes and take him around the track a few times. I want you to show Savannah how the tryout will work." Townsend goes with another groom to get Lucky Strikes out of his stall.

While waiting, Jack squats and scratches his dogs' ears, muttering to them, "You stinky dogs, you. You're handsome devils, and, Athena, you're a beautiful girl. Give me a kiss." The dog licks and slobbers on his face. He peeks up at me a few times, but I tighten my gloves and pretend not to notice him.

Several minutes later, the groom named Whitfield reappears with Minerva. She's a chestnut, about sixteen hands high, and might be the most beautiful horse I've ever seen.

"She's a great horse," Whitfield says. "She's raced in fifty-three races. She's won eleven, and placed or shown in thirty-five."

She bends down to scratch her nose on her knee.

"Come on, pretty girl," I whisper to her. "Help me through this."

• • •

I'm standing in the clocker's tower with Gael, Dad, and Jack, watching Bryant Townsend breeze around the track atop Lucky Strikes, one of Mr. Goodwin's prized horses. The stallion won the Preakness three years ago.

"That's complete shit, Townsend! Complete shit! You can do better than that!" Gael is five feet tall, but when he yells, he might as well be the Hulk.

Townsend finishes seven furlongs (nearly a mile) in 1:35. That's insanely fast. It's like he was riding a rocket, not a Thoroughbred.

And Gael thinks that's complete shit?

Townsend may never learn how to talk to a girl, but he knows what he's doing on the racetrack. I take a deep, rattled breath and tighten my gloves. I can do this.

Gael turns to me and claps. "Your turn."

I jog over to Minerva. The mare smells of sweat and liniment, and she seems relaxed, flicking her ears at me. I secure my helmet, goggles, and vest before getting a leg up from the groom to mount.

"Thanks, Whitfield."

"It's Rory," he says.

"That's a girl's name," I tease.

"And being an exercise boy is a man's job," Rory snaps back. We smile at each other.

Weaving the reins between my pinky and ring fingers, I squeeze her flanks with both heels to get her moving. I follow the horse's movements, posting on her back, flowing with her body. Minerva knows racing is what she's all about—her graceful gait is measured and sure-footed. Heck, Minerva could probably train exercise riders herself, she's such a professional.

If I get the job, I wouldn't be the first female exercise rider at Cedar Hill—Dad told me two other women in their twenties work here every day, but I'm still enough of a novelty that a lot of the staff have stopped working to watch.

I steer Minerva out onto the track and wait for Gael's signal. He raises a hand and I use my outside leg to urge Minerva into a canter, warming her up over the course of a lap. The sound of her hooves relaxes my muscles and the trip is so smooth I feel like I'm riding a surfboard over gentle ocean waves.

When I pass the clocker's tower for the second time, I take off and we fly around the track. At the first turn, I urge the horse faster and into a breeze.

"Good job, girl!" I yell, as dirt splatters onto my goggles and face.

On the final turn, Minerva jerks her head to the side and I have to hold on to her reins as tight as I can, making sure she doesn't ride off the track and straight into the wild blue yonder. Getting her back under control makes us slow down and adds seconds onto my time. God. Do Jack and Gael think I'm complete shit?

As I cross the finish line, I pump my fist and whoop, glad I've shown what I can do. Even if I don't get the job, I tried my damned hardest. I pat Minerva's neck and brush her hair, whispering how beautiful she is as she whinnies and slows to a canter.

After cooling down, I dismount, wipe the dirt off my face, hand the horse off to Rory, and go face the music.

"So what's the story?" I say.

"I'd say she's got what it takes to start working," Gael says, cleaning his sunglasses on his shirt. "What do you say we get her started on Monday, Jack?"

"No," Jack says, and my heart plummets to the ground. "She's not starting on Monday."

"No?" I whisper.

A sly grin sweeps across his face. "No. I want you to start tomorrow, at River Downs in Cincinnati." He turns to face Gael and my father. "She'll warm up Star before the race. Then I'll decide if she gets the job or not."

"But," Dad starts, until Jack raises a hand.

"She'll wear a helmet and vest, and I know she'll take every precaution to keep herself safe. She says she's been around horses her whole life—let's see if she's ready for the next level."

"She's not ready to ride Star," Dad says. "That horse doesn't want anybody riding him."

"She handled him well today," Jack says. "She kept him calm, which none of the rest of us seem to know how to do. That's what he needs most before a race. And if the horse ends up liking her, then I want her taking care of him. Understand?"

Dad's not the kind of guy to take orders from teenage boys, but Jack moves and speaks with authority. Dad nods once.

"Thank you," I say to them, bouncing on my toes.

"Don't thank me," Jack says. "Just figure out how to keep Star calm. He needs a win bad."

"Ahem." We all turn to find Mr. Goodwin standing there with an eyebrow raised. "I didn't realize it was happy hour already."

Jack steps up to his father. "I might hire Savannah as an exercise rider."

Mr. Goodwin stares me down. "What?"

"She had an excellent tryout, and like I told you earlier, she caught Star on foot. Maybe she can figure out how to handle him."

"Savannah might be a good hand in the barns. It's probably best to assign her there," Mr. Goodwin says, and I shake my head quickly. I can't lose this opportunity! I can't get stuck working a crappy job after I graduate high school.

"I'm trying to shore up my investment with Star," Jack tells his father in a strong voice. "If your exercise boys can't control him, I'll find one who will."

A smile begins to form on Mr. Goodwin's face. "All right then," he says and claps Jack on the back. "You're the boss."

"We'll talk after Star's race tomorrow," Jack tells me.

I jump into my dad's arms and hug him hard. "Please let me do this. Please."

"Just promise me you'll be careful."

I pull away from Dad to find Jack smiling at me with no evidence of a smirk. Mr. Goodwin sees his son's smile too, and his expression grows darker. "Jack, shouldn't you be hitching the trailer so you can take Strawberry Fields to Kentucky?"

"Yes, sir."

"And did you call Abby Winchester?"

Jack rubs the back of his neck. "Yes, sir."

"Good."

Jack walks off with his father, not looking back. Even though he's supposedly the acting owner, it seems that Jack isn't completely in charge of everything.

Does his father control his every move?

There's No Place Like Home...Sort Of

After my tryout, Dad opens the door to Hillcrest. It's the middle of the day on a Saturday, so many of the maids, cooks, gardeners, and horsemen are hard at work. Still, a few people are watching TV or reading the paper in the large common area, which is filled with comfy couches and squishy chairs. Two younger boys are huddled together over a comic book. Fifteen people live in Hillcrest, hence my sudden-onset claustrophobia.

The second I cross into the kitchen, She Who Must Not Be Named is all over me, Mom-style. Must be the hormones. Cindy hugs me long and hard, and I get a whiff of apple shampoo. Her new blue maid's uniform stretches over her rounded stomach; my little brother or sister is growing in there.

She's nearly five months pregnant. Dad was really apologetic and embarrassed this happened, considering it's just gonna make things harder on us. He stayed single until about a year and a half ago when he started seeing Cindy, who's twenty-eight. She's nice enough, I guess, but I don't think of her as my mom.

I'm still pissed she got pregnant—it's not like they're married…or that we have the money for this. In a way, it's a good thing we left West Virginia, because at least here we get free housing. Maybe now Dad will have more money to spend on baby clothes and insurance and stuff. I may not like the situation, but I sure want the kid to have a better life than I did growing up.

Cindy brings my hand to her stomach. "He's real active today." I can't help but smile when I feel the baby moving.

"Wow," I say. "If it's a boy, we should name him Hercules."

"We are not naming the baby Hercules," Cindy says.

"How about Zeus then?" Dad asks.

"That sounds like a name Jack Goodwin would give one of his hounds," Cindy replies. "I heard one of his dogs is named Athena and one is Thor. He also let his little sister name one of his dogs Jasper, after the *Twilight* character."

"I think you should name the baby Yvonne," Yvonne says, sewing a man's shirt at the table. The Goodwins' Laundry Dictator wears her gray hair in a bun and her maid's uniform miraculously doesn't have a single wrinkle. She glances up, sees my clothes are splattered with dirt, and leaps to her feet as if she's twenty years old, not sixty.

"Get those clothes off, girl. Gotta get them in the wash before a stain sets."

"It's okay, I can do—" I start to say, but Yvonne gives me a death glare.

"Don't you dare go near my laundry room." I smile at the thought of Yvonne standing in front of a laundry room door, holding a battle axe, ready to fight off any intruders who want to do a load of whites.

"I know how to wash my own clothes," I say.

Yvonne wags a finger in my face. "One time I found Mr. Goodwin in my laundry room teaching Master Jack how to wash colors, and after I got done yelling at those boys, they looked like I'd caught one of them doing the nasty in the backseat of a car. They probably *wished* I'd caught them doing that." She grumbles, "Mr. Goodwin claimed he was trying to teach Jack an 'essential life lesson.' Sheesh!"

Dad cracks up. "Doing the nasty."

"Gross," I say. I never want to hear my dad say "doing the nasty" again.

"The moral of the story is *stay out of my laundry room*," Yvonne goes on.

"But laundry *is* an essential life lesson," I say.

Dad laughs, biting his knuckle. "Doing the nasty."

Yvonne wags her finger at me. "You let me handle the laundry and you go eat a ham sandwich." She points her finger at Dad. "Danny, you see the bones on your girl? She looks like she's never eaten before."

"Who wants lunch?" Cindy interrupts, as a grumbling Yvonne returns to sewing the shirt. It looks soft. Is it Jack's? I bet it would reach my knees if I slipped it on. God, I've become a laundry stalker.

Cindy brings sandwiches, chicken salad, and cookies to the table. Cindy takes a dainty bite of sandwich, looking nauseous. Her pregnancy has been awful; it's hard for her to keep food down. "What'd you find in town, Shortcake?"

I wince then quickly force a smile. Like Dad, Mom always called me Strawberry Shortcake because of my hair color, and it annoys me every time Cindy calls me by my nickname. It belongs to my parents.

"There's an arcade called the Fun Tunnel that has tons of skee ball lanes. I found lots of places to eat. I saw the school, Hundred Oaks. Looks pretty nice. But it's like five miles from here—I'll have to take the bus to school. I wish I had a bike."

Dad and Cindy glance at each other. I can see the gears turning in their heads. We can't afford a bike, and we all know it.

"I talked to Jack Goodwin earlier," I say. "He seems pretty down to earth."

Dad and Cindy glance at each other again. I swear, did they develop ESP or something?

She taps her fork on her plate. "Shortcake, I don't think spending time with Jack is a good idea."

"Yeah, yeah, I know. The Goodwins place a *high premium on their privacy*."

Cindy shakes her head. "It's not that…he sneaks girls into his room. The other maids say they never see the same girl twice. You're too good for him."

I snort. What a silly thing to say. I'm too good for a millionaire horse farm owner? Whatever. Besides, the first thing I discovered when I got here is that the household staff lives for gossip. They exaggerate everything.

"I'm sure Jack doesn't have a revolving door to his bedroom."

Yvonne tightens her thread and loops the needle through the cuff. "I heard from the gardener that Master Jack gave Candy Roxanne, that harlot of a country music singer, a tour of Mrs. Goodwin's rose gardens. And apparently one thing led to another and he was picking thorns out of his—"

"Yvonne," Dad says, his voice laced with warnings. He pats my hand. "You know Mr. and Mrs. Goodwin want us to keep our distance. I can't afford any problems with my new job. Not with a baby on the way."

"I got it, I got it."

Dad takes a bite of chicken salad. A piece gets stuck to his mouth, and Cindy leans across the table to sweep it away with her napkin. He gives her a quick kiss. Oh gag me.

Deep down I wish I had someone who would adore me like that. Back in West Virginia, I dated occasionally and fooled around with this guy Adam sometimes on weekends, but I've never had a boyfriend-boyfriend. Maybe this'll be the year I finally get one.

I can't help but think about how Jack treated me when he thought I was here with a senator. He flirted, he asked questions, he smiled at me. It felt effortless...but he wouldn't have flirted if he'd known who I was.

• • •

After I finish my sandwich, I head to Greenbriar to find Star. I should get to know the horse before warming him up tomorrow morning.

I jog past the mud pile where the farmhands burn manure and make it into fertilizer. Dad told me Mr. Goodwin sells it to soup companies; they use the fertilizer to grow mushrooms. Remind me never to eat creamy mushroom soup again.

The large wooden doors are wide open as I charge through a flock of birds mooching grain, and the intoxicating smell of hay and horse and manure hits me in the face. Sunlight fills the cool barn, warming me like a good hug.

I find Rory Whitfield grooming Star. He rubs the colt's nose then uses a soft brush to smooth his face. Rory is cute, but not my type. He's taller and lankier than Jack and hasn't fully filled out his frame yet.

"Hey," I say.

He gives me a grin. "Hay is for horses."

"Damn, I thought you might be cool. But with lines like that..." Rory laughs at my expression. "So you're a groom here?" I ask.

"Part-time. I'm still in school. I'm a senior."

"Me too. Starting Hundred Oaks on Monday."

"That's where I go," he says.

Rory steps away from Star to chat with me, and I find he's real easy to get along with, just like the guys in the barn I used to work at. Turns out that Whitfield Farms is right up the road from Cedar Hill. He has two parents, three brothers, and a barnyard full of animals. Like Cedar Hill, Whitfield Farms has been around since the Civil War, but instead of horses, they raise cows and breed dogs. In fact, Jack bought his three hounds from Rory's father a few years ago.

"Why do you work here if you got your own farm?"

He doesn't meet my eyes. "Demand for dairy has gone down, so my parents aren't really forthcoming with an allowance. I gotta work here if I want cash."

"I get you. That's why I want the exercise boy job."

Rory swivels to grab a different brush, breaking the cardinal rule of Horse 101: never turn your back on a horse. Star takes advantage of the situation and nudges Rory's shoulder, shoving him toward the stall door. Then the colt lies down on the floor and rolls back and forth across his straw bed like a puppy. What a prankster.

I laugh. "Good one, Star."

"Come on, boy," Rory says. "Get up."

The horse scrambles to his feet then trots around his stall. He's definitely a Thoroughbred: lots of energy with a dash of crazy. I love his goofy personality. Star walks over to me. He's long and sleek. Not an ounce of fat on him.

"Be careful," Rory says. "He's been biting."

Star rests his chin on my shoulder and I rub his neck. He smells super musky, which leads me to believe the grooms are having a hard time keeping him clean. He must act up during his baths. Rory grabs a shovel, scoops up Star's manure, then charges past me to dump it in a wheelbarrow.

"You are a handsome boy," I tell Star. He sniffs my hands and snorts and tries to bite my arm. I rip it away just in time. Thoroughbred racehorses aren't pets. They bite like sharks.

"No!" I say.

Star looks me in the eye and I stare right back, daring him to defy me again. The staring contest goes on for over a minute. I wonder if he's looking into my soul, finding something I don't know about. Pain roars through me when I think of Moonshadow and how frightened I am to get close to another horse, considering what happened to her. Finally Star breaks eye contact, leans forward, and nips at my hair, nickering.

"I win," I tell him, scratching his face. He likes that.

I help give him a bath and check his shoes, and find out he's a two-year-old colt. Rory confirms that Star is indeed a Ferrari of horses, a descendant of Nasrullah and Man o' War, super famous racehorses from way back in the day. Five years ago, his sire—his father—nearly won the Triple Crown. We never saw horses like

Star in Charles Town, because those races didn't have big prize money. Those races attracted minivan-like horses; they got the job done okay, but they weren't flashy or special. The only truly special horse I knew was Moonshadow.

I sigh and follow Rory out of the stall.

"Hey, do you want to hang out tonight?" he asks. "There's a party we can hit up. I'll introduce you to people."

"As friends or a date?" I'm not wild about hooking up with a guy I might be seeing on a daily basis around the farm. Could get awkward real fast.

"Just friends. You're, like, over a foot shorter than me. I'd break my neck trying to kiss you."

I decide I like Rory Whitfield.

"Yeah, sure. Tonight sounds good."

Jack suddenly appears in the barn. "Whitfield, could you excuse us please?"

Rory nods then heads out without another word. Jack's eyes meet mine and we stand in relative silence. Those damned squawking birds won't shut up.

"I want to apologize for my behavior this morning," Jack adds. "Dad always says a gentleman doesn't hit on his staff."

One point for me—I was right. His dad must control the puppet strings.

Wait. He was hitting on me?

My heart rockets out of control. He's cute, but I could never trust him. I'm sure all he cares about is his fortune, just like other rich people, like awful Mr. Cates back in Charles Town.

Jack goes on, "It won't happen again."

"Good to know," I say, copying his super professional voice.

He looks shocked momentarily then struts over to a stall. "Can you help me get Strawberry ready to be loaded into her trailer?"

"Of course." I move toward the mare's stall. "Where are you taking her?"

Jack blushes. "I'm taking her to stud up at Lotus Farms."

I choke back a snort of laughter, picturing Jack having to stand there staring at his watch while two horses get it on. He grins at my reaction, but it melts away quickly. Apparently running a horse farm means you are never allowed to smile.

A yearling pokes his head out of his stall to see what we're up to. I open Strawberry's tack trunk, pull out her treats, and change the subject.

"Jack, is there anything I need to know about Star before tomorrow's race? Like, anything I should do during our warm-ups?"

"Star is scared of something, and none of us can figure out what it is. Not even your dad or Gael knows. And if they can't figure it out, I guess we'll never know," Jack says, attaching a lead to Strawberry's halter.

Lots of horses are scared of silly things. I once knew a powerful stallion that was terrified of dandelions.

"What's Star's record this year?" I ask. "I haven't seen him mentioned in the *Daily Racing Form*."

Lines zip across his forehead. "He hasn't placed or shown yet."

"Out of how many races?"

"Six."

With Star's breeding, he should have at least shown by now. I cringe as I feed Strawberry a treat.

Jack nods at my reaction. "I'm trying to get some wins before the Dixiana Derby in October."

"What's the purse?"

"Tomorrow's is $75,000. The Dixiana is guaranteed $500,000."

I whistle. "How much was the stud fee for Star?"

Jack adjusts his hat, averting his eyes. "Over half a mil."

I whistle again but louder this time, making him laugh nervously. Paying for Star to be born was like ordering the most expensive thing on the menu. Most midrange Thoroughbred stud fees are around $250,000–300,000. I imagine that's what the Goodwins charge when other owners want to breed their mares with Cedar Hill stallions.

"It's one of Dad's tests. He gave me a budget and wants to see what I'll do with it." Jack shakes his head. "I hope Star can at least place tomorrow. Otherwise I've wasted a shitload of my dad's money...and I'll have failed his test."

"And then you won't get a sticker, huh?" I joke. Must be nice to have money to play with.

"I want my father to know I can handle running the farm. I don't want to let him down." He gives me a sad smile, sounding sincere about wanting to work hard, and I feel a hard pang in my chest for him.

A successful horse turns a profit. And Star hasn't even made back the money the Goodwins spend on his grain and horseshoes.

"I'm sure you made the right call on the stud fee. Breeding usually works out. Star ran so fast this morning, he probably would've made it to Cincinnati before tomorrow if he'd just kept on going."

Jack laughs quietly, and before I know what I'm doing, I reach out and touch his wrist, to show I support him. He coughs. Then I jerk my hand away. Shit.

I nervously lick my lips, hoping my being forward doesn't influence whether he gives me the job or not.

He takes off his hat to reveal disheveled blond hair that curls around his shirt collar. We're standing so close, I can see a red tint mixed in with the blond.

"You're easy to talk to," he says, turning his cowboy hat over in his tanned hands. They're strong and calloused, like they've hauled plenty of wheelbarrows. His big blue eyes peek up at me.

"Jack!" a girl yells. He shoves his hat back on as a younger girl who looks to be in middle school comes running up.

She latches on to his elbow like a barnacle. "I'm coming with you to Kentucky!"

"You can't come, sweetheart," Jack replies, wrapping an arm around her. "Have you met Savannah yet? This is my sister, Shelby."

Shelby says hello but goes right back to pestering her big brother. "I want to be with Strawberry."

Jack looks at me. "Shelby thinks that Strawberry Fields belongs to her, but Dad would say otherwise."

"I've been with Strawberry ever since she was a foal!" Shelby says. "And I'm not abandoning her today."

"This isn't something you should see," Jack says with a soft voice.

"Come on! I've seen cows do it over at Whitfield Farms."

Jack's face hardens. "The Whitfields let you watch that?"

"Er, well, Trey and I watched one day. His parents didn't know—"

"I'll be having a talk with Trey," Jack says, setting his hands on his hips.

"No, don't!" Shelby whines. "My life would be over!"

Trey must be one of Rory's brothers. Jack whispers to me, "Shelby has a crush on him."

"I do not." She pounds Jack on the chest with her fist.

"There's no reason to get violent," Jack says. "We all have crushes from time to time."

"Like your crush on Abby Winchester?" Shelby teases.

"I don't have a crush on Abby, okay? Shut up about that." Jack avoids my stare.

"She's sooo pretty," Shelby says to me. "She told me that last year she won Fairest of the Fair in her county."

"Of course she did," I mutter.

"If I can't go with you and Strawberry, will you take me to the movies tonight, Jack?"

"I wish I could, sweetheart, but I already have plans." He suddenly focuses on his watch. "I need to get going if I'm gonna make it back in time. See you tomorrow, Savannah."

He walks away without another word, leading Strawberry and his sister to the trailer. But then he glances back at me, smiles, and waves. I return the wave.

Who does he have plans with tonight? Does he have a date? And more importantly, why do I care?

The Goodwin kids are not what I expected...I figured they'd spent all their time taking tea and laughing hoity-toitily or something.

I open the door to Star's stall and slowly approach the horse, to continue getting to know him. "So, it's just me and you... want to tell me why you buck your riders?" He lets out a little snort and nudges my hand then tries to chow down on it.

"Hey, now!" I shove his face away from me. Sure, he's being snotty, but I'd take horses over humans any day of the week. Horses never give a damn if I have labels on my clothes.

Herds are sort of like high school—they definitely have their own social dynamic. There's always a stallion or gelding who thinks he's in charge. Out in the pasture, horses bully each other around food and water; lead horses get their fill before others get a bite or a sip, and if a horse that's low in the pecking order tries to butt in, he'll get bitten or kicked. And there's always a troublemaker or two, wallowing in the mud and teasing the fillies.

Once Star has calmed down and he's treating me with respect, I pet his ears and let him eat a treat out of my palm. I want him to feel safe with me so he'll let me ride him. "Good boy. Now, let's see, what are you scared of? Raccoons, obviously. Are you scared of fillies? What about mud puddles?"

I rub his head until his breathing slows and he falls asleep.

The Colors Were So Real

Later on Saturday evening, Rory is driving me down the streets of Franklin, giving me the grand tour.

"We have three Shell gas stations, but each has a different nickname. There's the *Social Shell*, where almost everybody goes to get gas. I always see somebody I know there. Then there's the *Secret Shell*, which no one notices, because it's not on one of the main highways. And the last is called the *Soviet Shell*, because it's usually out of gas and the snack shelves inside are always empty."

"Wow," I say with a laugh.

"Franklin was named after *the* Benjamin Franklin," Rory says.

"Oh yeah?"

"Yeah. He also discovered electricity and invented the carriage odometer and he's on the hundred dollar bill."

"I bet Benjamin Franklin never had to take the bitch seat in a carriage." Rory brought his Irish setter, Ava, along tonight and apparently she always gets the passenger seat so she can hang her head out the window. "I mean, isn't it ironic that I'm sitting in the bitch seat while the dog gets the best spot?" I say, making Rory laugh. "My mom would've liked your tour. She was real big into history."

"Where is she?"

"She died," I say quietly, and Rory gives me a sad look. I tell him about the cancer and how much I miss everything from her macaroni lasagna to the way she braided my hair to how she said *I love you* every night.

"That macaroni lasagna sounds amazing," he says, grinning.

"Oh, my mom kicked Martha Stewart's ass for sure." I tune the radio from rap to the hard rock station. "Ror, who is Abby Winchester?"

"I dunno." He smacks my hand away from the tuner and flips it back to the rap station.

I pick at a piece of duct tape holding the truck's upholstery together. "Mr. Goodwin sure seemed serious about Jack returning Abby's phone calls today. She's practically stalking him."

"Maybe Mr. Goodwin's doing some special business with her or something? I don't know her. She doesn't go to our school, unless she's a freshman."

"I see."

"Why do you care?"

I tell Rory everything: how Jack didn't know who I was and how he offered me a private tour.

Rory gives me a worried look. "Jack's a good boss…but you

shouldn't get your hopes up about him—he never has serious relationships. Well, except for this one girl—Senator Lukens's daughter. They dated last year. It didn't end well apparently." Rory pauses to drum his hands on the steering wheel. "So he wanted to take you on a private tour?"

"Yep. I bet he wouldn't make me take the bitch seat either," I taunt.

"Hush."

I scratch Ava's ears. "So my dating prospects are pretty bad so far. I mean, you're out because you might break your neck trying to kiss me. And Bryant Townsend is a real dick—"

"I'd rather you date just about anybody besides Douchey McDoucherson."

I howl laughing at Bryant's nickname. "Even, like, that guy who rules North Korea who wears pajamas all the time? You'd be okay with me dating him?"

Rory stops at a traffic light. "That sounds like a great idea for my next script." He pulls a scrap of paper from his pocket and the pen from behind his ear. He rips the cap off with his teeth and starts jotting down notes: *Hot teen girl kidnapped by ruthless commie bastard/she falls for him/he brainwashes her by impressing her with his knife collection!!!*

During the rest of my driving tour of Franklin, Rory tells me about how he wants to be a famous screenwriter one day. But I can't figure out what genre Rory writes. What movies have eight million explosions, twice as many deaths, and loads of gratuitous sex scenes?

We pull into the lot of a place called Tennessee Ballers and park next to a Mercedes convertible. Two pretty girls, a guy, and Jack are climbing out of the car as we speak.

Crap. Of course Jack would be here, haunting me. I swivel to face Rory. "How can we afford this place?"

"It's cheap, I promise," Rory says.

Walking up to the wooden doors, I realize Tennessee Ballers is an old flour mill. A drugstore across the street is now an empty storefront.

Inside Tennessee Ballers, I gaze around at the odd décor. The tables, chairs, and carpet are tasteful and clearly brand new, but different kinds of dead fish (bass? sturgeon?) mounted on plaques and pictures of famous football players cover the walls. A picture of the Hundred Oaks' football team from four years ago hangs right beside the cash register. The caption says the photo is from the Tennessee State Championship game. They had a girl quarterback? God, that's so badass.

Rory and I get in line behind one of the girls who came here with Jack. She's super tall with long blond hair. "Fish tacos at a place called Tennessee Ballers? Who came up with that?" I ask.

She turns, and a smile spreads across her face. "I know, the name is awful. I have to listen to guys make perverted comments every time I'm here."

Rory pats his stomach. "Man, do I love me some fish tacos."

"Ugh," the girl says, rolling her eyes.

The guy she's with grins evilly. "You love it when guys talk like that."

"I hate you. So much," the girl says to him before striding to the counter.

"You love me!"

"Who are they?" I whisper to Rory.

"That's Vanessa Green and Colton Bradford. Colton's dad is the mayor of Franklin. And Vanessa's really cool. Her brother used to go to Hundred Oaks but now he's in the NFL. First person ever from our school to make it."

Crazy. How is it I've only been here a few days and I keep meeting people who are way out of my league?

Vanessa studies the menu, but Rory is studying Vanessa like *she's* what's for supper. I nudge him with my elbow. "Is she why we're here?"

"No, we're here for tacos." Rory points his chin at the menu. Liar.

Jack slips an arm around the other pretty girl's waist as they check out the menu.

"And who's she?" I ask.

"Kelsey Painter. She's a cheerleader."

I'm so confused. Wasn't he calling Abby Winchester earlier today? What if his bedroom really does have a revolving door?

I daydream of Jack touching me like that. Gently dragging his fingers across my hip, zapping me with lightning. Wait a minute. He was flirting with me earlier today when he knew he had plans with this girl tonight? What an ass. And I'm an ass for even thinking about him.

I focus on the food. The menu is full of tacos, nachos, tortilla chips, rice, and beans. This place is dirt cheap. I can buy a taco and rice for like $3. Nice.

That's when Jack looks over his shoulder and sees me there. Our eyes meet and the side of his mouth quirks into a smirky grin.

"Savannah, hey. This is my friend Kelsey," he says, and I shake hands with the girl. "Savannah's living at my farm now."

"Can we get chips and salsa?" she asks, turning away from me.

"Sure." Jack seems startled that Kelsey just snubbed me, but I'm not. She clearly wants to jump him. Or already jumps him. Or something.

"You want to sit with us, Savannah?" Jack asks.

"Yeah, we do," Rory rushes to reply. His eyes flick over to Vanessa.

After I get my order, I join Jack, Kelsey, Vanessa, and Colton at a circular booth in the corner. Curious, I watch them out of the corner of my eye. Kelsey taps on her cell phone as her friends dig in. Between texts, she feeds chips to Jack, giggling like crazy. He eats the chips she feed him because his stomach is clearly doing the thinking—just like with 99 percent of all guys. But he glances at me as he chews.

"Oh my God, this rice is so good," Vanessa says, shoveling it into her mouth.

"I think it's 'cause they cooked it in straight-up butter," Jack says, practically inhaling his rice.

"I wish they served this stuff at Starbucks," Vanessa says.

"You only love three things in this world." Colton ticks them off on his fingers. "Starbucks, clothes, and meeting guys at Starbucks."

"That is so not true," she replies, throwing a tortilla chip at Colton's face. The chip sticks to his black T-shirt. He plucks it off and eats it.

Rory slides into my booth with his tray. "You guys are so rude. I can't believe you started eating before I was seated."

"That's what you get for being a perv, Whitfield," Vanessa says, sucking her drink through her straw. She shakes her cup. "I'm already out of iced tea."

"Maybe if you didn't drink like a horse," Rory says.

Vanessa rattles her cup again, trying to get more tea out.

"Let me get you more to drink. I won't be able to eat in peace if I don't," Rory says, leaping to his feet and snatching the cup out of her hand. He jogs over to the beverage station to get a refill. He comes back and passes Vanessa her tea. She takes one sip and nearly gags.

"This is warm. Where's the ice?" she asks.

"Oh, well I don't like ice, so I didn't get you any."

"But it's *iced* tea!" she says. "It tastes crappy when it's warm."

"Oh." Rory looks down at the cup. "Maybe you should put some ice in it then."

I silently laugh and Vanessa throws a tortilla chip at him, looking furious, but then it turns into a subtle smile.

"So," Jack says to me. "Tell me about yourself. What else do you like besides riding—"

I'm about to start talking when Kelsey starts bragging about the college party she went to last night. "It was an underwear party and everybody danced around in foam and we sprayed silly string everywhere."

Jack bites into his taco, looking perturbed at Kelsey.

Rory mouths "silly string," and his eyes light up. He digs the scrap of paper out of his pocket again and jots down *underwear and silly string.*

"Tell me about that girl from last night on your Instagram pictures," Colton says to Kelsey. "The one from the sorority you want to rush next year."

"She said she's going to study abroad this spring," Kelsey says.

"Never mind. Long-distance relationships are hard," Colton replies. "I couldn't handle dating that girl Ellen I met in Murfreesboro."

Jack rolls his eyes. "That's only thirty minutes from here."

"Yeah." Colton purses his lips and shakes his head. "She was just too far away. I can watch a whole episode of *I Didn't Know I was Pregnant* in that amount of time."

Because they've both been drinking like horses, Rory and Vanessa stand to go refill their cups at the same time. Rory purposely pushes a lever on the Coke machine, making orange soda spray on her hand.

"You ass!" She pushes on the ice button, grabs a cube of ice, and drops it inside his T-shirt. He jumps and wiggles around like an eel.

"He'll never get her into bed now," Colton muses, laughing.

Considering she's popular and wealthy, I don't think Rory will ever get her into bed even if he does behave like a perfect gentleman.

• • •

After dinner at the perverted taco place, we drive out to a huge field where a large bonfire is already blazing. Tiki torches are everywhere. I feel like I'm on that show *Survivor*, only instead of surviving on a deserted island, I have to survive a couple of hours with people I've never met before.

Trucks and four-wheelers are parked on the muddy grass. My heart speeds up as I scan the large group of kids, drinking, dancing, laughing, jumping around.

The second I hop down from Rory's truck, people from my new school are already staring at me. With a firm grasp on Ava's leash, Rory glides through the crowd, laughing and grinning at everybody. He seems like the All-American Guy, one of those people everyone wants to be friends with. When I get separated from him in the crowd, Rory reaches back through a cluster of people and grabs my arm, pulling me closer to him.

That gets the attention of the girls. And unlike the guys smiling and pointing me out to their friends, the girls are giving me Ultimate Stink Eye.

"Be careful tonight," Rory says quietly. He scans my tank top and skinny jeans.

We go get beers from the keg. Vanessa is silently drinking from a plastic cup. Some girl speeds over to Rory and jumps into his arms, squealing and hugging him.

I want to say something to Vanessa, but the second I open my mouth, I lose my nerve and take a sip of beer. I've never been all that good at making girlfriends, considering I grew up around horses and boys and more horses. Vanessa catches me gawking at her and moves closer.

"Where are you from?"

"West Virginia."

"Never been there."

"You aren't missing much. The only difference near as I can tell is that people here refer to all soft drinks as 'Coke.' Even if it's Sprite, you call it Coke. We refer to it as soda up north."

She laughs, looking around. "You aren't missing much here either. This party's pretty lame."

"Where'd your friends Colton and Kelsey go?"

"Colton went home already 'cause he was tired. He loves sleeping. And Kelsey's over there." Vanessa nods toward the edge of the circle where Kelsey is sitting on a log next to Jack, talking animatedly with her hands. He's roasting a marshmallow.

"Are they together?" I ask.

"Not yet...but I think she wants to try the whole relationship thing with him, even though he rarely dates seriously. He's too into his work. They've been friends a long time but they've never been single at the same time before...so it might work out. I dunno."

Is Jack about to be taken? That's not surprising. Still, a weird feeling of disappointment settles inside my chest. I ignore it.

That's when a beefy guy wearing a wrestling T-shirt comes over. "I'm Brent," he slurs in my ear.

"Oh yeah?" His hot beer breath on my skin makes me shiver—and not in the good way.

The guy cups my elbow. "Want to get out of here, new girl?"

"No, thanks."

"But you're hot." He spills beer on my boot. I give Vanessa a look that says "is this guy smoking something?" and she rolls her eyes.

"Get lost, Brent," she says, sipping from her cup.

"You got a boyfriend?" Brent clamps his hand on my arm.

I want a boyfriend—I really do, but I want somebody who likes me for me, not because I'm the new girl. I can't think of a good word to describe how this Brent guy makes me feel. Resentful? Flattered and angry? Flangry.

"Let go," I say, yanking my arm away from this drunk King Kong.

"Is there a problem here?" a low, rough voice says. Jack gently pulls me away from Brent, loosely wrapping an arm around me. "We're good here," Jack says pointedly, and Brent skedaddles toward the trucks. So much for Mr. Macho Wrestling T-shirt.

Jack touches my wrist, and the sensation of his skin on mine sends shivers up my arm. In the good way. Our eyes meet.

I pull a purple sucker out of my pocket and pop it in my mouth. I'm pissed at myself for being attracted to a rich boy. I turn to focus on anything else but him.

Great. Now everyone at this party is looking at me. *Way to make a good impression before school starts, Savannah.*

"You okay now?" Jack asks me quietly. When I nod, he pats my shoulder and rejoins Kelsey over on their log. She grabs his hand and threads her fingers between his, but he keeps staring at me. His gaze makes me nervous.

What if Jack had gotten into a fight with that stupid Brent kid and Brent punched him out? What if Mr. Goodwin had blamed me? What if Mr. Goodwin fires my dad before we even unpack our winter clothes?

With a new baby on the way, we can't afford to lose the free housing. Plus, this job is the biggest thing that's ever happened to my father. He's proud of it, and I want to help him succeed at Cedar Hill.

I resolve not to cause Jack Goodwin any problems from now on.

Rory reappears, drops a hand on my shoulder, and smiles at Vanessa. "Ladies, I have a surprise. Come with me." He ushers us down to the pond at the end of the big field. Ava barks happily and runs in circles.

"What's the surprise?" I ask, bouncing on my toes.

Rory grins then pulls up his shirt, revealing a muscular back and torso.

"The surprise is you're doing a striptease?" I ask. Vanessa glances at Rory's body. Then she does a double take before taking another sip of beer.

Two boxes are sticking out of his jeans. Sparklers! I squeal and run toward him. Smiling, he gives me a sparkler and pulls a lighter from his pocket. He lights it and I twirl in a circle, sucking on my purple sucker, watching my sparkler spit out green and red sparkly goodness, relishing the smell of summer on the air.

"Can I have one?" Vanessa asks. Rory stares at her for a sec before whipping a sparkler out of the box and lighting it for her.

"I'm a witch!" she yells, laughing, pretending her sparkler is a wand.

"Witches are sexy," Rory mumbles to me, not taking his eyes off Vanessa.

While we play with our sparklers, Rory starts launching bottle rockets. I love fireworks. You never know what's going to happen when they explode in the dark sky. Will it be a giant burst of light or just a dud? Will sparks rain down like glitter?

Jack touching me just now was like fireworks exploding right in my face. It was so, so dangerous.

But the colors were so real.

At the Races

Today I find out if I got the exercise boy job.

But first I have to ride a horse that doesn't like being ridden. A horse that bucks all his riders. Sure, I had luck with him when he escaped yesterday, but can I strike the jackpot twice?

We're at the barns at River Downs in Cincinnati, and the races start in a couple hours. Dad is standing off to the side, looking worried. I ignore him and concentrate on steadying my heartbeat. I tighten my gloves and pull a deep breath as Rory leads Star toward me. All I have to do is take Star through two warm-up laps and one at a full breeze. I can do this.

I suck in long breaths, working to rid my body of tension. If Star thinks I'm nervous, he's gonna be scared, and I've gotta show him that I'm in charge.

Rory stops about ten feet from me and attempts to hold Star still, but he's prancing and acting skittish. I charge toward Star with confidence and purpose. I rub his face and he whinnies for a sec, and then he sighs and lips my hair. I straighten his front leg so he will be easier to mount.

"You got this?" Rory asks, mimicking my dad's expression.

"I got this," I say, moving to the near side to mount. Rory hands me the reins, I get a leg up from him, grab the horse's mane, throw my other leg over his back, and slip my feet into the stirrups. Star prances in a circle and jerks away from Rory, and I might go flying.

"Whoa!" I say, and Star snorts. "Whoa."

I cluck my tongue and trot onto the practice track. Out of the corner of my eye, I watch as Dad joins Jack, Mr. Goodwin, and Gael in the clocker's tower. Jack waves and whistles, and suddenly I'm not so nervous. We circle the track twice at an easy speed and then it's time for the real show. I push the horse to a full gallop. Wind rushes against my face. We must be going forty-five miles an hour. That's well past the speed limit on the four-lane back in Franklin.

"Go," I shout to Star, gripping the reins tight. We fly around the track. I'm standing hunched over as I make the far turn, urging the horse faster. My guess is that Star starts slow but makes up his speed later, and now's when it counts. "Go, Star! You got this!" Ten seconds later we cross the finish line, and I bring the colt to a jog, patting his neck and smiling my brains out.

Jack is clapping and beaming.

"Time?" I call out to Gael.

Gael rubs his chin. "1:40. It's not completely terrible."

I pump my fist. To hear him say it wasn't complete shit must mean the horse did pretty well. I steer Star over to the hot-walkers ring, dismount, and hand him off to Dad.

"If he runs like this later today, he'll win for sure," Dad says, stroking the colt's mane, trying to get him to calm down. Star's ears twitch and point forward.

I get up on tiptoes to kiss my father's cheek, making him smile. "Do you think I'll get the job?"

"I'd wait until after the race to bring it up to Jack. He seems nervous out of his mind right now. But yeah, I'd say you've got the job if you want it."

I kiss Dad's cheek again then make my way toward the barns, my red braid bouncing against my back.

I'm super excited about Star's prospects for today but tired as hell. I shouldn't have stayed out past midnight when I had to get up at 5:00 a.m. for the four-hour drive. I spend the next couple of hours helping Dad and Rory in the barns, feeding the six horses and lead ponies we brought with us, keeping them calm. Exercise riders typically don't help in the barns, but I don't mind. I love being around horses.

When it's time for Minerva's race, I go with Rory to the paddock to help put her saddle on. When she's ready, Rory goes back to the barn and I start walking Minerva in a circle. Not only does this calm her down, it's a chance for spectators watching the race to check out the horses. They get to see which horses are looking good, which ones are moody, which ones have too many bandages on their front legs, and which ones are clearly injured.

Horses die every week at racetracks all over the country, and when I hear about it, I want to punch something. That's the one thing about this sport that really pisses me off—seeing abused racehorses. Some owners drug horses to make them stronger, which is totally illegal. I've heard of people who try to drug the horses' water, but they won't drink it. So to make them thirsty, they gave horses a salt lick, so that they have no choice but to drink the drugged water. It's so sad.

I keep moving Minerva around in circles. I use a rag to clean out the mare's mouth. "Good girl," I say with a yawn, not bothering to cover my mouth.

That's when Jack enters the paddock, wearing that sleek gray suit, a cowboy hat, and black cowboy boots. My heart starts pounding and my mouth goes dry as he adjusts his cufflinks. I glance down at my frayed T-shirt. It has a hole in it. And is that a mustard stain?

"You did well this morning." Jack pats Minerva's side and walks beside me, but doesn't say if I got the job or not.

"Thanks. Star is super, super fast. I don't see how he could lose today."

"Thanks, that means a lot. How's Minerva looking?"

"Good—"

"Jack!" a girl yells.

I look up into the grandstands to see a brunette waving a large hat at him. How ridiculous. Women hardly ever wear hats unless it's the Derby or one of the other big races.

Jack ducks out of the girl's line of sight. "Oh shit."

"Jesus," I say. "That hat is huge."

"Why do girls think giant hats look good?"

"Jack!" the girl yells again.

"Who is that?" I ask.

Jack looks physically sick. "Abby Winchester. I gotta escape!"

"*That's* Abby Winchester?" I ask, squinting. "Why is she wearing that?"

"No idea," Jack says, removing his hat and dragging a hand through his mop of hair.

"You know, I bet you could yell 'Rapunzel, Rapunzel, let down your giant hat' and climb up to her."

Jack laughs at my joke then groans when Abby yells his name again.

"Your girlfriend's gonna freak out the horses."

He gives me a look. "She's not my girlfriend."

"Then what is she?" And why does he want to escape her so bad? "Does she know you were with Kelsey last night?"

Jack stares at me for a long moment. Fear rushes through me. Why the hell did I ask that? Who am I to question my boss? We might attend the same parties, but he's the owner's son and I'm cleaning out his horse's mouth.

"Sorry," I say quickly. "I shouldn't have said anything."

Jack keeps looking at me. "Kelsey and I just hang out sometimes…it's nothing serious. I'm going to check on Star." He disappears from the paddock in the direction of the barns.

Minerva nudges my face with her nose, whinnying like she's worried about me.

"I'm okay," I tell her, exhaling deeply. "I'm okay."

• • •

The announcer announces that it's ten minutes to post time. Bryant Townsend mounts Minerva, and I head over to the fence so I can collect her after she finishes the race.

Rory joins me at the edge of the track to watch. "$100,000 guaranteed purse on this one."

"I know," I reply, grasping the white fence, white-knuckled.

If Minerva wins today, Mr. Goodwin will be $100,000 richer, and Rory says he tends to give good bonuses to the grooms, exercise boys, and trainers who work with his horses. Mr. Cates never did things like that. One point for Mr. Goodwin.

"I could sure use the money for college applications," Rory says. "They're expensive. Like, some of them are thirty-five bucks apiece."

"Damn. I didn't know that. Do you know where you're applying yet?"

Rory lifts a shoulder, staring out at the track. "I'm thinking

UTK. They have a good theater program. But I doubt I'll get any big scholarships like my brother Will did."

I don't totally relate, considering I'm not going to college, but I hurt for my friend.

Last night during the grand tour of Franklin, Rory confessed that most of the Whitfields' money goes toward taking care of his autistic nine-year-old brother. Special schooling doesn't come cheap, especially when farms are declining all over the country. Rory's older brother gave up attending a fancy college so they could afford special schooling.

"What happens if you can't afford college?" I ask. "Are you just gonna keep working on your screenplays or take over Whitfield Farms like Jack is gonna take over Cedar Hill?"

"I can't do it," Rory says quietly.

"Hmm?"

"I can't end up like my parents. You know, struggling with our farm. We haven't broken even in two years. I don't ever want to go through this when I'm older and have kids or whatever..."

"But who's gonna run the farm? Your brother, Will?"

"Frankly I don't care who runs it. It's a black hole."

"But the farm's been in your family since the Civil War!"

"I know that, but I've gotta do what's best for me. Some things aren't meant to last."

"But your family—"

"Would you drop it?" he hisses. He clutches the fence and I suck in a deep breath, staring at the scoreboard.

"I'm sorry," Rory says after a moment, giving me a quick, sad smile. "Just ignore your dick friend over here."

"It's okay," I say quietly, resting a hand on his arm. "I understand." But I don't. So his family has had a few bad seasons. So what? I'm sure it'll pick up. Family's too important to give up on them. Even if I'm annoyed that Dad got his girlfriend pregnant, I can't imagine leaving them high and dry.

• • •

Minerva wins her race against other fillies and mares, which means that Mr. and Mrs. Goodwin, Jack, Shelby, Bryant, and Gael go to the winner's circle and have their picture made with the horse.

When Bryant dismounts, Jack hands Minerva off to Rory so he can hot-walk her and lead her back to her stall. "I want you to watch Star's race with me," Jack says. "For good luck."

I nod. Mrs. Goodwin and Shelby disappear back to their box, but Mr. Goodwin stays put against the fence, thumbing through the race program. He says, "Thank God, they're gone. I need a hot dog."

Jack whispers to me, "Mom won't let him eat hot dogs, so he has to sneak them."

"Do you want one?" Mr. Goodwin asks Jack.

"That's the stupidest question I've ever heard." Jack adjusts his suit jacket. "Of course I want a hot dog."

Mr. Goodwin gently taps Jack's cheek. "How about you, Savannah?"

"Yes, sir." I reach into my back pocket to give him cash, but Mr. Goodwin waves me off. "Wait here so I can find you," Mr. Goodwin says, then goes over to the concession stand.

"Dad refuses to get a cell phone," Jack says. "That's why we have to stand here so he can find us."

"Why doesn't he have a cell phone?"

"Because he insists on living in the prehistoric era. I read this story about how apes in zoos use iPads and I showed the article to Dad, hoping it would make him want to start using a computer or a cell, but you know what he said?"

I shake my head.

"He said, 'I'm not an ape.'" We laugh together as Jack folds his arms on top of the white fence. "I don't see how he lives without a cell."

"I don't have one," I mumble. "And I get along okay."

"Considering how often mine beeps, I'm tempted to get rid of it myself."

I don't buy that for one second.

"If Star wins," Jack says, "I want you in the winner's picture, okay?"

I duck my head, grinning. "Okay," I reply. "So where's your girlfriend?"

Jack's face goes hard. "She's not my girlfriend."

"Whatever you say," I tease.

"You know, normally I hate giant hats on girls—I think whoever invented them should be rounded up and quartered—but today I love them."

"Oh yeah?"

"Yeah, because every time I see Abby's hat bobbing through the crowd, I can just turn and run off in the other direction."

I laugh quietly, wishing he'd elaborate on this whole Abby Winchester situation. Clearly something is going on between them, and whatever it is, it pisses me off because I like him—

I pinch my arm. Why can't I stop thinking about him?

Mr. Goodwin comes back balancing three hot dogs and his notebook in his hands.

"Don't tell my wife," he tells me, as if I would ever impose upon Mrs. Goodwin's *privacy*. We yank the aluminum foil back and chow down. I tap my boot nonstop, hardly believing I'm standing with Jack Goodwin at a race.

We finish, wad up our aluminum foil, and Jack checks his watch. "Whitfield should have Star in the paddock by now. Let's go check on him."

Dad is helping Rory to put Star's saddle on when we enter the paddock. Star prances and tries to rip away from Rory, and he attempts to bite Dad's arm. Dad raises an eyebrow when he sees me with Jack. I quickly shake my head, trying to show Dad that hanging out with Jack wasn't my idea. He asked *me* to stand with him during the race.

"Danny," Jack says, tipping his hat at him. "How's Star doing?"

"Fed and somewhat more relaxed than usual," Dad replies. "I think his workout this morning really helped him."

"Good." Jack steps up to Star's nose and whispers to him. It's really cute.

After Bryant mounts, I pat Star's neck. "You can do this, understand?" I tell the horse. Star lets out a snort and his tail flips in circles as he looks every which way, and I pat him again to try to soothe him. His breathing steadies as he looks me in the eye.

But the second Bryant steers Star toward the starting gate, the horse whips his head around again. What's it gonna take to keep him calm?

I move to walk with Jack.

"Shortcake, where are you going?" Dad asks.

"Jack wants me to stand with him during the race. For luck."

A grin slides across Jack's face and he mouths, *"Shortcake?"*

I'm tempted to flip him off, but one doesn't generally flip off the boss.

Dad does not look pleased. "I need you back in the barn right after, understand?"

I nod quickly and join Jack at the finish line. The scoreboard shows 9–2 odds for Star to win. Not bad. That means people are betting on him to win based on his pedigree and how he looked in warm-ups this morning and the paddock just now.

It makes me proud I played a role in those odds.

I'm leaning against the fence watching the horses and lead ponies trot around the track, doing a final warm-up before post time, when Jack starts tapping his hands on the fence like he's pounding a bongo drum.

"Calm down," Mr. Goodwin says to Jack.

"Can't," Jack says.

My palms go sweaty and I cross my fingers and my toes as the horses enter the starting gate. Star is in the seventh position. I glue my eyes to the green-and-black Goodwin family silks worn by Bryant and the horse.

The gates fly open.

"And they're off!" the announcer says, as the crowd goes silent. Hooves thunder across the dirt. It's a sight that's mesmerized me since I was a little girl, almost like seeing floats in a parade. The excitement of seeing horses fly out of the gate leaving a wake of dust is electric.

But Star broke late and now he's trailing the pack. Ten other horses are leaving him in the dust. A colt named Hard Money has the lead, followed by Desert Waves. The Name's Timmy is in third. "Go, Star," I say, not tearing my eyes off the green and black silks.

He starts to pick up speed at the 5/8 pole, and I jump up and down. This is Star's seventh race. *Seventh time's a charm.*

The pack reaches the straightaway and hurtles toward the finish line. Star is still in last place but he's making ground—he passes four horses in a late break, but it's not enough.

Jack slams his hand against the fence when Desert Waves crosses the line first.

"Maybe next time," Mr. Goodwin says, looking equal parts pissed and pitying.

"Damn," I whisper, not wanting to meet Jack's face. He brought me along today to keep his horse calm! To help him win the race! How will I get the job now?

"He should've won," Jack says, rubbing his eyes. "Shit."

Mr. Goodwin lays a hand on his shoulder. "Son, lower your voice, please."

"He shouldn't be losing. Not with his breeding! That's all horse racing is. Breeding!" Under his breath, I hear Jack mutter, "And I can't even fucking do that right."

I look at the crowd around us. People are staring at Jack. Here's the thing: regular horse races aren't like the Derby. They aren't like an NFL game. It's about gambling. People watch the races then they go inside and cash in their winning tickets, and then they bet again. They usually don't make a big scene.

"I can't believe it," Jack says, turning to face his father, letting out a string of curses. "Five lengths! He might as well have not run," Jack hisses.

"Shh," says Mr. Goodwin.

I feel bad for Jack, but I'm also scared I won't get the job now. I'll have to try out for another owner, maybe even work at another farm away from my dad. I need an opportunity to do something big with my life—I won't get stuck making minimum wage.

I turn to watch Bryant handing Star off to Rory to cool the horse down. Dad pats the horse's neck then walks over to us. "Savannah, I need you back in the barn now."

That's when Jack looks at me as if he just remembered I'm here. Blood races to my head. I really thought I could help with Jack's horse. Bile works its way from my stomach to my throat.

"Excuse me," I say to Jack and Mr. Goodwin, then follow Dad back to the barn. I yank a sucker out of my pocket. Now's not a good time to ask if I got the job.

Star did great in his warm-ups. So what went wrong? What's he so scared of?

I glance back just in time to see Abby Winchester hurling herself into Jack's arms. He looks over her shoulder, staring at me. Why in the world is he hugging her?

I pop the sucker in my mouth, shove the wrapper in my pocket, and get ready for the long drive home.

Why Can't Things Stay Simple?

After the races, at twilight, I'm hanging out by the Greenbriar pasture, watching Star graze. He's chomping on grass, not a care in the world. I unlock the fence and head into the pasture.

Star sees me, trots over, and invades my space, pushing against me.

"Nuh uh." I get right back in his face, showing him who's boss. I push him away, making him move several feet from me. Dad always says that horses have short memories and that I should never worry about hurting their feelings. They'll always come back, because they want to feel safe, they want to feel taken care of.

So why doesn't Star feel safe? What's he scared of? With his bloodline, he should be an expert racer already. Instead he panicked and got a shitty start out of the gate.

I cluck my tongue and snap. "Star, c'mere."

He looks up and walks over, keeping a bit of distance from me this time. I reach into my pocket and pull out a treat, rewarding him for showing me respect. As he eats from my hand, his breathing slows and a stillness settles over his body.

I start examining him, looking for injuries. Monitor his breathing. I rest my head against the withers and listen for his heartbeat.

Sometimes, it's almost like I can hear a horse's voice. This one time, I could tell a mare was sick because she kept rubbing her head against mine and whinnying. Turns out she had an infection that could've made her go blind. And I caught it just in time.

"Why are you so skittish?"

I stand there with Star while he grazes and stare up at the sky, praying to Mom. Is she up there listening to me? I pray that even though Star did bad in his race today, I get the job.

All of a sudden, Star's tail starts whipping around and his ears lay back. He's nervous or angry.

"Hi," Jack calls out, waving from outside the fence, his hounds running circles around him. Jack looks comfortable in a T-shirt, track pants, and a baseball cap turned around backward. A good outfit to curl up in on a Sunday night.

Star pins his ears. Does the horse not like Jack, or is it the three rambunctious dogs at his side? I'd hate to tell Jack that his horse doesn't like him.

"Can we talk?" Jack asks.

Nodding, I pat Star's neck and exit the pasture.

"You did really well today." The fresh smells of Jack's cotton T-shirt and soap waft up to my nose, luring me into a trance. His eyes are bright sapphires under the moon.

"I'm sorry he didn't win. I can't believe it, honestly."

"Me neither. He did better in your warm-up than he did in the damned race." Jack purses his lips and looks at the next pasture over, where mares are grazing with their young. "We should probably get the horses inside."

Jack and I mount Appaloosa ponies and herd the horses toward the barns. A rush of happiness fills me when he gently coaxes a yearling into his stall. I love how he respects and takes care of his animals, and his fluid riding skills show he's a true horseman. The stars glitter against the deep purple sky. It feels like it's just me and Jack for miles and miles.

Much too soon, the horses are safe and cozy in their stalls, and I have no excuse to spend more time with him.

"Lock that gate," he calls.

"Yes, sir." I finish the chore and meet back up with Jack.

"Don't call me sir."

"Aren't you the boss?" I tease.

He scratches the back of his neck, looking pained all of a sudden. "I'm probably gonna score a big fat F on this test."

"Why do you say that? Everyone respects you." Gael told me a story about when Jack was fifteen and his father was out of town and couldn't be reached, Gael was wrestling with whether to euthanize a prized gelding that broke his femur on the track. Jack made the call to put the suffering horse down.

"I don't know who'd buy a horse I breed considering how bad Star's turned out."

"He's a fast horse," I reply. "He just has some growing up to do."

"He should be better than this. He's bred from the Man o' War and Nasrullah lines."

"He just got a bad start out of the gate."

"Star's been gate-trained a couple times already." We're standing so close, I can count the freckles on his nose. See the flecks of gray in his blue eyes. "I love Star, but my father thinks I should sell him to recoup some of the cost. Cut my losses."

A memory of Moonshadow roars into my thoughts. *Moonshadow bucking and squealing, trying to get away from strange men she didn't know, trying to get back to me.* I swallow hard and try to focus on the present.

"Please don't sell Star," I say quietly. "Crotchety as he is, I like him."

"It's a good thing I'm the boss right now 'cause I can't sell him. I can't fail on my first big stud fee deal. Nobody will respect me as an owner...Maybe your workouts with Star will get him in shape for the race at Keeneland next weekend."

I move closer to Jack, getting in his space just like pushy Star. "Does this mean I got the exercise rider job?"

He steps closer, invading *my* space this time. "I think it's pretty obvious you've got the job."

"Yay!" I squeal and jump into his arms, wrapping my arms around his neck. My heart swells at the trust Jack is putting in me. He clears his throat and I immediately let go, mortified. "I'm sorry."

He gently pats my shoulder. "So we'll see you tomorrow morning, then?"

"Yes, sir."

"Stop calling me sir." He laughs softly and gazes into my eyes, and it feels like everything stops. The wind stops rustling the grass. We both stop breathing. The only thing that keeps on are the twinkling stars.

Heat floods my body as he takes a step closer and gently pushes me against the white fence. "Hey," he says. His fingertips graze my cheek. He stares at my lips, setting me on fire. Holy shit, what is happening!

I grab his shoulders to hold myself up, breathing hard, inhaling a mix of honeysuckle and soap. The fence scrapes against my back. What would Jack say if someone caught us here?

I push him away before anything happens.

"What's wrong?" he murmurs, as if in a daze, locking his hands around my waist.

"Jack, no."

At the word *no* he jerks his hands away and holds them up. "Wow, you really don't want to kiss me, eh?"

"You're my boss."

His eyes flutter open wide and he takes a step back. "Shit, I'm sorry. I wasn't thinking."

Of course he wasn't thinking. He doesn't have to worry about what other people would say. *"Why is the rich, gorgeous Jack Goodwin kissing a girl like* her? *He must be using her because she works at Cedar Hill. She's convenient."* He doesn't have to worry about his father getting fired if he's caught kissing me. On top of that, after he badmouthed Abby Winchester today, he let her hug him! So how can I trust anything he says? Just like all rich people.

Jack nervously scratches his nose. "I'm sorry. Can we pretend this never happened? My dad'll be pissed at me."

Without a word, I abandon Jack by the pasture, haul ass back to Hillcrest, and rush into my shoebox of a room, slamming the door shut behind me, rattling the picture of my mother hanging by the door. I reach my bed in two steps and collapse.

Jack Goodwin just tried to kiss me!

It's not that I'm nervous about the prospect of hooking up. I've fooled around before—I even had a regular thing going with this guy Adam. We almost slept together once, but not even the cheap wine coolers we drank before made it feel right. I want my first time to be with someone I love and respect.

I cradle my stuffed bear. If I'd stayed out by the pasture, if I hadn't pushed Jack away, he would've kissed me.

And I'm not sure what I think about that.

• • •

I have five days to get Star in shape for his next race.

If he doesn't win this time, there's a good chance Mr. Goodwin will convince Jack to sell him, and I can't let that happen. *Not again.*

So, on Monday morning before school, I meet Gael for my first day of work as an exercise rider at Cedar Hill.

"Congratulations on the job, drama mama."

I give him my death glare as he gives me my schedule. I'm to take Minerva, Star, and Echoes of Summer out for exercise. I will ride each horse for about twenty minutes before handing the horse off to a hot-walker to cool down before it gets a bath and food.

First I take Minerva out onto the track, warm her up, then turn the other direction and race around the turf to avoid a traffic jam with other riders warming up.

When I'm just getting finished with Minerva, Jack appears on the edge of the track, riding Wrigley. He pulls his cowboy hat off, waves it at the staff, and puts it back on. Most guys my age would still be sleeping at 5:30 a.m., but Jack's up early to see what's happening on the track and in the barns.

When I trot past, riding Minerva, I discover that Mr. Serious is back. He avoids my eyes and tips his hat. "Good morning, Savannah."

"Good morning, *sir*."

Thank the heavens he didn't bring up last night's almost kiss.

I drop Minerva off with a hot-walker then retrieve Star from Greenbriar. He flicks his ears forward and approaches me but doesn't get too close. He's starting to respect my space.

"Good boy." I take his lead and direct him out onto the track. He seems happy and carefree today. We trot around the track two times and then head over to the clocker's tower.

"I'm ready," I tell Gael so he can time me, and Star and I take off. I feel like I'm riding a ballistic missile. "Woooo!" I maintain perfect control, so it's a great run. When I'm finished, Gael and Jack are clapping, and Mr. Goodwin has joined them. He whistles and claps too.

"Time?" I call out to Gael.

"1:41," he replies. "It's not complete shit."

"It was brilliant!" Jack shouts. Mr. Goodwin gives his son a weird look.

I wave to Jack, dismount, and whisper to Star that he did a wonderful job. But the second I pass Star off to a hot-walker, the horse starts whinnying and slapping his tail around. Instead of going to get Echoes of Summer, I rush back over to Star, relieve the hot-walker, and cool the horse down myself. Star nickers and nips at my face as we walk in circles over and over.

I only have five days to get this horse ready to race.

What's wrong with him? Why does he only respond to me?

• • •

After work on Monday morning, Rory drives me to my new school, and on the way, I dig into his new screenplay.

"But this doesn't make any sense," I say, waving the script. "Your character just met the girl two minutes ago. Why would she sleep with him?"

"True love. She saw him and just had to have him."

"Girls don't sleep with guys two minutes after meeting them."

"But it's like, every guy's dream!" Keeping one hand on the wheel, Rory taps his other hand on the paper. "That's why this script will sell. Men will love it."

"Well, I wouldn't pay for a movie ticket to this. You need to edit."

"I'm so glad I met you. Nobody else wants to read my screenplays."

"I'm sorry no one wants to read your porn," I tease.

"Hey, now. It's high-brow porn."

My heart starts thumping hard the moment we pull into the parking lot, where Rory says the seniors park in the back corner. I peer out the truck window at a sunken area of concrete filled with water, weeds, and mud.

"Why is there a lake in the middle of the parking lot?"

"Because the school spends all its money on the football team."

Rory adds that everyone calls this area of the parking lot *The Swamp*, and for some unknown reason it's cool to park there.

I hop down out of the truck, and Rory links my arm in his as we walk past a group of smokers and then the skaters. He helps me check in at the office and points out the cafeteria and the bathroom, but then abandons me at my homeroom because he absolutely has to meet up with the drama teacher. He swears this will be the year the teacher finally agrees to produce his original play, *Call Me When Your Mom Is Back in Town*.

After homeroom, in which I talk to absolutely nobody, I navigate through the crowded hallway. My first class of the day is Crucial Life Lessons, a required course for seniors, where we'll learn, you guessed it, "Crucial Life Lessons." Is that stuff like how to balance our bank accounts, warnings not to sign up for credit cards, and the difference between 87 and 93 octane gas?

I enter the classroom and grab a seat toward the back. The name Coach Lynn is scrawled across the whiteboard. Vanessa Green comes in, takes the seat right in front of me, and turns around.

"I had fun Saturday night," she says. "I think I have a sparkler addiction now."

"I had fun too—"

Jack Goodwin appears in the doorway.

"Oh shit," I mumble.

He sees me and swaggers past girls trying to speak to him and lazily drops into the desk next to mine, props his foot on his thigh, and shakes his cowboy boot. I guess he isn't allowed to wear a cowboy hat in school; his hair curls around his collar.

"You did fantastic this morning," Jack says, leaning toward

me and smiling that lopsided smile. "I know Star'll do well this weekend at Keeneland. I know it."

"Thank you." I smile, bowing my head a little.

"So you and Whitfield, huh?" He drapes his arms across the desks in front of and behind him. Vanessa swivels slightly, listening in.

"What?" I reply.

"I saw you walking in the parking lot with him," Jack replies.

"So?"

"So I'm wondering if you guys got a thing going on."

"Naw. He's too tall. He'd break his neck trying to kiss me."

Vanessa laughs.

Jack gazes into my eyes and my pulse thumps harder and harder. Is he gonna bring up the almost kiss?

"So he's just a friend?" Jack asks.

"Right."

That's when Rory enters the classroom and grabs the seat right in front of Jack.

"Hey, Ror," I say. "Jack thought that we're dating."

Rory screws up his face. "The other night after the party? S fell asleep on the drive home. Her snoring is terrible. She's like a troll or something."

"Hey!" I say.

"A troll, huh?" Jack whispers to me. "I thought you were a Shortcake."

I feel my face flaming pinker than Strawberry Shortcake

her damned self. I swivel around and concentrate on Vanessa's straight blond hair.

As Coach Lynn begins to take roll, Jack leans across the aisle toward me.

"I wish this class taught us real life lessons," he whispers.

I open my notebook and uncap my pen, pretending to get ready to take notes, which is ridiculous because I hate taking notes. "What kind of lessons?"

"Like how to woo women. Or how to get over a really bad hangover."

"Aren't you already an expert in both of those areas?" I whisper back.

"Yeah. It would be an easy A, you know?"

I roll my eyes, but can't help but smile.

Coach Lynn announces that we have to write a two-page paper about where we see ourselves in five years, and everybody starts groaning.

"Where will you be in five years? Still in college? Grad school? In the military? Married? Kids? Working at the car factory?" The teacher looks at me and says, "Will you be working on a farm? Each of you will be required to write a two-page paper."

"Two pages?" Rory whines.

"Oh, just write that you want to be a gynecologist," Vanessa mutters.

Rory bursts out laughing at that, and Vanessa smiles back

at him. He holds Vanessa's gaze for a second longer then faces the whiteboard.

Jack slips his pen behind his ear and leans across the aisle toward me again. "I hope this class has a lesson on how to decide if you want a tattoo or not."

"Ha!" I laugh, blushing.

"Do you have a tattoo?" he murmurs.

"Maybe...If you tell my dad, I'll kill you."

He holds his hands up. "Your secret is safe...as long as you tell me what this tattoo is and where it's located." His eyes move from my chest to my butt to my stomach.

"You're getting colder," I whisper when he starts eyeing my ankles.

"What is it? A butterfly or a heart or something?"

"You're getting even colder."

"Is it a dragon?"

"Brr. You're really cold."

He grins. "Dammit, tell me where your tattoo is!"

"What?" Rory blurts, turning around, looking me up and down. "You have a tattoo?"

"Shhhhhhhh!" says some brownnoser kid.

Coach Lynn sighs. "Face the front of the room please, Jack and Rory."

Rory swirls around. Jack stretches his legs out to either side of the desk in front of him and smirks, continuing to eye me. Dad would kill me, so I pray Jack and Rory don't say anything.

I honestly can't believe I told Jack about the horseshoe tattoo on my hip. Maybe a little part of me wanted to tell him—to show him I'm not some little girl that can be pushed around.

Truly though? Maybe I want him to think of me as sexy.

If Pie Cured Confusion

Between periods, I'm disappointed to discover that Rory and I aren't in the same lunch because his drama course is interfering, and of course he'd rather do that than eat with me. Ugh, nothing's worse than eating alone.

When I head into the cafeteria, I find Jack slipping quarters into the Coke machine, holding a tray loaded up with a burger and fries. I skirt the edge of the cafeteria and make a break for the picnic tables in the courtyard. Outside I grab a seat in the corner, unsnap my Velcro lunch bag, and pull out a sandwich, carrots, a cookie, a juice carton, and one of those soups you can drink.

I open one of Mom's history books—*A Compendium of Poetry.* I don't like poetry all that much, but reading her books makes me feel closer to her and lets me pretend she's right here beside me. I set my bookmark on the table and start reading the section where I left off. It's about Robert Frost. It says one of his most famous poems is "The Road Not Taken." I don't completely understand some of the lines in the poem, but the last section makes me sit up and pay attention:

I shall be telling this with a sigh
Somewhere ages and ages hence:
Two roads diverged in a wood, and I—
I took the one less traveled by,
And that has made all the difference.

Mom highlighted that one section in yellow. Did she feel like she lived life to the fullest? Did she take the right path for her? I bite into my sandwich and chew, thinking.

That's when I hear him. "What is *that*?"

I turn to find Jack salivating over my sandwich. "Roast beef."

He straddles the picnic table bench and sits. "Split it with me."

"No." I take a big bite, smacking obnoxiously.

He laughs. At school he's so different from how he is on the farm where he's the boss. "Where'd you get the lunch?"

"Yvonne," I say through a mouthful.

"Yvonne made you lunch?"

"She did."

"She's never made me a lunch."

"Probably because you've never asked her to, brainiac."

"I'll be speaking with her as soon as I get home." He sits up straight and pops open his Coke. "I want a roast beef sandwich."

"Boys," I mutter. When I move to open my thermos, Jack snatches my roast beef sandwich off the table. He takes a huge bite, grinning, before I can stop him.

"Give me that!" I say, grabbing it back. A piece of roast beef slips out onto the bench. In retaliation, I grab a handful of his fries and stuff them in my mouth.

That's when Brent, that bonehead from the party the other night, walks by, staring at me. Girls at the next table over see I'm sitting with Jack and give me dirty looks.

"This sucks," I say to myself.

"What does?" Jack asks, scooping up ketchup with a fry.

"Everyone's looking at me like I'm a science experiment gone wrong. They don't even bother to say hi. They figure they know everything they need to know based on what I look like."

"People are assholes."

"Yourself included?"

"Guilty as charged." He holds his hands up, laughing. "You are really pretty…" He drags a hand through his blond hair. "But you're kind of like a great book…you know, you pick up a book at the bookstore because it has a beautiful cover…but it's what's inside that pulls you in."

That might be the nicest thing anyone's ever said to me. I give him a small grin and his eyes meet mine.

That's when Vanessa, Kelsey, and Colton enter the courtyard. Kelsey stops dead when she sees me sitting with Jack.

"What?" she mouths at Jack. He stiffens as his friends saunter over. Colton and Vanessa are bickering.

"Any idiot can be on *The Price is Right*," Colton says. "*Jeopardy!* shows that you're smart."

"But you get to spin the big wheel on *Price is Right*," Vanessa says.

"I wish they could incorporate that wheel into *Jeopardy!*" Colton muses, biting into his burger.

"You guys remember Savannah, right?" Jack asks. "She works on my farm. We were just going over some business."

Once Kelsey hears that, she stops glaring at me and turns her attention to her cell phone, glancing up at Jack a couple times. Vanessa smiles but can't get a word in, because Colton launches into a speech about how, if he were to go on *Jeopardy!*, he'd bet it all and make it a true Daily Double.

"Listen, I wanted to talk to you about Star," Jack says to me. "Do you have any idea what's wrong with him?"

"No," I lie, remembering how Star got upset when Jack came around. I don't want to say anything until I'm sure I'm right.

Jack pops another fry in his mouth. "Tomorrow before school, before you exercise Star, can we try gate training him again?"

"Yes, sir." The words are out of my mouth before I can stop myself.

"Smart ass," Jack says with a grin. "Stop calling me sir. For real."

Kelsey glances up from her phone, looking at me as if I said I love doing homework. "You call him sir?"

"Yes, ma'am," I snap, and she turns her focus back to her phone. Jack covers a grin by sneaking another bite of my sandwich. I yank it away. "Give me that!"

I bite my lip, excited about the prospect of hanging out with him tomorrow morning. I tell myself it's only business. But if it's only business, then why are all these girls giving me dirty looks because I'm sitting with Jack?

My heart can flutter all it wants—that's not gonna change the fact that Jack is not in my league. How could we ever have a good working relationship if I were to let him have his way with me, and then things go back to the same ole same ole?

I steal one more of his fries, just to show him who's boss.

• • •

Dad and Cindy want to take me out to dinner tonight to celebrate my first day of senior year. Neither of my parents got a high school degree, so this is a big deal for me. Of course, Dad's idea of "going out to dinner to celebrate" is not the same as mine.

"Really?" I ask, as we park in the dumpy parking lot of a dive diner called Foothills.

"I said the same thing, Shortcake," Cindy says, making me wince. "I told him we should go to the Cracker Barrel, but your dad never listens to me."

"Do boys ever listen?"

"No," Cindy replies.

Dad tries to hide his grin as we climb out of his ancient truck. "Mr. Goodwin told me Foothills is the best place in town."

The F and the T of the neon sign are burned out, so it looks like we're going to OO HILLS diner. The bell jingles as we open the door. We order coffee and breakfast for dinner, and after we finish eating eggs and bacon that are surprisingly amazing, we pick songs out on our private little jukebox until Dad clears his throat.

He reaches across the table and takes Cindy's hand in his before he speaks. I feel my eyes grow wide at the sight of them holding hands. Holy hell, what's coming?

"Savannah—"

"Are you sick?" I ask quickly, wanting to rip the bandage off.

"No," Dad says. "Why'd you ask that?"

"Mom," I choke out, as my heart races out of control. When my parents told me Mom had cancer, we went to McDonald's as a special treat.

Dad puts an arm around my shoulder and pulls me closer. "I'm not sick," he says quietly, glancing over at Cindy. "It's the exact opposite. We went to the doctor this afternoon for a gender ultrasound."

"Let's order pie and have a toast with our forks," I say, raising a hand to wave down a waitress.

"Shortcake, don't you want to know if it's a boy or a girl?" Cindy asks.

Part of me wants to know, and part of me doesn't. "Whatever it is, we're still getting pie." I wave my arm at the waitress. She's standing behind the counter yapping on her cell phone.

Cindy's face falls and Dad gently curls a hand around the back of my neck.

"Savannah..." Dad's tone brings my attention back to him instead of pie procurement.

"I guess Cindy's gonna need a double order of pie," I say, trying to delay the conversation. If things were different for my family, I wouldn't mind so much that they're having a baby. "So what is it?"

Cindy grins shyly. "It's a girl."

"Oh."

"What's wrong? Talk to me," Dad says, kissing the side of my head.

"I was thinking about tomorrow," I lie, not wanting to discuss the baby. I lightly run my fingers over spilled salt on the sticky table.

"What's tomorrow?" Cindy asks.

"I ate lunch with Jack Goodwin today, and he asked me to work with Star personally on starting gate training."

"And?" Dad asks.

"I said okay. I told Jack I'd meet him first thing."

"Shortcake, there are other boys out there," Cindy says slowly, shaking her head. *Does she have to call me that?*

"It's one thing to work with his horse, but I don't want you around him," Dad says. "I don't want you to upset Mr. Goodwin."

What if they knew he nearly kissed me last night?

Cindy nervously taps her knife on a plate. "Have you been spending time with Jack? At breakfast this morning, I overheard him telling his little sister how much you impress him and that you're a good role model."

A *role model*? Talk about the last thing you want a guy to say about you. "He was talking about me?"

"What's going on with you and Jack?" Dad asks in a rush.

"Nothing," I say, my face flashing hot.

"Shortcake, you know we don't need any drama right now. Not with a baby on the way." How unfair. He's the one who got his girlfriend pregnant.

My mind is all screwed up because I loved eating lunch with Jack, and I like working with him and Star, working toward something together, and I can't sort it out in mind, and I'm gonna have a sister who'll go through the same shit that I've been through—growing up eating the free lunch, not having much for dinner, and wearing yard-sale clothes—and I can't even flirt with Jack without feeling guilty, because Dad and Cindy are having a baby they didn't plan for.

"I'm just helping with Star," I say. "That's all."

"You don't need to work with Star on the gate," Dad says, sipping his coffee. His hand shakes as he sets the cup back on the table. "I'll talk to Jack in the morning and take over Star's training personally if he's that worried about the colt."

"Dad, it's okay. I can handle it...Can we get some pie over here?" I call out.

The waitress finally hangs up her phone, and soon we're toasting my new sister over rhubarb pie.

If pie only cured confusion.

• • •

The next morning I meet Jack at Greenbriar barn at 5:00 a.m. The sun is just starting to peek over the horizon, and the grass is still damp with dew.

"Morning," he says, tipping his hat, giving me a grin that makes my palms go sweaty.

Along with Star, we bring Mr. Goodwin's stallion Lucky Strikes with us to the gate. This horse won the Preakness and the Breeders' Cup a few years back. People who don't know horseracing think the Kentucky Derby is the most important race in the world, but the Breeders' Cup in California attracts the best horses of all. It had a $5 million purse last year.

"Tie Lucky Strikes to that hitching post," I say.

I hand Jack two bags full of baby carrots and sliced apples; then I mount Star and steer him to the starting gate. He whinnies, his ears go flat, and he backs up. I rub his neck and comb his hair, murmuring nonsense to him. "It's okay," I say quietly. "It's just a gate. It's not scary. It's okay."

I pat his neck again. "Jack, come in here quietly, shut the gate behind you, and climb up next to me."

Soon he's standing on the side of the gate, resting a hand on Star's head. Star is going crazy, whipping his head around every which way, banging against the stall.

"Feed him an apple slice," I call out, and Jack follows my orders. Star munches on his apple. "Feed him another," I say again, holding the reins steady.

"God, you're a taskmaster."

"Feed him another."

"It's cramped in here," Jack says loudly, wiping sweat off his face.

"Remind me never to work on a submarine," I say, both overwhelmed and intoxicated by the smells. This early in the morning before baths, Jack and Star both have their own muskiness going on.

Star won't stop snorting, so I decide to take an extreme course of action. "Star!" I transfer the reins to one hand and grab Jack's hand with the other.

"What the—" Jack gazes down at our linked hands and glances around, as if making sure we're alone.

"See, Star? Jack's my friend. Be nice."

We stay inside the gate, holding hands, until Star's breathing calms down and he's still. I think I've bored the hell out of the horse.

"That's probably enough," I say. "Let us out of the gate, and now we'll do the same thing with Lucky Strikes while Star watches."

Back outside the gate, I call for an exercise rider to mount Lucky Strikes and ride him into the gate. I stand with Star, feeding him apples and carrots, while Lucky Strikes moves in and out of the gate, over and over. Then I feed both Star and Lucky Strikes apples out of my palm, loving how their lips tickle my hand.

"Did you get your training style from your dad?" Jack asks.

I nod. "Dad always says that horses learn by watching other horses. And all guys love food, right?" I hold up the bag of carrots and apples.

"True."

I wipe sweat off my forehead with the back of my hand. "I need to exercise Star before school."

Jack smiles and nods. "Thanks again."

I take Star out on the racetrack and ease him into a jog, thinking of how patient and kind Jack was this morning. At Gael's signal, I bring the colt to a full gallop and race him around the track, waiting for the speed to make my brain go numb.

• • •

After the workout, I pull my gloves and helmet off and look up to find Jack standing beside the clocker's tower with a mug of coffee. "Two sugars and cream?"

I set my helmet and gloves on the ground, take the cup, wrap both hands around it, and sip slowly. "It's perfect."

He smiles. "I thought Cindy was lying to me. She didn't seem happy when I asked her how you take your coffee."

"She didn't lie to you," I say, sipping again.

"I figured you might like it black or something. Black for a badass girl."

I give him a look. "Well, thanks, I think."

Jack's hounds circle around us as we walk back to the house arguing about black coffee versus coffee with delicious sugars and creams until he reaches for my elbow. "Listen," he says quietly, turning me to face him as we reach Hillcrest. He places a hand above my shoulder against the house. My heart bangs against my chest. "I want to say thank you for helping me. It means a lot to me."

I should tell him that he has a huge staff of people willing to do anything for him, because the Goodwins pay them, but somehow I know he considers what we did this morning more personal than regular ole work. He smiles, and I find myself staring at his lips.

Then Yvonne waddles up with a laundry basket under her arm and Jack tries to take it off her hands, but she swats at him. "Don't even think about it." She wags her finger at him, and then motions for him to lean down so she can kiss his cheek. Then she kisses my cheek and heads inside where I can hear her getting on to Cindy for not drinking some special prenatal green tea she concocted. Jack and I laugh at Yvonne together.

"Anyway," Jack says. "I have to finish balancing the accounts before school."

He takes off for the manor house, and I sip my coffee. Mmm. Perfect.

• • •

I shower and dress for school, and while I'm sitting at the table trying to finish my stupid geometry homework, the maid bell starts ringing. Cedar Hill has several bells that date back to the Civil War. Each bell indicates if one of the Goodwins needs something. The chef bell, for food or coffee; the maids', for laundry, bedding, or cleaning issues; the gardener, for gardening issues.

You know, in case there's an emergency gardening issue.

The maid bell ringing doesn't make any sense—none of the maids are down here right now. They're making beds and serving breakfast and doing other things maids do. Then the phone rings. "Savannah," Cindy says in a weak voice.

"Is something wrong with the baby?" I rush to ask.

"I'm not feeling my best…I'm so tired," she replies. "I need … Paula up to work breakfast instead of me."

… nbered it's her day off."

… fore school—"

ts

eath.

"No, no," Cindy says. "Mrs. Goodwin doesn't like it when the help track mud in the house."

"I've already changed clothes." I peek down at the pink Converse Dad gave me for Christmas last year. "I'm coming."

I jog up to the manor house and barrel into the kitchen. Cindy's sitting at the island, wiping sweat off her face. Jodi, the Goodwins' chef, is frying an omelet and writing down notes at the same time.

"I can't serve breakfast," Cindy says, on the verge of tears. "I don't know how I'm gonna make it another four months. I'm so tired."

"You should take some time off."

"I need the money," Cindy whispers, shaking her head. "You know I need a root canal and I won't be able to afford it for a long time and I want to buy your little sister clothes and start a savings account and—"

"Shhh," I say soothingly. She Who Must Not Be Named should be able to take time off if she needs to. But with Dad still paying off Mom's medical bills, having enough money to take time off seems like a fantasy. What the hell are we gonna do after she gives birth?

"Jodi? What do I do?" I ask in a harsh tone.

"Refill their coffee. Mr. Goodwin drinks his black. So does k. Mrs. Goodwin drinks tea. Shelby likes hot cocoa with l hipped cream, so make sure she has enough."

ickly wash my hands in the sink and take a deep b

"Come back to grab Shelby's omelet," Jodi says.

I tie on an apron and grab the coffeepot before striding into the dining room. A chandelier hangs above the table made of a deep cherry wood. Sunlight illuminates the room through the floor-to-ceiling windows. Shelby is doing the word search in today's paper. Mr. and Mrs. Goodwin look up at me.

"Short-staffed today," I say, holding up the coffeepot.

Mr. Goodwin sets his paperwork down. "Is everything okay?"

"Cindy's a little under the weather. She's really tired. And Paula has the day off."

"Oh, of course," Mr. Goodwin says, returning to his papers. He's reading printouts of the *Daily Racing Form*. Dad and I read it every day so we can stay up-to-date on the best horses and jockeys and their news.

"Welcome to the team," Mrs. Goodwin says, toasting me with her teacup.

"Thank you, ma'am," I say. I saw her at the races on Sunday, but this is the first time she's spoken to me. I can see where Jack and Shelby get their good looks from—Mrs. Goodwin is exquisite.

Jack chooses that moment to enter the dining room, looking fresh in a pair of dark jeans, cowboy boots, and an Oxfor button-down shirt with the sleeves rolled up to the elbows course. His hair is still wet from the shower.

He sees me standing there and stops moving. Avoids God. This is the most. Embarrassing. Moment. Ever his mother's cheek before taking a seat and placing a napkin on his lap.

"Morning, sweetie," Mrs. Goodwin says to him, smiling as she sips from her teacup. Then she goes back to sorting through the pile of mail in front of her. It's probably invitations to charity balls, political fundraisers for her brother who's the governor of Alabama, and cocktail parties, or it's about her cookbook.

Apparently every year she develops recipes for a special cookbook—*Entertaining with the Goodwins: Prizewinning Recipes from Prizewinning Cedar Hill Farms*. She sells them for charity. We have a copy on the Hillcrest common room coffee table.

I move to pour hot coffee into Jack's cup. Dear God, don't let me spill.

"You know," he says under his breath. "Just because I brought you coffee doesn't mean you had to bring some to me."

I freeze as Mr. and Mrs. Goodwin exchange glances with each other. I move to pour coffee in Mr. Goodwin's cup, but he puts a hand over it.

"I'm fine. I've had enough."

Jack selects a muffin from the breadbasket. "Dad, I'm selling he Big Society yearling."

"To who?"

ushy Branch Farms in Georgia. Got Paulsen up to $320,000."

d boy," Mr. Goodwin says with a smile, making Jack glow with pride.

Jack sorts through the mail at his place setting. He opens an envelope and pulls out a card. The embossed initials on the paper read AW.

"Crap," Jack mutters, dropping the card on the table.

"What is it, dear?" his mother asks.

"It's just a card from Abby Winchester. I saw the AW on the front and thought it was about A&W Root Beer."

"You goof," Shelby says.

"I love root beer," he replies, sounding sad and overly emotional about root beer. Boys.

Mr. Goodwin opens his mouth, presumably to talk about AW of the Abby Winchester variety, not the root beer, so I go back into the kitchen. Jodi hands me a tray loaded up with the omelet, little bowls of something I don't recognize, and another basket of scones and muffins. I reenter the dining room to another interesting conversation.

"I want pink streaks in my hair," Shelby says as she licks hot cocoa off her upper lip.

Mrs. Goodwin sets her letter opener down. "No."

"C'mon! I want pink hair for my birthday! Carla got blue streaks and Whitney has purple streaks and I think I would look good with pink!"

"No," her parents say simultaneously. Mr. Goodwin never looks up from the *Daily Racing Form*.

I put a bowl at each spot. It looks like some sort of wonderful egg casserole bacon mash-up? I bet it totally rocks the socks off the Fruit Loops I had for breakfast.

"Dear," Mrs. Goodwin says to Jack, "what do you think of the cheese grits brûlée?"

He shovels it into his mouth, talking with his mouth full. "Delicious."

She claps. "You're not just saying that?"

Jack looks like a goddamned bulldozer scooping it up. I'd say he likes it.

"Trust us. It's wonderful," his father says, glancing up from his paperwork to smile.

"Maybe try adding some sour cream to the grits," Jack says.

"I'll tell Jodi," Mrs. Goodwin replies, nodding as she writes a note about sour cream. "Can you look over the draft cookbook again after school?" she asks Jack.

"Of course," he says. "I hope you added the surf 'n' turf option like I suggested."

He helps with the cookbook? Who knew? I thought his activities consisted of:

1. Womanizing
2. Thinking about horses
3. Torturing me

Now that they've been served, I hover between the kitchen and the dining room, waiting on everybody to finish. Mrs. Goodwin goes with Shelby to help her get ready for school, leaving Jack alone with his dad. I'm about to leave to go finish my math homework when I hear my name. I feel guilty for eavesdropping, but I can't help it.

"What were you doing with Savannah Barrow this morning?" Mr. Goodwin asks.

"Trying to get Star used to the starting gate," Jack replies.

"Is that all you were doing?"

"Yeah, I swear."

I peek around the corner to see Jack taking a gigantic bite of muffin, so big it looks like he might choke. I lean up against the wall, making sure to keep out of sight.

"It doesn't look good when a businessman dates his staff. Or uses them for any other activities."

A pause. "Savannah had some ideas for training Star, that's all."

"Anything new?"

"Not really. Same stuff we usually do."

"Did it work this morning?"

"The horse seemed calmer than usual. He's been clocking excellent times during his workouts. Savannah just knows how to control him."

"Don't get your hopes up that Savannah can make a difference with the horse. I haven't decided if she's talented. I still think you should sell Star."

I breathe in and out, suddenly panting. *Please don't sell Star. Please don't sell Star.* He might end up with a cruel owner. Just like Moonshadow. *Please don't sell Star. I can't bear to lose one more thing.*

Mr. Goodwin says, "Don't forget, we have that dinner tonight. I'll have Yvonne get a suit ready for you."

I peek around the corner one more time to find Jack rubbing his eyes. He sighs, picks up the *Daily Racing Form* papers, and stands as he chugs the rest of his coffee.

Jack didn't stand up for me when his father questioned my talent. I guess it's not surprising. I just started working as an exercise rider here. I haven't proven myself.

I slowly take off my apron.

• • •

Out the kitchen window I watch as Jack's big shiny red Ford truck coasts down the driveway toward the main gate. I pull a deep breath and walk back into the dining room where Mr. Goodwin is poring over *The Tennessean.*

"Sir?"

His head pops up and he smiles. "Yes, Savannah?"

"May I have a quick word?"

"Of course." He folds the newspaper, places it next to his empty bowl, and looks up at me expectantly.

"I'm sorry Cindy wasn't here to serve breakfast this morning. She's normally not a flake—it's just she wasn't feeling well and

I'm sure it won't happen again. I know we haven't made a good impression our first week here. I hope you won't take it out of her paycheck since I worked—"

He waves a hand. "No big deal. I understand you've got a new little brother or sister on the way?"

"A sister, yes, sir."

"How are you liking living here? Is your bedroom okay? Everyone treating you nice down in Hillcrest?"

The paint is peeling off my bedroom walls, but Dad said we can wait until we've been here awhile to fix that. "Everything's great, sir. I mean, except for that Yvonne won't let me wash my own clothes."

"Join the club." He smiles. "Anything else? You probably need to be getting on to school."

I toe the fancy Persian rug with my pink Converse. "Sir, I was wondering. My dad and Cindy have a whole lot going on. Lots of bills and debts and stuff."

"Yes," Mr. Goodwin says slowly, narrowing his eyes.

"I'm wondering…since Cindy will need to take more time off for the baby, can you please keep my paychecks instead of docking it from hers? At least until the baby is born?"

"If that's what you want. But I wish you'd save it for yourself instead." Mr. Goodwin studies my face. "Let your father handle his debts."

"I want to do this." *I won't let my little sister grow up like I did.*

"I'll make it happen." A sly grin forms on Mr. Goodwin's face. "Tell me something, Savannah. Do you know what's wrong with Tennessee Star?"

"I've got a possible idea, yes, sir."

It surprises me when Mr. Goodwin doesn't quiz me further. Instead, he winks. "Can't wait to see if you're right at the race this Saturday."

Blinded by Inspirational Posters

The evil Coach Lynn is making us run laps around the track in gym class. It's eighty gazillion degrees outside and my arms and legs feel like Silly Putty by lap three.

Vanessa Green slows way down so she can run beside me. "Wow, you're in dead last," she says. "I guess your horse-riding skills don't translate to running."

I swipe sweat from my upper lip. "Yeah, totally different muscle groups."

"I hate gym," Vanessa says, wiping sweat off her brow.

"Really? Isn't your brother like the best athlete ever? Like Superman or something?" He's in the NFL.

"Don't let him hear you call him Superman. Ty's head's already big enough since he started dating Gabriella Marsden."

"The supermodel?"

"Yeah, she has nothing interesting to talk about though. It's like he went to a supermodel factory and said 'I'll take that one please. The one with the extra-long legs and the big boobs and the hair that falls past her butt.'"

We laugh together, and at that moment, Jack and Colton sprint by. Jack turns, bows, and says, "Ladies," before streaking off again, his long hair flopping in the wind. He's so hot, my breath catches in my throat and I cough.

"You think he's cute?" Vanessa asks.

"Who doesn't?"

She shrugs. "He's hot, but he's not my type. He's too pretty."

I laugh at the irony. The most beautiful girl at school doesn't want the beautiful boy.

"Hey," Vanessa starts. "Do you know if Rory Whitfield is dating anybody?"

"I don't think he is."

"Oh…I wondered if you and him…?"

"Naw. Why?"

"Just wondering…" She gazes across the track. Rory and Jack are now racing each other, trying to be King of Gym Class. "He's cute."

"But you're like, *you*, and he's Rory—he's my friend, and you could date whoever you want and I don't want him to get hurt and you're super popular," I say, flustered as hell.

"So?" she says.

"Would that supermodel be dating your brother if he weren't an NFL quarterback?"

Her nose crinkles. "Who knows? Who am I to decide something like that? If you like somebody, you just like them, you know?"

"Do you really like Rory?" I ask.

"I'm not sure. I mean, I've known him forever, but it's not like I've thought about getting to know him better and kissing him or whatever…until lately, I guess."

"I'm sure he's thought about it," I say, and Vanessa flashes me an excited grin.

"Really? What'd he say?"

I laugh. "He hasn't said anything to me. It's just the way he looks at you."

"Good to know. Thanks," she says, and we finish running our laps together. On the last lap, Colleen and Jaime, these snotty girls, run by and give me strange looks.

"Bitches," Vanessa says.

"Bitches," I agree.

We bump fists and head into the locker room to change clothes. I've never been all that great at making girlfriends, but I like Vanessa. I smile over at her as I pull my gym bag from my locker.

Crazy that she's interested in Rory, considering they come from very different lives. What will the other kids say when they hear about this? Will they wonder why Vanessa would date a farmhand?

That's when it hits me: even if other people had a problem with it, Vanessa wouldn't give a damn. I wish I could get away with not giving a damn.

• • •

After study hall in the library, I drag my fingers across locker doors on my way to the art room.

I discover Colton fast asleep on the sofa outside the guidance counselor's office. Vanessa wasn't kidding that he likes to sleep. When I look at the wall above the couch, I'm blinded by inspirational posters: CONFIDENCE, WINNING, COURAGE, TEAMWORK, DESTINY, CHARACTER.

Oh, my eyes. Why can't there be an inspirational poster for BADASS?

Thinking about Rory and his dreams of going to college, I open a pamphlet about the ACT. I scan the information, reading about upcoming test dates and facilities and—

Shit.

Just taking the test costs $50.05! Why is *nothing* free? Or at least cheap! How are poor people supposed to plan for the damned future if everything costs so damned much? How can Rory afford the testing costs plus the application fees?

And what the hell is the five extra cents for?

I slip the pamphlet back in its slot and turn away, and run smack into Jack. He's drinking a Capri Sun and carrying a blue camping cooler.

"Yvonne packed you an entire cooler?" I ask, giving my Velcro bag a dirty look.

He grins. "Sure did. She gave me string cheese. And a juice pouch!" He toasts me with the Capri Sun.

I shove his chest. "She gave you string cheese!"

"I might have one left," he says with a wink.

"I want it!"

"You wouldn't share your roast beef with me yesterday."

"Yeah, well, you ate half of it anyway."

"What were you looking at?" Jack asks, nodding at the wall of brochures. "Deciding when to take the ACT?"

"Oh, um, no—"

"Did you already take it? I've taken it twice but I'm gonna take it again because Dad thinks I can do better," Jack says, sipping his juice pouch.

"I haven't taken it."

"You can borrow my study guides if you want. I've got a whole box of them."

"I'm not taking the test."

"You're taking the SAT then?"

"No…I'm not applying anywhere, so there's no reason to take the tests."

"But what about college?" Jack asks.

"Why would I go to college? I can work as an exercise rider and make plenty of money. You have to, like, pay for college."

"But don't you want more?" Jack asks, furrowing his eyebrows.

"I do. That's why I applied to be an exercise rider. Plus, a high school degree is worth a lot."

Jack stares at me for a long time, sucking on his Capri Sun.

"Are you going to college?" I ask.

He looks shocked at my question. "Yeah. Probably nearby, so I can keep an eye on the farm. Maybe Vanderbilt. I'm gonna major in business and get my MBA, like my dad did."

At my old school in Charles Town, only about half the graduates ended up going to college. The rest went on to work at the casino or a hotel, or got married.

Jack continues, "I have no idea why you wouldn't go to college."

I suck in air through my nose, dumbfounded that he doesn't understand how little money I have. Is he clueless?

"My family could never afford it." Hell, Cindy can't afford to take one morning off work. Not to mention the root canal she needs.

He sips from his Capri Sun again. "Don't your parents want more for you?"

"My dad's really proud I've made it this far. I mean, he doesn't have a high school degree or anything…neither he or Cindy went to college, and no one in their families have ever been…My mom died, you know?"

A sad smile crosses his face. "Yeah, my father told me. We were really sorry to hear about that…What was she like?"

I swallow the lump in my throat and blink tears away. "Well, she sang when she vacuumed. She was a real bad singer. Like, worse than the horrible singers on *American Idol*." Jack laughs with me. "And she made Mickey Mouse pancakes every Sunday morning. She loved history."

"I'm sorry I didn't get to meet her," Jack says softly, gazing down at me.

The bell for fifth period rings. Jack reaches into his cooler and whips out the last string cheese and hands it to me before taking off down the hall.

I peel the plastic off the cheese, put it between my teeth, and yank it away, chewing.

• • •

After school, I spend a good hour grooming Star and feeding him, and then I decide to walk to the very edge of Cedar Hill and skirt the lake over to Whitfield Farms. I climb the fence and walk past cows and pigs and ducks and other animals up to Rory's farmhouse. I ring the doorbell, he lets me in, and we go to his room. His dog Ava is lounging on the rug, panting with her tongue hanging out.

Old movie posters cover his walls. It seems all posters in his room must feature one or all of the following:

1. An explosion
2. A woman's cleavage
3. George Clooney

Rory flops down on the floor and resumes playing some crazy racecar game called *Ho Down in Hoochieville,* where he drives around and picks up hookers.

Pig.

I drop onto Rory's bed and sigh. "You've gotta ditch the *Star Wars* bedding if you ever expect to get laid."

"The right girl will accept me, Darth Vader and all," Rory says, thumbing his controller.

Trying to block out images of Sunday night's almost kiss and trying to forget how Jack said I could go to college—which further proves he and I will never work out—I cuddle with Rory's Chewbacca stuffed animal and watch him play his video game that is effectively setting women's rights back a hundred years.

"I heard you ate lunch with Jack yesterday," Rory says.

"It was more like he wanted to steal my roast beef sandwich."

"I'd bet $20 that you'll hook up with him within a month."

I fall backward onto Rory's pillow, thinking about the past few days. Jack could be a first-class womanizer who's way out of my league...but he has a soft side. He calls his sister sweetheart and helps his mom with her cookbook. He brought me coffee just the way I like it. But I won't be one of the supposed one-night stands the maids talk about. Hell, he could've hooked up with both Kelsey and Abby last weekend, and that was after flirting with me! But he's so nice...and he wasn't paying all that much attention to Kelsey at lunch...

"You're on. That'll be an easy $20. I'm not gonna hook up with him," I say.

Rory pauses his game. "Just be careful. He won't give you the kind of relationship you deserve."

My friend is telling the truth, but embarrassment washes over me nevertheless.

"Well, just for that, I'm not gonna tell you the great gossip I've got on you, Ror."

"Me?" He starts playing his game again. "Did someone tell you how I acted out a scene from *Call Me When Your Mom Is Back in Town*—"

"No, no," I say. "Somebody likes you."

"God, I wish we could send that girl to Antarctica or something. I can't stand how Evelyn Treanor stalks me between classes and tries to pinch my butt. Who does that—"

"It's not Evelyn."

Rory's pimp character picks up a hooker in a monster truck. "Who is it then?" he asks, sideswiping a pimpmobile.

"Vanessa Green."

He drops his controller and whips around, his mouth falling open. On the screen, his monster truck runs into a 7-11, flinging a bunch of bystanders into the air and causing a massive explosion.

"Bullshit."

"Nope. Should I talk to her or anything?"

Rory pulls his bottom lip between his teeth. "I'm interested, but you don't have to say anything. I'll handle it myself."

"What are you gonna do?"

"I dunno," Rory replies with a shrug. He pushes his bangs off his forehead. "I'll just wait and see what happens."

But doesn't he want to be in control of something like this? Doesn't he want to put himself out there?

"Would you take her to dinner or something?" I ask. "A girl like that—you gotta take her somewhere fancy in Nashville, not Tennessee Ballers. Where are you gonna get the money for a date like that?"

"I'd find the money."

He abandons the hooker game to stand and pace around the room, pausing to check his floppy brown hair in the mirror. I love that Rory says he'd find the money. It's black and white for him: if he wants to take a girl on a fancy date, he'll find a way to make it happen.

Would Jack ever take a risk for me?

An Honorable Man

"Shit."

Jodi, the Goodwins' chef, is pacing back and forth across the Hillcrest common room. Cindy still isn't feeling well. She's lying on the couch while Dad massages her feet and makes her drink water. He thinks she's dehydrated. The other bad news is that we're short-staffed for Mr. Goodwin's fancy dinner party tonight.

If Cindy calls out of work sick tonight, it sure won't make our family look good. It would truly suck if Dad lost his new job.

"Mom, let me help," Ethan, Jodi's thirteen-year-old son, says. "What can I do?"

"If you owned a tux maybe you could serve," Jodi replies.

"Let me take Cindy's place," I interrupt, standing up.

Everyone stares at me. Working in the kitchens during a fancy Goodwin dinner is the last thing I want to do, but I can't let Cindy get fired.

"You can be a server," Jodi says, nodding at me. "Just follow Paula's lead and you'll be fine."

"I'm so sorry," Cindy says to me, clutching her stomach. Dad gives me a kind smile, looking grateful as he places his hand over Cindy's.

"It's not a problem," I say, but it is. I can't imagine serving Jack twice in one day.

Cindy loans me one of her maid uniforms, because unlike at breakfast, I have to put my Goodwin game face on. The blue dress hangs below my knees and if I look straight down, I can see my bra.

Super embarrassing. God, why did Dad have to get Cindy pregnant?

Up at the manor house, Ethan is helping his mom plate the salads while Mr. and Mrs. Goodwin greet their guests in the parlor. Paula is filling carafes with wine. Jack is hiding out in the kitchen, sneaking bites of everything Jodi is cooking. He pops a shrimp in his mouth and she smacks his hand. "For the third time, get out of my kitchen!" Ethan and I crack up when Jack steals a piece of cornbread behind Jodi's back.

Jodi hands me a water pitcher and tells me to go fill the glasses in the dining room. I pour water into a glass and I'm moving on to the next place setting when a handsome guy I've never seen before stumbles through the doorway. He appears to be twenty or so. His black suit, blazing red tie, and shiny shoes just scream *power*.

"Where's the goddamned bathroom?" he says.

"Down the hall to your left," I reply quietly, taken aback by his behavior. I start toward the kitchen to see what else Jodi needs me to do but he takes me by the elbow and turns me around. I smell alcohol on his breath.

"I'm Marcus Winchester." He puffs his chest out like he's more important than Prince William then scans my body. "I can't believe the Goodwins keep you hidden away."

You have got to be kidding me.

"Excuse me," I say, cradling the water pitcher against my chest, and try to head toward the kitchen, but he doesn't let go of my arm.

He looks down at my uniform, well, more specifically, down my dress, because it's way too big.

I have a sudden urge to throw this water on Marcus—but if I do that, my dad and Cindy might get fired and we would have to leave before the baby is born and we might not find more work and where would we live and oh holy God—help.

"I'm needed in the kitchen."

"You're needed here." Marcus laughs softly, squeezing my arm harder. "Don't you want a kiss? I'll give you another chance, even though a bad girl like you doesn't deserve my forgiveness."

Who the hell does he think he is?

Marcus leans in and I'm debating whether or not to toss the water on him when Jack appears in the doorway.

"Jack," I blurt.

Marcus releases my arm and I step away, panting, my tongue heavy and dry. I shake my head at Jack, trying to show him that Marcus is the last thing I want.

"Marcus, meet Savannah. She's one of my good friends," Jack says with the hint of a threat in his voice.

I step away, my hands shaking as I continue pouring water into glasses. I breathe in and out. It's only a couple hours. I can handle a couple of hours. My hands go from shaky to earthquaky in a matter of seconds and I can't imagine how pissed Mrs. Goodwin will be if I drop this glass pitcher on her hardwood floor.

"You're friends with your servants?" Marcus asks, raising his eyebrows. His eyes are red and hazy. "My servants clean my toilet."

Jack grabs Marcus's elbow. "C'mon, we've got a great bourbon collection you should see."

A minute later, Jack reappears by my side and takes the water pitcher from my hands.

"Did Marcus hurt you?" he murmurs, placing the pitcher on a sideboard.

I hate that Marcus questioned whether Jack could be friends with a servant like me. And all I can think about is how Jack looked at me today when he found out I'm not going to college. Like I'm this pathetic little bee, swarming around, with no thoughts and dreams of my own. Marcus Winchester and his I'm-a-rich-person-so-I-can-do-whatever-I-want attitude reminds me of horrible Mr. Cates.

"Why would you invite such a Neanderthal to dinner?" I ask.

"Dad's working on a business deal with his father." Jack pulls a handkerchief out of his suit pocket and dabs it on my face, and I cover his hand with mine, searching his eyes. It feels nice being comforted by him, and I wish I could stay in this moment, but I can't. I'm pissed.

"So it's okay if Marcus humiliates me because your dad does business with his father? That sucks."

Jack's face drops and he furrows his eyebrows. He takes his hand off my face then walks around the table and finishes pouring water into each glass. Him taking over my chore is a nice concession, but can that really make up for what happened?

"You don't have to do that," I say.

"I know," Jack replies. "But Dad's always harping on me about how I should learn to do stuff for myself before college starts."

"Is that why he tried to teach you how to do laundry?"

"You heard about that, huh?" He leans around the flower arrangement to grin at me.

"I hear everything," I say, sniffling into his handkerchief. It smells like him. "The maids gossip about you all the time in Hillcrest."

"Oh yeah, like what?"

"I heard about the walk through the rose garden with the country singer and you picking thorns out of your—"

"I've been looking for you, son." Mr. Goodwin appears in the dining room wearing a gray suit like Jack's. "I want you to talk to

George about business school—" He gazes from me to the water pitcher in Jack's hands. "What's going on here?"

I hold my breath and bite down on the handkerchief.

Jack lays a hand on his father's shoulder and speaks quietly to him. I hear the words "Marcus" and "dickhead."

"Are you okay?" Mr. Goodwin asks me.

"Yes, sir." I nod quickly.

"Do you wish to be relieved? I'm sure we can find someone else to serve us."

"No, sir. I'm fine." *Cindy needs the money.*

"Good. Why don't you head back into the kitchen to see if Jodi needs anything."

It's not like I expected Mr. Goodwin to throw Marcus out of the house, not with a big business deal with Marcus's father on the line, but I can't help feeling a tiny bit betrayed anyway. But this is how our world works—rich people like Marcus and Jack can do as they want, while people like me serve them coffee and hope they will treat us nicely.

I leave the dining room and hide in the same cranny I did this morning to calm down, but also to hear what else they say in case they mention selling Star again.

"I see the way you look at Savannah," I hear Mr. Goodwin saying quietly.

What?! How does Jack look at me?

Mr. Goodwin goes on, "You better not do that tonight during

dinner. You know how much I want this deal with Winchester… and I'd rather you not piss off his daughter by being more interested in Savannah than her."

"I know Dad…Savannah and I…we've just been working on a school project together."

Lies.

"And that's it?"

"Yes, sir."

"What's this project?"

A long pause. "We have to tell the school where we want to be in five years."

"And where do you want to be?"

"Getting my MBA and working for you. I hope I'll have a winning horse by then."

"What else?" Mr. Goodwin asks.

Jack pauses for several seconds. "When you were my age, where did you want to be in five years?"

I peek around the corner to see Mr. Goodwin checking his tie in the window reflection. "In a woman's bed, I imagine."

Jack laughs. "That's where I want to be in five years too."

"I dare you to write that on your project." Mr. Goodwin straightens Jack's blue tie and dusts his shoulders off. "Please be on your best behavior tonight. Don't eat all the bread before anyone else gets any, okay?"

"You're a cruel man, Dad."

"No, I just really like Jodi's bread."

I rush to the kitchen, breathing in and out. I set the water pitcher down and bury his handkerchief in my apron pocket. *Forget about him, Savannah.*

• • •

I'm cradling a wine carafe as everyone files into the dining room.

Mrs. Goodwin and Mrs. Winchester are wearing chic suits, and Abby Winchester and Shelby look straight out of a movie with their sparkly cocktail dresses. My awful blue maid's uniform makes me want to jump out the window. A man with stark white hair, Mr. Winchester seems like one of those guys whose ego fills an entire room. Jack steps forward to shake his hand. "It's good to see you, sir."

"I'm sorry we didn't get a chance to speak in Cincinnati the other day." The man searches Jack's face and fiercely squeezes his hand. Looks painful.

"I was busy with my horse," Jack says.

Mr. Winchester sips his drink. Looks like he's been checking out the famous bourbon collection. "I'm sorry he lost. He should've won, considering his pedigree. Sometimes the breeding doesn't work out like we hope it will."

Embarrassment stains Jack's face redder than the wine I'm holding. Mr. Winchester drops his hand and Jack moves to pull out Abby's seat and helps her to sit down. She smiles at him over her shoulder as he scoots her chair in. She really is pretty, and elegant, but she looks breakable, like one of Cindy's angel figurines.

I fill wine glasses while Mr. Goodwin and Mr. Winchester start talking business. Marcus makes eyes at me from the other side of the table.

"I'm looking forward to your sister's birthday party this weekend," Abby says quietly to Jack. "Maybe we'll have a chance to explore your farm? Alone?"

"I don't know if we should do that," Jack says slowly. "Not alone."

"Oh? Why not?"

"Well, um." He pauses to cough. "It's haunted."

I purse my lips so I won't burst out laughing. Cedar Hill is *not* haunted.

"Whose ghost is it?" Abby asks.

"Um, there are three ghosts?" Jack says.

"Three. Hmm." She playfully narrows her eyes at him.

"Yeah, there's a woman in a white dress. Um, her name is Moaning Myrtle."

"You stole that from *Harry Potter*."

"Damn," he mutters.

She glances over at Mr. Goodwin and Mr. Winchester, who are busy arguing about who makes better trucks: Ford or Chevy. "You could protect me from the ghosts," she says, and leans toward Jack. His face suddenly goes stark white. I was wrong. Maybe we do have ghosts at Cedar Hill.

Is she touching him under the table? Jesus Lord.

"How long have you owned Paradise Park?" Jack rushes to ask Mr. Winchester. His voice sounds squeaky.

Mr. Winchester stirs his cocktail. "The racetrack has been in my family since 1877."

"It's amazing that it hasn't been sold and resold over and over again," Jack says.

Mr. Winchester seems impressed by the observation. "Many tracks do change ownership, yes, but my racetrack is an important part of my heritage."

"Then why do you want to sell it?" Jack asks Mr. Winchester.

He wants to sell Paradise Park! How can he just give up a track that's been in his family for more than century? That's crazy. If Mr. Goodwin suddenly decided to give up Cedar Hill, I'd cart him straight to a psychiatrist.

I pause and stare. Mrs. Goodwin clears her throat and nods her head, indicating I should get back to work. I set the wine bottle on a sideboard and begin helping Paula pass out salads.

Mr. Winchester smiles at Jack. "None of my kids want to take over the business and I want to retire. I want to play golf and spend time with my kids and my grandkids." He reaches out and touches Abby's hand. "I've spent too much of my life away from my family. There's nothing more important."

"I agree," Jack tells Mr. Winchester, and Abby swoons so hard I'm surprised she doesn't melt into a puddle.

I go back into the kitchen to get another bottle of wine and a breadbasket. When I reenter the dining room, Mr. Winchester is speaking again.

"I want my track to go to a family that has integrity," Mr. Winchester goes on. "I want somebody who will treat it as his own and take care of it."

"Yes, sir," Jack says, sneaking a glance at his father. Mr. Goodwin's face is stoic, unmoving.

"Honor is important, wouldn't you say?" Mr. Winchester asks as he shakes his glass, rattling the ice. I can't believe a man like Winchester has honor if he allows his son to treat girls like shit.

Jack looks up at my face before saying, "I agree, sir." Abby sees him looking at me and scrunches her eyebrows together.

"I remember when I met your father," Mr. Winchester says to Jack. "It was at my track, and he was a teenager. Your father kept saying how much he loved Churchill Downs and how he wanted to own his own racetrack. I liked that. And that's why I'm willing to entertain your family's offer for Paradise Park."

I suck down a gasp. Mr. Goodwin and Jack sit there with impassive looks on their faces, quintessential businessmen.

So the business deal is that Mr. Goodwin wants to buy a commercial racetrack. Wow. I can't even imagine owning my own horse and they want to buy an entire track? Is this why Jack has to suck up to Abby Winchester all the time?

What if Mr. Winchester wants Abby to marry Jack, so they can keep Paradise Park in the family, so to speak?

That's when Mr. Winchester snaps his fingers and points at his wine glass. After I've refilled his glass, he doesn't thank me. Marcus gives me a lewd glance, licking his lower lip. Perv.

The Winchesters are the epitome of *rich people*.

How do the maids serve people like these assholes all the time?

• • •

Later that night back in my room, I carefully dig my memory box out from my top dresser drawer, open the lid, and pull out a weathered envelope that's spotted yellow with age. Before she died, my mother wrote me a letter and asked Dad to give it to me on my sixteenth birthday.

She told me how smart and beautiful I am, and that I can do anything I want if I work hard enough, that I can go down in history.

I needed to hear those words after everything that happened today.

All I can think about are Marcus's eyes staring down my dress. Mr. Goodwin basically telling Jack I'm not good enough for him. Why is it, when something bad happens to you, you can never forget about it no matter how much you want to?

When Mr. Cates announced he was selling Moonshadow, I cried and begged Dad to find a way to buy her so she could stay with me. I rode her every day before school and groomed her after. Moonshadow took care of me after Mom died and I helped her move on after her foal got sold. I was her home, and she was mine. Even though Mr. Cates said Moonshadow wasn't worth the cost of grain to feed her, Dad still couldn't afford to buy her.

And then she was gone and later I heard what happened to her…

I shake my head quickly, squeezing my eyes shut.

These terrible memories are branded in me, and every time they pop up in my mind, my body goes cold and clammy and I wish I could yell at somebody.

I wish I could go back in time and demand that Mr. Cates keep Moonshadow, tell him I'll work for free for as long as it takes to save her.

Before I know what I'm doing, I'm running out of Hillcrest in the direction of Greenbriar, ripping through the cool night air. At the barn, I light a lantern and move to the fourth stall on the right. A pair of brilliant brown eyes meet mine. Star keeps his distance until I cluck my tongue, and then he's right there beside me, nuzzling his nose against my neck, zapping the bad memories away.

The Race and a Change of Pace

"You can do better than that! That was complete shit, Barrow. Complete shit!"

Gael shouts at me as I pass the clocker's tower, and I'm grinning like crazy. I steer Star over to them, his hooves crunching the dirt.

"Shut up, Gael. You know that was perfect." Dad shakes his head at my behavior, but Gael laughs. "What was my time?"

"1:43," Dad says, giving me a smile. "Star did really good."

"You hear that, buddy?" I say, rubbing the colt's sweaty neck. Star pins his ears and snorts when Dad reaches out to rub his nose.

My father laughs and shoves the colt's face away from him. "I know why you and Star get along so well. You were a brat just like him when you were a toddler."

I smile as Star jerks his head around. He swishes his tail back and forth.

"Let's get you some food," I tell the horse, clucking my tongue to urge him into a canter, passing the grandstands and the giant green Rolex clock. On the way to the barns, I see Jack standing with his father. His dad writes in a notebook while Jack yawns and checks his watch. Neither of them cheers for me and Star, and that's okay—everyone's getting used to the rapport I have with the horse. We're last week's news.

This week's news is whether Star can get his first win today here at Keeneland. He's running in The Dogwood, a race for horses that haven't won more than two. I'd say he's got a good shot, considering his breeding and all our hard work. The purse is $85,000. This should be easy peasy, considering how well he's run in the past week.

An outrider on an Appaloosa pony comes trotting up to me. She smiles and pats Star's neck as the pony and Star sniff each other.

"He's a beautiful horse," the woman says, letting Star smell the back of her hand. The colt nips at her fingers, acting silly. He nickers and nuzzles her thigh. "A flirt too, huh?"

My eyes narrow. "Not usually."

"Good luck today," the outrider says to Star, and I squeeze the horse's girth with both heels to move us toward the barn.

I meet Dad and Rory there, cool Star down, and help groom the horses before their races. I have a good feeling about today. Keeneland is a beautiful track—it's near the Maker's Mark distillery, and it's nestled in the most beautiful rolling green hills you've ever seen. Scotland can kiss Lexington's ass, that's for sure.

In his job as acting owner of Cedar Hill, Jack entered Lucky Strikes in a race called The Fort Harrod, which has a purse of half a mil. Every time I've seen Jack this week, he's been talking about it, and it's clear he wants to impress his father by taking risks and getting some big wins.

About half an hour before Star's race, Bryant Townsend comes into the stall to see how we're doing. As soon as he steps inside, the horse charges him.

"Whoa!" I yank Star back by the bridle. "No." I pull him over to the window where he can look at the trees.

"I'm beginning to take this personally," Bryant says to Star, tightening his gloves.

"I wouldn't. I think I know what's wrong with him." And considering I've seen horses scared of lawnmowers, bicycles, and dandelions, what I'm about to tell Bryant isn't much of a stretch.

Dad and Rory poke their heads in the stall. "You know why he's skittish?" Dad asks.

"Men freak him out."

Dad's eyebrows shoot straight up. "Hmm...Whitfield, Townsend, get out of here and let Savannah get the horse ready herself. We'll meet you at the paddock."

I feed Star some grain and let him have a bit of water before I throw his saddle and silks over my shoulder and we trek out to the paddock. When I get there, I find Dad talking quietly to Jack.

"Shortcake, tell Jack what you think's wrong with his horse."

"I think he's scared of boys..."

A confused but intrigued look crosses Jack's face. He narrows his eyes at Star.

"Dad, help me get him saddled up," I say, but Jack shakes his head at him, pulls his phone from his pocket, and walks away as he talks. Wow, I never figured Jack would turn away from a problem. Dad keeps his distance as I begin tacking the horse up. I tie his lead to a post and move to his near side to start saddling him. I put his saddle pads on, but Star is becoming increasingly difficult to control without help from a second groom. He starts prancing and acting silly again.

That's when Jack reenters the paddock with Shelby, who's wearing a skirt and leather boots. He beckons me with two fingers. I leave Star tied to the post and go see what they want.

"Did you know Shelby turned thirteen today?"

"I didn't," I reply. "Happy Birthday!"

Her cheeks blush pink. "Thank you."

"And now that she's thirteen, it's time she started working," Jack says, hugging her from behind.

"What? I'm not working on my birthday!"

"Yes, you are."

"You can't make me."

"I'm boss of the farm this year," Jack says.

"If you make me work, I'll tell everyone you still sleep with your little Raggedy Andy doll under your pillow."

The horsemen stop talking. The horses stop moving. Everyone looks at Jack. I burst out laughing along with everybody else.

"Raggedy Andy?" I say.

His cheeks puff like a chipmunk's. "Can you help Savannah, please?" he asks his sister, exasperated. "We really need your help."

"You do?" Shelby asks.

"I think Star hates boys," I say. "And I need help tacking him up."

"Oh. Well, why didn't you just say so, Jack? I figured you wanted me to muck out a stall or something." Shelby sashays over to Star in her skirt.

Other horsemen in the paddock seem amused that a horse owner's daughter is taking charge. Star behaves like a polite gentleman while Shelby and I finish getting him saddled up. And before I know it, it's post time.

Bryant Townsend mounts the horse, and sure enough, Star starts acting like a brat as they trot up to the starting gate.

Jack beckons for me to walk with him up to the finish line. Our fathers and Gael trail behind us, and Shelby returns to the grandstands to sit with her mother.

"Stand with me," Jack says. Then he drops a hand onto my shoulder and squeezes, not taking his eyes off the starting gate.

The gates crash open and the horses erupt into the race. Star comes out clean and charges ahead with the other horses. "Yeah!" Jack screams. The pack makes the first turn together, leaving a wake of brown dust. The field spreads out on the backstretch. Star stays with the lead group as they navigate the far turn.

"You got it, boy!" I yell.

Red Delight streaks to the front of the pack. Getting the Dream falls back into third. Star moves forward into the seventh position. On the straightaway, as they're charging for the finish line, I'm gripping Jack's arm and bouncing up and down.

"Go!" I scream, and I swear, Star looks over at me and kicks it into high gear. He manages to pass Raising the Flag and Mixed Appeal but ends up in fifth place overall. Dammit.

I crouch to the ground, covering my eyes. How could he lose? I kept him calm all the way up until the race. He was happy, he was fed, he was raring to go.

"1:47," I hear Gael saying.

Damn. He added four seconds onto his time. I dig the heels of my hands into my eyes and pray that Mr. Goodwin doesn't make Jack sell Star. Pray, pray, pray.

I feel gentle hands cupping my elbows and pulling me up from the ground. Jack lifts my chin and looks in my eyes. "How much do you weigh?"

My eyebrows pop up. "What? Wh—"

"Just tell me—what do you weigh?"

Why is he asking me this? I know exactly what I weigh (102 pounds), but I won't let on that I care. "I dunno, a hundred pounds or so?"

"Do you have a jockey's license?"

I shake my head.

"Get her an apprentice license," Jack tells Gael. "Start the paperwork tonight."

My mouth drops open.

"No—" Dad starts.

"I want to see what she's got during a real race," Jack interrupts.

"Son, Savannah has no experience—" Mr. Goodwin says.

"She's better than most men," Jack replies. "Do you think I'd allow Gael to put just any exercise boy on my horse? Clearly it's been working out during practice, and that's why Gael and Danny are gonna start training her for real tomorrow morning. I want her trained up and ready to go before Kentucky Downs, understand?"

Kentucky Downs is next week. Oh God.

"But she's a girl," Dad says.

"Girls have been jockeys before," Jack says. "A woman won the Santa Anita Handicap two years ago. And Rosie Napravnik has over a hundred wins."

My heart slams into my chest.

Dad shakes his head. "It's too dangerous and I want more for her—"

"This would be more for her," Jack says, standing up tall. "If she's able to get her license and win a race, she'd get a percentage of the purse."

I've never heard Jack speak so authoritatively. Mr. Goodwin rubs his chin, looking from his son to me.

"Are you just going to stand there?" Dad says to Mr. Goodwin.

"Star is my son's investment and he's in charge. I gave my opinion, but he makes the calls."

"She's my daughter," Dad growls.

"She's getting her license—" Jack says.

"Over my dead body—"

"Stop!" I yell, and the men turn to face me. Boys. They can't even be bothered to ask what I want. "Dad, I'd love to get my license. Riding is what I want to do—"

Dad slaps a scowl on his face. "Savannah—"

"What's wrong with getting a license? I could start training and see if I'm good enough. I want to see Star win."

Gael nods. "I'll do the paperwork today. Since she's over sixteen years old and I'll sponsor her, it won't be a problem to get an apprentice license in a hurry. She can start training first thing in the morning."

Dad says to Jack, "Savannah has no experience and you want her to race a priceless horse—"

"He isn't priceless," Jack says. He's several inches taller than Dad, but my father is smart, quick, and strong, so he doesn't even flinch at Jack's display of Alpha maleness. "I paid a lot for him to be born and I want to see him win some races. I want Savannah trained as a jockey. Go big or go home."

He nods at me, and I bounce on my toes. Racing horses is even better than being a full-time exercise rider. I could fly!

Not to mention I could make a percentage of the purse! I could help Dad pay off debt from Mom's medical bills. I could help give my little sister a better life. I clasp my hands together, excited at the prospect of racing horses for a living. Why have I never thought about this before?

To get a full-blown jockey's license, I think I'll have to race in something like forty races as an apprentice under instruction of a trainer.

"I want you back in the barns right now," Dad says to me in a low voice. "We'll talk about this in private."

I've never seen him so pissed. I turn right around and hightail it toward the barns.

"Savannah!" Jack calls out. "Tomorrow! Five a.m."

Whether Dad likes it or not, I'll be there.

• • •

Back in the barn, I pace back and forth across Star's stall, waiting for Rory to get done hot-walking him.

Dad appears and leads me away from the horses before he rips into me.

"This is way too dangerous to even think about. Isn't being an exercise rider enough for you?" Dad asks, grasping my shoulder.

A few weeks ago, yeah—it was enough. But I never imagined I'd stand by the racetrack and dig into a hot dog beside horse owners. I never imagined Jack would question why I'm not going to college. I never imagined a guy like him might try to kiss me.

"It seems like I should try," I say. "You just said a few minutes ago that you want more for me. Well, this would be."

Dad kisses the top of my head and embraces me tight. "Remember the Derby last year? Seven jockeys got thrown from their horses. Seven! Jockeys die every year. And Aaron Riddle was paralyzed not long ago. He'll be on a respirator the rest of his life. Max Jackson fell off a horse and broke his collarbone, his legs, his arm, and had a brain bleed! Do you know what that would do to me if I saw you like that? I've already seen your mother die—" Dad chokes on his words.

"I get what you're saying. I really do. And I'd hate to hurt you. This sport has never been safe or easy. But when you already have nothing, shouldn't you take a risk to try to find something better?"

"But people get hurt—"

"Those jockeys weren't riding a Goodwin horse," I say, working to keep my voice steady. Cedar Hill Farms isn't located in Tennessee just because. The Franklin area is full of limestone, and it runs into the water supply, and it gives the horses stronger bones. That's why the best horses in the world live in Tennessee and Kentucky.

I go on, "You know Mr. Goodwin would never put an injured horse on the track. That reduces my risk right there. And I'd never get on an injured horse. That's why so many jockeys get hurt—they ride a horse that shouldn't be on the track in the first place. You know that, Dad."

He throws his head back, thinking. He knows I have a point. "I don't know what I'd do if anything happens to you."

I can tell he's thinking of how we lost my mother. But we have to keep moving. I mumble, "This could be good for us. For our future."

His eyes meet mine and he goes very still. "Before we agree to your being trained, I'm gonna talk to Mr. Goodwin about insurance options."

I hug him as hard as I can.

"And we're stopping at Arby's on the way home," he adds.

"Ugh, you know I hate Arby's."

Rory appears with Star and asks, "Did somebody say Arby's?"

I spend the next hour helping to bathe and brush the horses before we set out for home. My whole goddamned life has changed in a day. And I kind of like the high.

The Dance, Truth or Dare, and Beef Jerky

It's Saturday evening and I could be out at a perverted taco restaurant, but I'm hiding behind Shelby's birthday tent. Just call me Super Loser.

When I got home from Keeneland earlier today, a large white tent was set up in the clearing between the racetrack and the manor house. Decorators and servers were busy arranging dishes and flowers and lights.

One section of the tent is decked out like a nightclub, complete with a large neon sign that blinks SHELBY over and over like the window of a liquor store. The tablecloths are black and blue. Middle schoolers are dancing and sliding across the dance floor in their socked feet. A DJ is teaching them to dance.

I salivate when I see the chocolate fountain.

The other half of the tent—the side for adults—is elegant, with silk gold tablecloths, succulent flower arrangements, and a champagne fountain.

Good God, how many food fountains do these people

have? Is there a ranch dressing fountain? Where's the Diet Coke fountain?

If I went to college, would I be the kind of person who gets an invite to a Goodwin party?

Jack is standing on the adult side of the tent, holding a cocktail glass filled with amber-colored liquor. His blond hair is slicked back with gel and it's like he was born to wear that tux. He's talking to an older man, giving him his full attention. I've seen him in the newspaper. I think it's the Tennessee governor.

When Jack finishes speaking with the governor, he looks across the tent. I follow his line of sight to Abby Winchester, who's sitting at a table and staring at Jack. Obviously.

He sets the cocktail glass on a server's tray, rubs his palms together, and heads for Abby. The Fairest of the Fair.

The band begins playing a slow song. Jack leads her out onto the dance floor and pulls her up against his chest. They move fluidly, and unlike me, she clearly knows how to do fancy dances like the waltz. He laughs at whatever she's saying, probably making her feel like she's the only girl at the party. Like how I feel when I'm around him.

My heart pounds so hard it hurts. He said nothing was going on with Abby, but he's dancing so close to her they could share skin. Is a business deal worth that much to him?

I trudge back to the Hillcrest common room and sit down at the computer we all share. I start messaging with Vanessa Green, chatting about Keeneland today, telling her how I'm getting an apprentice jockey's license.

At the same time, I scroll through my Facebook wall. Looks like a few juniors I met this week are going to the Back to School dance tonight in the gym.

Savannah Barrow: are you going to this dance?

Vanessa Green: NOOOO. seniors don't go to the back to school dance. we only go to homecoming, winter wonderland, and prom. homecoming is in October. it's a big deal. Guys ask girls in fancy ways—like last year this super hot senior asked kelsey by hiring an airplane to fly a banner over the school that said, *Kelsey, will you go to Homecoming with me?*

Savannah Barrow: did she say yes?

Vanessa Green: obvs. who wouldn't?

Savannah Barrow: I wish I could go to the Back to School dance.

Vanessa Green: LOL. No you don't.

Savannah Barrow: But I do. Come with me!

Vanessa Green: NO. Are you crazy?

Savannah Barrow: I can get Rory to come...

Vanessa Green: ....I'm in.

Even though Rory's working on a new screenplay, it only takes me about five seconds to convince him to come with us. Two weeks ago, I never could've imagined I'd hang out with a girl like Vanessa Green. I never even considered a girl like her might like my friend.

My life is changing so fast, I wouldn't be surprised to wake up tomorrow to find the sun rising in the west.

• • •

"I'm too old for this shit," Colton says, as we all take off our boots and shoes. It's against the rules to wear them on the gym floor.

When Vanessa told Colton she was coming to the dance with me and Rory, he insisted on coming because his father the Franklin mayor is having a reelection event at their house and Colton hates glad-handing.

Rory mutters to me, "This better be worth it. I was making good progress on my new screenplay, *Tattoos of the Clinically Depressed.*"

"I hate dances," Colton says, lifting his nose in the air like he just smelled a pile of manure.

Vanessa rolls her eyes at Colton. "Go take a nap over there, then," she replies, pointing at the bleachers.

His eyes light up. "Great idea." He hustles over to the bleachers, sits down, leans his head back, crosses his feet and arms, and places his ball cap over his eyes.

"When we first met," Vanessa says, "I asked Colton what his hobbies were, and he replied, 'Sleeping and TV.'"

We laugh together as I take in the scene. "We are definitely the oldest people here."

"We're gonna be wearing Depends undergarments before you know it."

I laugh with her. Rory looks over at us, and when he sees her smiling, he smiles too.

"We could do what my brother and his friends used to do," Vanessa says.

"What's that?"

"See how fast we can get kicked out of the dance."

"Seems pretty easy. All you'd have to do is whip out a flask or something."

"Yeah," she says. "But that's boring." She crooks her finger, beckoning Rory. He raises an eyebrow. *"Let's dance,"* she mouths.

She and Rory meet in the center of the gym and start dancing like I've never seen dancing before. Popping and locking, doing the robot, grinding against each other. Kids crowd around them, laughing hysterically.

"These young minds are gonna be scarred for life."

I whip around to find Jack standing there in a white T-shirt and faded jeans, barefoot. His hair is still slicked back with gel. I swallow, wishing I could touch his biceps and run my hands across his shirt. He looks yummier than a ranch dressing fountain.

"What are you doing here?" I ask, folding my arms across my stomach. "What about your sister's party?"

"Colton texted and said you guys were coming to the dance and I'd rather do anything than watch a bunch of middle school kids try to act sexy." He looks around the gym. "But I sure as hell don't know why you're here."

I roll my eyes. "Because I like dancing."

"Oh yeah? I'm a great dancer."

"And humble too."

He gives me a look.

"I know you're a good dancer," I say with a strong voice. "I saw you with Abby Winchester tonight."

"You were spying on me?"

"Yeah."

"You stalking me?" he asks with a laugh.

"You lied. You said nothing was going on with her."

"Nothing *is* going on with her." Jack finds my eyes. "My dad wants to buy Paradise Park from Abby's father."

"I know."

He goes on, "My father thinks that if I piss Abby off, her dad will call off the deal."

"That's kind of sick. And what kind of businessman would base a decision on his daughter's feelings?"

Jack shrugs. "I know…but my dad wants this deal so bad. Winchester is so big on honor and family and stuff."

"Honor can't mean all that much to him considering Marcus's behavior."

"Savannah…"

"How can I trust that you aren't treating me great to my face so I'll take care of your horse? What if you hate me behind my back?"

"I could never hate you." He raises his hand to my cheek, but he drops it before making contact with my skin. "The stuff with Abby is embarrassing, you know?"

"Your dad expects too much of you." I poke him in the chest. "When is this deal gonna be over, anyway? How long do you have to keep the Winchesters happy?"

Jack drags a hand through his long hair. "Dad says Winchester'll be making his decision in the next couple of weeks. We should know soon if he accepts Dad's offer. It can't come soon enough, you know?" He looks over at Rory and Vanessa. "So what's going on there?"

"I think they're gonna hook up tonight."

"Ohhh realllly." He cups his mouth and yells, "Way to go, Whitfield!"

Rory flips Jack off.

"Dance with me," Jack says, striding to center court before I can give him an answer.

Kids quickly move out of his way as Jack stalks toward the middle of the gym. He parts people like the goddamned Red Sea. Girls stare at him like they'd kidnap baby zoo animals in exchange for a dance.

Jack beckons me. I shake my head, smiling slightly. When that doesn't work, he waves his hand around like he's using a lasso. He pretends to capture me and tugs the imaginary rope, pretending to pull me out onto the floor.

"Really?" I say.

"Really," he mouths back, beaming.

I join Jack, Vanessa, and Rory, and we all start doing the worst dances anyone's ever seen. A lot of the junior guys glance my way, checking out my skinny jeans and the sparkly tank top I borrowed from Vanessa.

I can't stop laughing when Jack does "the robber." It's a dance where he mimes stealing things off shelves and shoving them in a make-believe bag.

"Let's get our picture made!" Vanessa says, pointing at the über cheesy setup next to the girls' locker room. Couples pay $10 to have their pictures taken together, *because everybody wants to forever remember* the Back-to-School dance in the high school gym. I groan as Vanessa grabs my arm and gestures for

Rory and Jack to follow. Colton is still snoring away over on the bleachers.

The photo background is about the weirdest setup I've ever seen. It has a strobe light, a disco ball, and a giant, inflatable drum set.

"Wow. Fancy *and* seizure-inducing," I say.

We do this ridiculous pose where Vanessa and I pretend we're a couple. She puts her hands on my waist and I stand with my back against her. The guys stand to either side of us, gaping, with eyes wide as supper plates.

Jack gives Rory a fist bump. "This is my dream come true."

As we're having the picture taken, Vanessa pinches my butt. I squeal and rip away, crashing spread-eagle into the inflatable drum set.

"Badoom-chh," Rory says, as Vanessa and Jack die laughing.

The photographer rolls his eyes and checks his watch.

Jack helps me to my feet and leads us back out onto the dance floor. Vanessa starts grinding against me, well, trying to, but it's kind of impossible because we're doubled over laughing. Which of course gives Jack the opening he needs to do some really inappropriate dance moves. He pretends to do a strip tease, unbuttoning the top three buttons of his shirt.

Dr. Salter, the principal, comes up and taps Jack on the shoulder.

Jack says, "Oh shit!"

Jack, Rory, and Vanessa take off running, so I dart after

them, unable to keep the smile off my face. We're all laughing hysterically. We grab our shoes and boots, sprint out of the gym, and we're jogging toward the parking lot when Vanessa says, "I forgot Colton! He probably slept through all of that."

She skips back inside, her blond hair swinging back and forth.

Jack is wiping his eyes, he's laughing so hard. "Did you see the look on the principal's face?"

"Now he's going to associate me with you!" I say, laughing. "He'll think I'm some sort of stripper or something thanks to your dance moves."

"You're not a stripper." Jack loops his thumbs through his belt loops, giving me a wicked smile. "Me, however…"

"How many times have I told you you're not a stripper?" Colton says, walking up with an arm around Vanessa. He yawns.

"In my heart, I'm an exotic dancer," Jack replies.

"What. A. Dumbass," Vanessa says.

"We should go down to Miller's Hollow," Rory says, taking Vanessa's hand. I want to jump up and down I'm so happy for him. "I'll go pick up some food," Rory adds.

Colton yawns again and checks the time on his phone. "I'm going to bed."

"Ride with me," Jack says to me, jingling his keys.

"I should probably ride with Ror—"

"Ride with Jack," Vanessa whispers to me. "Please?"

Rory looks so enamored with her, he'd probably go skydiving naked if she asked him to.

"Okay," I say to Jack, and we're off.

He opens the passenger-side door and helps me step up into his Ford truck. The excitement of being in his truck makes me tap my feet. It's huge, with all-leather beige interior. It's nothing like Rory's beat-up hand-me-down truck, with injured seats patched with duct tape. But Jack's truck has some character of its own. Like, loose change is everywhere—in the cup holders, in the ashtray, on the floorboards. How can he just throw money around like this? A horse figurine hangs from the rearview mirror. His key chain holds a picture of his three hounds.

The truck smells like him, like cologne, and the seats are warm and cozy. We ride down the dark highways into the country, and he keeps the radio off and rolls down the windows, so we drive with only the sounds of trees rustling and cows mooing to entertain us.

Miller's Hollow is a wooded area way out past the baseball fields. It overlooks a dark pond. The cool night air is fresh and a little bit fishy, and the smell of pine makes me feel like Christmas.

When Rory and Vanessa arrive after getting snacks, he pulls out a paper bag full of beef jerky, chips, candy, and Cokes. Rory turns his truck radio up loud, blasting music, and we start dancing again. We all come from such different places, but we've all ended up at Miller's Hollow tonight. And it never would have happened if I hadn't taken a risk, if I'd stuck to the status quo, deciding to like people only based on where they come from, not who they are.

Vanessa dances in a circle, pouring Skittles into her mouth. "Let's play Truth or Dare."

"Okay," Jack says, chowing down on beef jerky. "Truth or Dare, Rory?"

"Truth."

"Have you ever held hands with a girl?"

"Yes," Rory replies. "Truth or Dare, Jack?"

"Truth."

"Have you ever farted in class and blamed it on somebody else?"

Rory and Jack start snickering like little boys and Vanessa and I roll our eyes at each other.

"You guys are ridiculous," Vanessa says. "I want to play for real!"

Jack grins. "Fine. Savannah, truth or dare?"

The last thing I need is for Jack to ask me questions. "Dare."

"I dare you to kiss Vanessa on the lips," he says.

"No!" I exclaim as Vanessa shakes her head, looking disgusted.

"You are my hero." Rory gives Jack a fist bump then fishes his notepaper and pen out and starts jotting down notes.

"Great, now we're gonna end up in a pervy movie script, Vanessa," I say.

"Fine." Jack smirks. "If you won't kiss Vanessa, then make out with Rory."

Rory's head pops up. He looks sick.

"C'mon," I say. "That'd be weird."

"Make out with Rory," Jack says, "Or you've gotta take a truth."

I cross my arms. He's goading me into taking a truth.

"Fine," Rory says. "Let's get it over with." He has a mischievous look on his face. He whispers in my ear, "I've been wanting to practice my stage kissing for drama class!"

"Oh hell."

Rory twirls me around in a grand sweeping movement, but right as he's about to kiss me, he slides his hand between our mouths and makes all these overly dramatic movements, whipping his head around like an angry horse. From an outsider's perspective, it might look like kissing…or Rory devouring me whole.

"Ow owwww!" Vanessa squeals.

I start giggling against Rory's hand, and when he pulls away from me, Jack and Vanessa are clapping.

"Bravo!" Vanessa says, laughing her ass off. "Rory." Her eyes pierce into his. "Truth or dare."

"Dare."

"I dare you to dance with me."

"Bo-ring," Jack says.

Vanessa pulls Rory against her chest, and laughing, he leads her down closer to the water, where she wraps her arms around his neck and he kisses her deeply. That's no stage kiss. I look away, smiling.

"I guess they're out of the game indefinitely," Jack says. Vanessa and Rory are full-fledged making out now.

"Game's over, I guess," I say, and walk over to the clearing, where I can better see the stars.

Jack appears beside me, sticks his hands in his pockets, and gazes at the moon. "Truth or dare?"

"Dare."

"I dare you to admit if you wanted to kiss me last week."

"That's against the rules!"

My heart explodes, pounding like a train engine. Did he really just ask that? Is he under the influence of beef jerky or something?

It's like, whenever we're not at Cedar Hill, we're normal. Normal people, normal friends, flirting like crazy. Playing waitress at his dinner party the other night seems a million miles away. He's not my boss out here under the stars.

"So what's your answer?" Jack asks.

I feel like I'm on a bridge, about to bungee jump, wondering if the cord is strong enough to hold me. Jack's blue eyes find mine.

"Yes."

Without a word he leads me down by the banks of the pond, where we sit. My body's doing all the thinking as I curl my legs up beneath me, touching my knees against his warm thigh.

He touches my collarbone and gently sweeps his fingertips over my necklace. "What's this?"

I suck in a deep breath and carefully remove the horseshoe

necklace from his grasp. It's a cheap thing, really. It came from Claire's and probably didn't cost more than a few dollars. But it's worth everything. "It's the last thing my mom ever gave me."

Jack traces the necklace with a finger. Then he unclasps his watch, turns it over, and rubs his thumb across the engraved initials. *JCG.*

"It's my grandfather's," Jack says.

"History is important to you," I say quietly, touching the watch.

"My family, Cedar Hill—they're my whole life."

I lean closer, snuggling under his arm, and rest a hand on his strong chest. Our breathing races out of control. He brushes my hair behind my ears and kisses my neck until I'm shaking all over.

"Truth or dare?" I whisper.

"Dare."

"I dare you to kiss m—"

His mouth captures mine and teases me into a long kiss. He weaves his hands in my hair and pulls me closer as I run one hand over his knee and cup his neck with the other. His pulse slams against my palm. His strong hands sweep over my shoulders and thighs, leaving me tingly and warm and feeling beautiful. I wish *this* had been my first kiss. It's perfect.

At some point, Rory comes over and says that he and Vanessa are leaving.

"I'll take her home," Jack says, barely coming up for air.

Cindy warned me about Jack and his supposed one-night

stands, but we never come close to that, even though I wouldn't mind him going up my shirt or climbing on top of me because I want to *feel*. His fingers don't wander under the hem of my T-shirt or below my waistband, and when he drives us home, he walks me to the door of Hillcrest, and after quickly gazing around to make sure we're alone, he slides his hands around my waist and kisses me goodnight.

I like him a lot.

If I had a genie in a bottle and wished for the perfect night, it couldn't be any better than this.

You Can't Help Who You Love

On Sunday morning after training, I walk over to Whitfield Farms so I can talk to Rory about what happened last night and get a guy's advice on what happens next. Should I tell Jack I really like him? Or should I be realistic and never bring it up again? Was last night a one-time thing because of our beef jerky-infused haze?

I ring the doorbell to the farmhouse and an older version of Rory answers the door. Same mess of floppy dark brown hair. Same tall muscular frame.

"Are you Will?" I ask, and he nods. I wasn't expecting to find him here since Rory said he's going to law school in Atlanta.

"You must be Savannah, the girl who's beating the hell out of the other exercise boys on the track, huh?"

"I guess."

A small boy appears beside Will's leg. "Hey, bud, can you run find Rory and tell him he's got a visitor? He's out in the barn." The boy jets toward the back of the house and Will motions for me to follow him.

"I hear you're getting a jockey's license," Will says. I grin and walk into the kitchen, where he's making a sandwich. "Want one?"

"No, thanks."

"Dessert?"

"Now you're talking."

He rummages in a cabinet and slides a package of Chips Ahoy across the island to me.

"So what are you doing here?" I ask. "Rory said you're in law school in Atlanta?"

"My wedding's next week. My *fiancé*'s at her final wedding dress fitting with my mom and her mom. And I was forced to act as chauffeur."

I smile and clap my hands together. "What does her dress look like?"

"I haven't seen it. That's bad luck, Savannah."

"Well, what do you hope it looks like?"

"You're just as bad as the moms," Will says, continuing to grin. He adds tomato and lettuce to his ham sandwich, and slices it down the middle, creating triangles.

They're getting married next weekend at Whitfield Farms—the same day of the races at Kentucky Downs, and according to Rory, Mrs. Goodwin has been going nuts discussing wedding decor with Mrs. Whitfield. The bride's family doesn't have much money and the Whitfields have had several bad seasons so they haven't taken many of Mrs. Goodwin's suggestions, but I'm sure it will be a beautiful wedding.

I feel something pawing at my leg. I discover a red puppy at my feet. "Aww." I lift the puppy into my arms, but he starts barking like crazy and going nuts, so Will reaches across the table to take him from me. The dog immediately calms down, licks Will's face, and gives a big yawn.

"The dog hates me," I say, laughing softly.

Will takes another bite of his sandwich and talks through a mouthful. "It happens." He jiggles the puppy up and down on his knee.

"This reminds me of Star," I say. "The horse doesn't like boys. What's wrong with him?"

Will laughs. "Nothing's wrong with him. He can't help it. It's just like with people. Sometimes we like certain people more than others and it's just the way it is."

I like Jack. A lot. And I wish I could stop liking him but my heart doesn't want that.

"So do you really think the Goodwins are gonna let you be their jockey at Kentucky Downs next week?" Will asks.

"I hope so."

"Damn." Will bites into his sandwich, smiling. "If that weren't the day of my wedding, I'd love to see you race. I've never seen a girl jockey."

I pause to eat a chocolate chip cookie. "What made you decide to go to law school?"

He feeds the puppy a small piece of ham. "Well, I mean, teachers had been telling me since sixth grade that I was going to college. Because of my grades, you know?"

No teachers have ever been like that with me. I guess my grades are okay, but nobody's going out of their way to tell me what to do with my life. Wait. I take that back. Adam, the guy I fooled around with in West Virginia, worked in the kitchens at the Best Value Inn next door to the casino, and he often said I could use him as a reference if I wanted to apply for a clerk position at the front desk.

"...and I'm going to law school 'cause I want to fight the big corporations that are buying up farmland and putting us small farms out of business."

"Do you ever wish you had stayed here to work on the farm?" I ask.

He shakes his head. "Going to law school will be better for my family in the long run."

I raise my eyebrows. In a way, he's making an investment for the future, kind of like how I'm becoming a jockey.

That's when Rory comes crashing through the back door with the small boy at his heels. "Cheerio is—" He stops to catch his breath. "Cheerio is about to drop her calf. Can you come help me and Bo?" Rory asks Will. "Dad is still down at the co-op."

Will nods, stuffing the rest of his sandwich into his mouth. Still chewing, he hands the squirming puppy to me. It barks like crazy.

"You'll come to the wedding, right? With Rory?" Will asks, pointing at me. "We could use some girls to even the party out. We don't have a single girl cousin but we have about eight thousand guy cousins!"

I laugh. "Oh yeah?"

Rory puffs his chest out. "I'm Best Man."

"I bet ten bucks he loses the rings," I say.

"No bet," Will replies.

"Hey!" Rory says, grinning. "By the way, I called it. I knew you'd hook up with Jack Goodwin." He rubs his fingers together, asking for the twenty bucks I owe him. I groan, and Rory tells me he'll come find me later, after he's done helping to birth the calf.

Instead of taking the road back to Cedar Hill, I decide to walk through Whitfield Farms and along the lake where I come upon a flock of geese. I love them. When they mate, they stay together for life. It's so sweet how they can barely stand being two feet apart. One time Dad and I saw a group of seven geese swimming together: four boys and three girls. I asked Dad where the fourth girl was, and he said she'd probably died or got lost.

What I wouldn't give to feel that sort of all-encompassing love. But is it safe? The boy goose will have to spend the rest of his life with a broken heart. Was the short time he had with the girl goose worth it?

I hope so. I wouldn't trade the time I shared with my mother. Or with Moonshadow.

I walk alongside the lake and soon I'm on Goodwin land again. Jack's three hounds bound up to me, barking playfully. I glance around, expecting to find Jack because he's always with his dogs, and spot him sitting on a picnic table next to a pile of rocks. One by one, he hurls the rocks into the lake, watching them splash.

A grin spreads across my face. Remembering last night's kisses makes me shiver all over again. I take a deep breath, waiting for him to see I'm here. But it looks like he's in a dream world. His eyes are hazy and withdrawn.

I pull a deep breath through my nose and make my way over to the picnic table. The hounds flop down in the dirt and roll around like roly-polies.

Jack keeps staring at the lake, but he smiles when I sit down next to him.

"Hi," I say.

"Hey."

"It's beautiful out here."

"Thor, Athena, and Jasper like the water." He gestures at the hounds. "We come here a lot."

"They seem like good friends to you."

"They are. Although Jasper isn't so much a friend as a frenemy."

"Did you just say frenemy?"

"This past summer? I decided to take a swim in the lake. I took off all my clothes except my underwear, and then Jasper stole my shorts and T-shirt. I had to walk in the house wearing wet boxers."

I laugh, and Jack laughs too as Jasper looks up at us and cocks his head, probably wondering why we humans said his name. "And then Yvonne started yelling at Jasper, telling the dog that only she's allowed to handle the family's laundry."

"I'm sorry I missed that. You know, the part about Yvonne yelling—not you in your boxers…oh, um." My skin heats up and I shake the sexy images out of my head. "Would you stop trying to distract me?"

"Talking about my underwear distracts you? If only I'd known that sooner." Jack grins fiendishly as he leans toward me, grabbing my wrist and rubbing it with the pad of his thumb.

I dip my head and move toward his mouth, wetting my lips. But he suddenly pulls away and focuses on the lake. I hold my breath.

"So, you and me…last night." He exhales deeply.

"I liked it…"

"I did too…but I don't know how this is gonna work out. I'm not saying it can't, but I don't know how it will…"

I yank away from him and stuff my hands between my knees again. Why did I lean in? Why was I so presumptuous to think he'd want to kiss me again?

"My father called me to his office a little while ago," Jack says, nervously rapping his knuckles on the picnic tabletop. "He said that Mr. Winchester called to say thanks for dinner. Mr. Winchester said that I impressed him. And my dad was proud of me for that...and proud that I'm becoming a responsible farm owner...a good man."

"And?" I ask quietly. A slimy feeling washes over me.

"And I don't want to disappoint my dad...you know? I wasn't a gentleman last night."

"My dad and Cindy would kill me anyway," I say defensively. "The maids say you have one-night stands all the time."

Jack pauses for a long moment, looking me head-on. "I don't have one-night stands all the time, no matter what the maids say. I've only slept with one person. And I cared about her."

That's one more person than I've slept with. But I'm glad to hear he's not the total man whore the maids made him out to be. He must've slept with Senator Lukens's daughter, the girl Rory said he dated last year. Or was it the country singer? Never mind, I don't want to know.

"I can't mess up this Paradise Park deal for my dad," Jack says. "It's his dream to own a big racetrack!"

"And what do *you* think? What do you want?"

"I like you...a lot..." He pauses to rub his lower lip with his thumb. "But I'm not sure we can have anything—I'm not sure what I can give you...besides last night, I mean. I do like you so much but dating somebody who works for me wouldn't look right—"

Thank God we didn't go further than kissing. Why did he woo me with kisses that taste better than lollipops when he knew it could never work out? How dare he treat me like a poor loser? This is why I don't trust rich jerks!

"—and my parents would be disappointed." Jack sighs and rubs his eyes. He looks upset.

I love my family too. It could be nice to have a connection with my baby sister when she's born. Thinking of her, and thinking of Jack's love for his family, brings me back to reality. Ensuring my dad keeps his new job is what's most important right now. Not being with Jack. This is why I was trying to keep my distance in the first place.

But it hurts. Bad.

I want to scream at him for kissing me, for leading me on, but I don't want to be a mean, vindictive girl. That's not who I am. I don't need a guy to validate me. And on top of that, I don't want to ruin what we do have: a great working relationship.

"Hey," I say quietly. "It doesn't sound like either of us can handle a relationship right now..." My voice cracks with emotion. I like him so much. "So let's just keep hanging out, keep being friends, keep working together. I've really liked getting to know you better, and I don't want to lose you," I say in a wobbly tone.

His eyes find mine. "I don't want to lose you either."

"Good. Let's just go back to where we were, okay?"

I stand and charge toward the manor house, and seconds later Jack bounds up to walk beside me. The three hounds circle us, barking and playing, oblivious.

I slap a fake smile on my face, sniffling. I pull a cherry sucker out of my pocket, rip off the wrapper, and stick it into my mouth, but it doesn't bring the relief I need so badly.

Hold on Tight

At daybreak on Tuesday, day two of my jockey training, I begin exercising the horses. Now that it's September and the humidity is fading into fall, my skin isn't slick with sweat like dew coating the grass, but I'm still hot as hell.

I steer Echoes of Summer out onto the track and click my tongue, urging her into a trot. An exercise rider who works for another horse owner calls out, "Women don't belong on the racetrack! Go make me breakfast!" The rider smiles goofily and the guys around him start chuckling. I ignore them and ride on by. Assholes.

At the 3/8 pole, Bryant Townsend rides up beside me and gives me a look.

"What?" I say over the sound of hooves slamming the dirt. "You come to tell me girls shouldn't be jockeys?"

"I came to tell you don't even think about stealing any more of my business. Yeah, Star hasn't won yet, but now I won't get *any* money off him."

I look straight ahead, continuing to trot. What Bryant says makes me feel somewhat guilty—jockeys only make money when the horses they ride win, and when Jack asked me to become Star's jockey, that meant Bryant would lose business if Star were to win.

"I need this chance," I tell Bryant.

"Just don't agree to race any other horses. I have a car payment and bills to deal with." Bryant speeds up, leaving me to think about how lucky I am to have a place to live.

After I finish exercising Echoes of Summer, second up on my schedule is Star. Sweat drips down my face as we trot around the track, warming up.

Three other exercise riders are right beside me when a baby raccoon appears on the top of a fence post. A colt screams and jerks his head. Then two of the fillies do the same thing. Which of course means that Star goes ballistic at forty miles per hour.

I hold on tight as Star rears onto his hind legs. Oh shit. "Star," I say in a soothing voice. "It's okay. It's okay." But I'm terrified. Star returns to all fours, sidesteps, and jerks his head again, whinnying, and I kick his sides and try to urge him forward, but he won't budge.

The next time he jerks, he uses such force I can't hold on. He pitches me sideways off his back. I free my feet and leap, making an emergency exit. Avoid Star's hooves. Attempt a shoulder roll. Land on the track, right on my butt, kicking up dust. Star takes off, the stirrups banging against his sides. The wailing alarm sounds. Other horses dash past me. I'm sitting on the interstate without a car. Outriders begin to chase after Star as I bring myself to a sitting position, and right then a speeding colt clips my shin with his hoof and I scream in pain.

I fall to the dirt, clutching my leg.

"No, no, no!" Jack sprints up to me and slides onto the track like a baseball player into second base. "Are you okay?"

I don't respond. I hold a gloved hand out toward him. It's shaking.

Jack squeezes my hand and shuts his eyes, panting. "Don't ever do that to me again," he says under his breath. Is he talking to me or to the horse gods?

"Go get Star," I mutter, clutching my leg.

"No," Jack says.

Dad and Gael follow behind Jack, and seeing the horrified look on Dad's face makes my eyes water. It's been a long time since I've fallen off a horse. My leg feels like I got wacked with a crowbar. Damn.

It takes a few minutes for my heart to stop racing and my body to stop shaking, but I think my leg and butt are okay.

Mr. Goodwin jogs up. "Do you need to go to the hospital?"

"I'm fine," I say through clenched teeth. "I just had the wind knocked out of me." There is no way I'm giving up my chance to race this Saturday! "What you need is a damned raccoon exterminator already!" I tell Mr. Goodwin, making him and Jack chuckle.

"I'll get right on that," Jack says.

"Maybe you should go to the doctor," Dad says, but I shake my head.

"I didn't hit my head or anything, and nothing hurts except for my leg and my butt," I whisper, embarrassed. Horsemen around the track are staring at me. People fall off horses all the time—Dad is just being a drama queen. I don't want him to have to pay for an emergency room visit just because my butt is sore. I'd know if I broke something. My leg is gonna have a nasty bruise tomorrow, that's for sure.

"We need to get you off the track," Mr. Goodwin says, looking over at the gates. "We've got about twenty riders waiting."

Cedar Hill is a business, after all. I lurch to my feet, and Dad tells everyone that he's keeping me home from school to make sure I don't have a head injury.

"Dad, don't. That'll make me look like a complete pansy."

"You're staying home."

"If she's staying home from school, I'll bring over some film for her to watch," Gael says, winking at me. He knows Dad is overreacting.

"I'll carry her back," Jack says, slipping an arm under my knees and the other under my shoulder blades, lifting me off the track. Mr. Goodwin gives his son a look, but Jack doesn't pay attention.

"Put me down," I tell Jack through clenched teeth. "Nobody's gonna take me seriously if you're carrying me all over the place."

He immediately drops me back to my feet and a pang of pain engulfs my shin. I hiss and hop on one foot.

My dad starts rubbing his eyes and wiping sweat off his face, glancing between Mr. Goodwin and Jack. I can see Dad's pulse racing beneath the skin of his neck.

"Son, get her off the track," Mr. Goodwin says, and Jack grabs my arm and pulls me toward Hillcrest.

"Can I still race on Saturday?" I ask, hobbling.

Jack avoids my question. "Let's go check out that leg."

He leads me back to Hillcrest and escorts me to my bedroom. There, he looks around my super tiny room. It's only big enough for a twin bed and a small dresser that doubles as a nightstand. A framed picture of my mother hangs beside the door. Yellow paint is peeling off the walls and the only sunlight filters through a tiny rectangular window near the ceiling. The twin bed has the same bedding I've had since I was eight—Strawberry Shortcake.

Jack chuckles at my bedspread as we plop down. "I knew you were a Shortcake."

I want to dive under the covers and die from embarrassment. I need a new comforter immediately.

After helping me remove my gloves and vest, Jack pulls my boots and socks off, lifts my legs onto his lap, peels my pant leg back, and examines my shin. He whistles at the big purple welt forming. "You should ice it, but it doesn't look serious—"

"Son," Mr. Goodwin says, appearing in my doorway with

my father. Both men stare down at my legs in Jack's lap. "You need to get back on the track and let the horsemen know why we have a twenty-minute delay this morning. You need to do your job, *understand*?"

The emotion disappears from Jack's face, he removes my feet from his lap, and he suddenly stands. "Yes, sir."

"I hope you feel better, Savannah," Jack says seriously before leaving, clicking the door shut.

Dad watches Jack disappear then sits down on my bed. "What happened out there? How did you lose control?"

"Star's strong and he was scared."

My father shakes his head. "I don't want you riding that horse anymore."

"No—"

"Don't argue—"

"The only reason the Goodwins are training me as a jockey is to ride Star—"

"And you think they'll let you now after you lost control of the horse and fell?"

"That happens to everybody! And raccoons were involved! This happened to a rider on the third day we were here, for God's sake!"

Dad clenches the Strawberry Shortcake comforter in his fist and shuts his eyes.

I can't give up the chance to make a better name, a better

future for myself. The fact I'm still using the same kid bedding just proves I need better opportunities. Sometimes you've gotta take risks to get something better.

"Please," I say. "I'll do anything. Please let me keep working."

"I've gotta get back to work," he says. "Stay in that bed."

"Dad!" I call out, but he leaves without another word.

God, is it all over after less than a week? I bury my face in my pillow. What happened this morning scared me...but not having a future in horseracing scares me just as much, if not more.

Midafternoon when I'm icing my shin for the fourth time, Gael brings film for me to watch and I move to the common room because I don't have a TV. It brings a smile to my face that Gael isn't gonna let me quit just because I fell.

"When I was a jockey," Gael says, "I fell at least once a month. And I didn't even have raccoons to blame."

Later in the day, Dad sits on my bed with me. "I'm sorry I yelled at you this morning," he says. "But you need to get your body in better shape so you can ride at high speeds if you want to keep your job."

"I can keep it?" I exclaim.

Dad runs a hand through his hair. "What happened this morning wasn't your fault."

"Yeah, it was those goddamned raccoons."

Dad pats my knee. "Hey, watch your mouth, Shortcake."

"Can I race this weekend?"

"We'll see...but you need to start doing more workouts with Gael. And don't think I won't hesitate to stop your training if I don't think you can handle it, understand?"

I hug his neck, promising myself I'll be extra vigilant from now on. He's right—this job can be the difference between life and death.

Dad hands me a packet of papers. "Jack came by. He brought your schoolwork."

"Groan," I say. "He must not know me very well if he thinks I actually want to do my homework."

On top of the papers is a thick beige note card embossed with Jack's name in gold ink. *John Conrad Goodwin IV*. What guy has his own stationery? It even smells like his cologne. Jesus Lord.

The note reads,

> Star says he's sorry. For his punishment, I'm withholding carrots and he isn't allowed to play in the pasture with the fillies for a week. That'll teach him a lesson. I'd go crazy if someone took away my favorite food and access to girls. Feel better soon -JG

I laugh silently at the note. But couldn't he have told me this in person?

"What's going on between you and him?" Dad asks.

I bring the note card to my mouth, to chew on the corner. "We're working with Star. That's all," I lie, wishing I could erase last weekend's make-out session from my mind.

"Make sure that's all it is," Dad says, giving me a stern glare. "I had a hard time keeping him out of here this afternoon. I told him he couldn't see you 'cause I didn't want you stressed out in case you got a concussion this morning."

So that's why he sent a note.

"Jack only wants to get in your pants," Dad says.

My hands fly to cover my eyes. "God, Dad! Shut up!"

"Mr. Goodwin would never allow his son to date you."

It hurts hearing Dad say that. Because I know it's true. I've heard it from Mr. Goodwin's own mouth.

"You know the maids' stories about all the girls Jack messes around with in his room. And like Cindy told you, you're too good for him."

I might have thought that a week ago. But a week ago, he wouldn't have sent me a card and collected my homework. I smell the card again, enjoying his cologne, thinking of his funny words. I really like who he is as a person.

Regardless of what anybody says, I'd give him another chance if he wants to try to make us work. But still, which Jack is the real Jack? The farm owner at home or the sweet goofball who emerges when we're alone?

My First Race

Even though I majorly crashed and burned Tuesday morning on the track, Jack still wants me to race Saturday at Kentucky Downs. Other than him, it's all I can think about during the day. Gael has me riding for hours a day now, and my arms and legs feel like noodles thanks to his weight training.

But late at night, when I'm alone with my thoughts, while Dad and Cindy are cuddling together on the couch and Rory is immersed in his writing or spending time with Vanessa, I think of Jack. I should've known better than to make out with him, but everything felt right, and I've always heard you should live in the moment. When she was my age, I doubt my mother thought she'd lose her life at thirty.

On Thursday night after everyone has gone to sleep, I climb out of bed in my pajamas and go to the common room. I flick on the lights and sit down at the computer.

I type *colleges in Tennessee* into Google. A school called Belmont pops up as the first choice. I tap the link and a picture of a brick building surrounded by lush green trees fills the screen. I click on the admissions homepage and scroll through the requirements. Looks like they suggest a minimum GPA of 3.5. Mine is 3.2. School has never been my forte. I'd rather shovel manure than do algebra.

Holy shit—the Belmont application fee alone is $50. Is it that pricey at every school? Didn't Rory say some cost $35? Applying to five schools like this one would cost $250. Other than people like Jack, who can afford that?

Still. The pictures of the dorm rooms, the quad, and students having fun at basketball games make my heart speed up a little.

"Why are you out of bed?"

I quickly exit out of the browser and swivel to face Dad, who's standing there holding a glass of water.

"Couldn't sleep," I say. "What are you doing?"

"Cindy was thirsty. What were you looking at on the computer?"

"Um, nothing really."

Dad sits on the couch armrest. "It looked like you were on a college website."

I slowly lift a shoulder, cracking my knuckles. "Just messing around."

"I didn't know you were interested in college. I thought you were gonna work as an exercise boy."

"I am," I say quickly. There's a long still silence, as Dad's eyes leave mine and focus on the glass of water.

"You've changed a lot in the few weeks we've been here, Shortcake…I barely recognize you anymore since we moved. I never imagined you'd be interested in jockeying or college."

I sigh and push the button to turn off the computer monitor.

"Don't get me wrong—I'm proud of you, but I don't know anything about college," Dad goes on. "I guess we could ask Mr. Goodwin what he knows but I don't know how we'd pay for—"

"No, no," I say. "Don't talk to Mr. Goodwin." I can't handle the idea of being more in debt than we already are. What I need to do is keep making money. That wouldn't happen if I went to college.

"Dad?" I ask. "Are you going to marry Cindy?"

He gives me a sad smile and cradles the glass in his hands. "I'm going to ask her when I have enough money to buy her a ring."

The memory of Mr. Winchester snapping his fingers at me to refill his wine glass pops into my mind. He was wearing a large ruby ring encircled with diamonds. He didn't even say please and thank you. Probably doesn't care who he hurts, just like Mr. Cates. *He didn't care that he sold Moonshadow to a bad man who whipped her and made her race, even though she wasn't in shape.* I bite down on the inside of my cheek so I won't cry, so the pain won't swallow me.

"You'd better get to bed, Shortcake. You've got training in the morning."

I climb back in bed and mentally run through my game plan for Saturday's race, but as I begin to nod off, lush images from the Belmont website fill my head, flooding my dreams with color.

• • •

Friday afternoon after I've visited Star in the pasture, I meet Gael in his office in the manor house to watch racing film.

I've never been to the second floor of the manor house before, but I know from Cindy that Mr. Goodwin's office is up here. She vacuums and dusts it every day.

I swallow as I pass large, closed, double wooden doors. I peek inside the stall manager's and the estate manager's offices, finding them hard at work on their computers. A glass chandelier that looks like it's from France or something blinds me with its bling. Mr. Goodwin's personal assistant is typing on the computer and talking on the phone. She points me down the hall. While looking for Gael, I discover that Jack has his own office too.

What seventeen-year-old has his own office?

I peek inside to find him talking on the phone about a stud fee deal and flipping through a large book at the same time. His office is very…clean. And tasteful. Jack has a flat-screen TV that's muted and tuned to the horse-racing network. Pictures of his family and friends cover the walls, along with famous horses and horsemen, including an autographed photo of Ron Turcotte, the jockey who rode Secretariat and had over three thousand wins… until he got hurt in a race. He's in a wheelchair now.

I leave Jack to his work and knock on the door to Gael's office. His office is very…much the opposite of Jack's. It's like a giant snow globe exploded in here. Paper is everywhere. Red Bull and Diet Coke cans litter every available surface.

Gael leaps to his feet like he's on a pogo stick. "Barrow! Sit right here." He clears a spot for me on his sofa and plops down next to me with a remote control in his hand.

Gael rubs his cheek, looking over at me. "You ready for tomorrow?"

I clutch my knees. "I think so."

"You're great on a horse and great during practice, but racing in a race is a whole new ballgame. You gotta respect it. If you're not careful and you don't know what you're doing on the track, you could die."

My stomach jumps into my throat when I think of what could've happened the other day. What if the horse's hoof had struck my head and not my shin? Riding a 1,200-pound animal at forty-five miles per hour is a rush. A dangerous rush.

"This footage will help you learn what to expect and know how to deal with any contingencies that might come your way," Gael says.

He pushes play and I spend the next two hours watching races. Elite races, smaller races, really fun races, really horrific races. I want to cover my eyes when riders fall and get hurt, but that would show weakness, so I stare straight ahead, trying to keep my eye on the goal.

That's hard after watching the Preakness Stakes where Barbaro pulled up, broke his hind right leg, and had to be euthanized.

• • •

Saturday morning, as usual, I'm up before dawn.

But today is different. Today is the annual Kentucky Downs Handicap. Normally people train for years before their first race, but Jack fast-tracked me. I hope I do okay today…I kind of feel like a poser.

Gael told me to sleep in and get my rest because I'm racing later in the day—at noon sharp. But I couldn't stay asleep thanks to prerace jitters. I'm so jumpy, it's like I've already had my coffee even though I haven't drunk a drop. Kentucky Downs is about thirty miles north of Cedar Hill. In the past week, Kentucky Downs has held eight races. Over $1 million in purse winnings have already been given out, but today's three races are the biggies.

Star is competing in the Juvenile Downs, a race for two-year-olds. The purse is $75,000, and the winner will make 70 percent of that, with the rest going to the runners-up. That means if Star wins, I'll get 5 percent of $52,500. $2,625. That's more money than I've seen in my entire life.

Jack is also entering Lucky Strikes in the Kentucky Turf Cup, which has a purse of $200,000. In the Goodwin world, these races are small potatoes, but Star needs a win. And I'm hoping I can help him with that. I don't have any illusions I will win my very first race, but I pray we won't come in dead last. I need to prove that I've got what it takes, that I've got something special.

While the Ladies Marathon race is going on, I sit on a stool in the barn, breathing in and out, talking softly to Star, who's busy eating grain.

Then all of a sudden the Marathon must be over, because Jack appears at the stall, rubbing his hands together as he keeps his distance from Star. He's wearing a sleek gray suit, white shirt, no tie, and cowboy boots. The no-tie look makes me tingle all over. I want to kiss the triangle of tanned skin exposed at his neck. Jesus Lord, all this anxiety over the race is making me a perv.

"Hey." Jack takes off his hat to muss his hair, looking everywhere but at me. "You feeling good?"

"Pretty good. A little tired. I've never been in the sweatbox before." The morning of a race, most jockeys go in this super hot room called a sweatbox and sweat all the extra fluid out so they'll weigh less for the race. "It was so relaxing I felt like I was on a beach somewhere."

Jack laughs softly. When he finally meets my gaze, his blue eyes pierce into mine, and I wish we could have a repeat of last weekend's kissing session. That would help me relax. A glance at his lips makes it hard to tell where my stress from the race ends and the sexual tension begins.

"You've read all the notes Gael gave you? You know all about the other horses, their jockeys, and their trainers?"

"Yes." I straighten my posture, trying to look impressive, which is hard when Jack stands a full foot taller than me. "I'm all set."

Jack blows air out and rubs his hands together again. "Thanks for doing this."

"Thanks for letting me do it," I say softly.

"You look good in the Goodwin colors," he says, scanning my black and green riding silks.

"I look like a damned Slytherin."

He laughs, looks around, and takes a step closer, wetting his lips. He gently pecks my cheek, sending a jolt up my legs and down my arms and between my thighs.

"I got you something for good luck," he whispers in my ear. He reaches into his pocket and pulls out a purple swirl lollipop.

"Yaaaaaay." I take the sucker, and before I know what I'm doing, I slip my arms around his waist. He sucks in a breath. Clenches up.

Crap. He doesn't want this. I take a step back, pissed at myself. I can't believe I gave in to instinct.

"I'm sorry." My cheeks are burning.

He looks away. "I need to tell you something. There's gonna be press here today. Press specifically for you."

"Me?" I blurt.

"Yes, you." His mouth slides into a small smile. "You're a big deal. This race is nothing compared to some of the big Kentucky races, but still. You don't see girl jockeys all that often at races in general. Especially ones so young."

I was already nervous enough. I drag a hand down my red braid and bring it to my mouth to chew on it. I pull a deep breath.

"Thanks for telling me," I say. "I'd hoped you were gonna tell me something else."

"Oh yeah? What?"

"Nothing," I say, shaking my head quickly.

He gently pulls the braid from my mouth, grasping my hand for a sec. The heat from his skin soothes my nerves and makes me want to dive right back into his arms. Jesus. When did I become such a horn dog?

That's when Rory brings Echoes of Summer back from her race and Jack disappears. Rory looks from me to where Jack vanished and starts beat-boxing, making music like you'd hear on his video game, *Ho Down in Hoochieville*. "Bowchicawowow."

I flip him off.

I pause and breathe deeply as I unwrap the sucker and stick it in my mouth.

"How'd she do?" I ask as Rory pushes Echoes of Summer into a stall.

"Third place," he says, grinning. "Not bad for an old lady."

I pat her muzzle. "She's only seven. I'd hate to hear what you call me when I'm not around."

Rory yanks a wrinkled booklet from his back pocket. "Hey, I got the race program. Your name's in it!"

I dash over to him, stick the sucker Jack gave me in my mouth, and thumb through the program. There I am.

HORSE	JOCKEY	TRAINER	OWNER
Tennessee Star	S. Barrow*	G. Solana	J. Goodwin/Cedar Hill Farms

* Denotes Apprentice Jockey

I close the program and cradle it against my chest.

And before I know it, before I can get my heartbeat under control, Rory has Star's tack thrown over his shoulder and we're heading up to the paddock, passing by other barns and the drug-testing pavilion. I finish the lollipop during our walk and throw the stick away.

Dad, Gael, Jack, and Mr. Goodwin meet us there as we're securing the colt's saddle.

Dad squeezes my shoulder. "You know you don't have to do this, right? We can always send Townsend out instead."

I tighten my gloves, glancing around at the other jockeys. They all look relaxed, chatting and joking with their trainers and owners. I blow air out through my mouth and bounce on my toes.

"I got this," I tell Dad. Jack and Rory exchange a smile at my words.

I mount Star and we make our way out onto the track. Kentucky Downs is old and the grandstands are small like the bleachers at the Hundred Oaks softball field; most spectators are hanging around the fence and on the infield. Or they're inside at the casino.

The cheering starts the minute Star begins to trot across the grass. A bunch of reporters are taking pictures of me. The flashes make me see spots. I hope Star isn't scared of cameras. I groan, praying my picture won't accompany a front-page article on how I blew it at Kentucky Downs.

Dad appears to my right, riding an Appaloosa pony. Star sniffs the pony and rams his head into Dad's side, acting bratty.

"Don't hesitate to pull up if anything goes wrong," Dad says, and I nod, chewing on my braid. "I love you."

"I love you too," I reply.

When it's post time, I meet two hands at the starting gate and they push Star inside the fourth position, locking the gate behind us. Dad disappears off the track.

Seven furlongs. Just under a mile. I can do this. I breathe in and out. In and out. In and out. The crowd cheers. It sounds like pressing a seashell to my ear and listening to the dull roar of an ocean.

The bell rings and the gates crash open.

Star blasts off. It's a clean break out of the gate. We shoot to the front along with two other horses.

"Go!" I shout, holding on tighter than ever before. The nine sets of hooves slamming the grass sound like a train speeding away with my heart.

I glance to my right and left. Sergeant Major, a speed horse, is right next to me. He'll lose his energy soon—I can already hear the colt huffing and puffing. On my left is Lazy Monday, who has good endurance. I've gotta make sure Star doesn't get too tired, too fast, so I ease up a little on the first turn.

On the backstretch, I move up on the outside. For a moment, we take the lead. Then in a blink of an eye we're back in the third position. But as I'm entering the final turn, a colt named Winning Waves sneaks up on the inside. He bolts past me. Dirt from a mud hole splatters on my face and chest.

"Come on," I urge Star. He gradually increases his speed, but he's losing his breath. We begin to pass Winning Waves. The horses are neck and neck.

On the home stretch, we're fighting against Winning Waves. Two other horses are in front of us. The crowd is going wild. Cheering. Clapping. I'm loving the rush. "Go, Star! Hurry up!"

I cross over the finish line right before Winning Waves. A horse named Gina's George is announced as the winner.

We lost by two lengths! Damn.

But we came in third place. Star has never done that before.

I hug his neck. "Good boy, Star. Good boy." He nickers and sighs.

I make my way over to the scoreboard to check our time. Reporters snap photos of me and I grin as I push my goggles up on top of my helmet. Third isn't bad for my first race. Then I see my official time on the scoreboard. My practice this morning was faster by three seconds. I rub my eye and take a deep breath, working to swallow the disappointment. *Third is good*, I remind myself. But will Jack be angry?

Over at the paddock, Rory is smiling as he reaches out to take the reins and control of the horse, and the next thing I know, Jack is pulling me down and wrapping me in a tight hug as more photographers take my picture.

"I'm so proud of you," he murmurs. "Thank you."

I bury my face against his chest, laughing, getting dirt all over his suit. We spin around in a circle and I've never felt so close to another person, not even when we were kissing.

I love that we worked together to make this happen. I've never felt so strong, like I could lift a boulder. Like I could do magic.

"I want you to be my jockey in the Dixiana Derby."

"Shit, for real?" I exclaim. That's only like three weeks away. It's a huge race at Paradise Park with a half a million dollar purse!

"I do," Jack says. I leap into his arms and we jump around like kids during recess.

"Jack," Mr. Goodwin says loudly. "We all want to talk to Savannah."

Jack releases me and grins. Out of the corner of my eye, I see that our fathers are actually smiling. Wait. We were just hugging like crazy, and they aren't freaking out?

"Let's go see your mother, son." Mr. Goodwin leads Jack toward the bleachers. He and I look back at each other, beaming.

"You did good, Shortcake," Dad says, squeezing me close to him. "I wish your mom could've seen it."

I wrap an arm around Dad's waist, get up on tiptoes, and kiss his cheek.

I came in third friggin' place.

Hell. Yeah.

Taking the Road Less Traveled

Church bells ring at Westwood Chapel for Will Whitfield's wedding.

Rory, his younger brother Trey, and two other guys I don't recognize dressed in tuxedos are serving as ushers, seating the female guests.

"Wow, you look great," Rory says, sticking an elbow out. "I'm glad you got all that mud off your face."

"You ass."

"You aren't supposed to say ass in church, S."

Smiling, I take his arm and let him escort me to a pew. I'm still giddy from the race a few hours ago. I'm on such a high, I feel like I could slam dunk a basketball. Jack wants me to be his jockey in the Dixiana Derby!

Along with an ace bandage to mask the hideous bruise on my shin, I wore a green silk dress that belonged to my mother. It's really beautiful and not mom-style at all.

The Goodwins sit a few rows in front of me. Jack sits between his mother and Shelby with his arms stretched around them across the pew.

I run my fingers over the beige wedding program laced with blue ribbon. It reads:

Parker Anne Shelton + William Connor Whitfield

Vanessa walks into the church and looks around, clutching her wedding program. I wave at her then pat the seat next to me. One of the ushers—a guy with loose curly blond hair that reaches his shoulders—sees Vanessa and gives her a big hug before escorting her to my row.

"Thanks for letting me sit with you," she whispers, rolling and unrolling her wedding program. "I wasn't sure if I should come."

"Why not?"

"I mean, Rory invited me, but it's not like we've been going out all that long. I haven't met his parents yet."

"It's fine—his family will love you. Besides, I just met Rory, like, a month ago, and they invited me. Who was that guy who you hugged? The super hot one."

"Oh," Vanessa says with a smile. "That's Sam Henry. He played football with my brother in high school—but don't even think about going after him. He was single for like a year, but he's very much taken again now."

Will steps out in front of the crowd. A few guys whoop at him, and he pumps his fist, making a lot of the little old ladies in the congregation gasp in horror.

"Oh my God, Will is so hot," Vanessa mutters to me. "Maybe when the minister asks if anyone objects to this union, I'll jump up and down and holler a lot."

"I bet Will's fiancé would tackle you."

"True."

"Rory would probably tackle you too."

"I wish." She fans herself with the wedding program.

Rory joins Will at the altar; he keeps patting his breast pocket every three seconds—I guess he's terrified he'll lose the rings, and if I were Will, I'd be a bit worried about that too.

Instead of organ music, a guitarist begins playing and a beautiful girl with long black hair starts down the aisle, being escorted by a man. They both stop on Parker's side of the aisle, and the guy doesn't sit down or move to Will's side. I open my wedding program. A girl named Kate Kelly is Maid of Honor. And for some reason a guy named Drew Bates is a bridesmaid…? I giggle, loving that she has a guy bridesmaid dressed in a tux.

"Rory looks nice," I tell Vanessa.

"Agreed. He should wear tuxes all the time."

"Even on the farm?"

"Even on the farm."

Suddenly everybody stands and we turn to watch Parker walk down the aisle, carrying a handful of wildflowers. Her creamy dress is very simple and made of lace. It has short, capped sleeves and hangs above her knees. When I get married, I don't want anything extravagant—I want a dress just like that. She's not wearing a veil and her long messy brown hair reaches her waist and is all over the place. Will beams and looks like he might cry.

The ceremony is short, but hilarious. Rory, of course, misplaces the rings and spends over a minute searching his pockets. Parker and Will don't seem to care, as he cups her face, laughing. They never stop smiling, even when the minister accidentally calls Will "Bill."

And then it's suddenly over with a "You may now kiss the bride" and for some God awful reason, Rory yells "Get 'er done," which makes Vanessa bury her face in her palms. The guys in the congregation leap to their feet and cheer and basically act like a pack of hooligan monkeys.

Rory and I ride in Vanessa's Mercedes to the reception in the Whitfields' backyard. Glittering lights hang inside a big white tent and tea lights dot the tables. They serve fried chicken and mac 'n' cheese and lots of other yummy foods on the buffet. An awesome band plays rock music as people alternate between eating and dancing. If I ever get married, I want a wedding just like this.

There really are, like, eight thousand male Whitfield cousins here. With all the floppy brown hair, it's like a boy band convention, and a bunch of them want to meet me, the "girl horse jockey."

Rory sneaks two entire bottles of champagne over to us and

smuggles the evidence under the table. He and Vanessa start drinking the champagne, giggling like crazy as they feed each other bits of food. I accept a tiny bit of champagne—I don't want to mess up my training tomorrow morning with a hangover.

Rory and Vanessa keep stealing kisses and somehow end up snuggling under the table with their contraband champagne—and with the options being 1) sit alone at our table, 2) sneak under the table with them (awkward!), or 3) get the hell out of Dodge, I find myself outside, circling the dinner tent, looking back and forth between the dancing and the stars.

The beautiful Maid of Honor is dancing closely with a guy who dared to wear flip flops. A ginormous engagement ring glimmers on her hand. I wish my life could be that perfect. Will and Parker are swaying right next to the couple, laughing and talking to them. The hot usher, Sam Henry, is dancing nearby with an extremely tall blond girl. She looks very much absorbed with the hot usher. For good reason.

Jack is dancing with his mother, twirling her around. I gaze over to Mr. Goodwin's table to discover him sneaking a hot dog while his wife is busy. It's like Jack knows I'm thinking of him, because he looks over his mom's shoulder, gazing at me. Scanning me up and down, studying my forest-green silk dress. He slowly starts to smile and holds up his pointer finger, telling me to wait.

What's that supposed to mean? What am I supposed to wait for?

That's when Will Whitfield jogs up and I hug him and tell him congrats.

"Have you seen Rory?" he asks, scanning the tent. "It's nearly time for the toasts."

"Uh, you might check under that table over there. He's drinking champagne with Vanessa Green."

Will's mouth forms an O. "Maybe we won't have a toast from him then."

"That's probably a good idea. It'd probably just be a repeat of 'Get 'er done!'"

"My mom is gonna kill him for that."

"Who's that couple who was dancing with you and Parker? The beautiful maid of honor girl."

Will looks over his shoulder at them. "Parker's best friend, Kate, and her fiancé. We've been friends with them for years. Since right after high school, actually."

"Oh yeah?"

"It's funny. I nearly went to prom with Kate, but I liked Parker more. I can't imagine what life would be like if I'd made a different choice. It would've been so easy…but so wrong, you know?"

I nod, feeling my eyes burn. It's like that Robert Frost poem I read in Mom's *Compendium of Poetry* book. *Two roads diverged in a yellow wood…* The narrator had to choose which path to take—just like we all do.

An older guy, one of the eight thousand Whitfield cousins, approaches, smiling.

"This is my cousin, Alex."

"Hey," the guy says, shaking my hand. "I'm about to take Meemaw home," he tells Will and gives him a guy hug. "Congrats."

"By the way," Will says to me, "there's a new litter of Springer spaniel puppies in Tanglewood barn. They were born just this morning to my dog, Ash. Maybe one of them will like you," he says with a chuckle before heading back over to his new wife. His cousin Alex smiles at me. A genuine, sweet smile.

"I wish I could stay for a dance with you, but Meemaw is getting tired. I'm her ride."

"Aw, that's cute."

"You know what they say—*grandmas before girls.*"

We laugh together and he glances at his watch.

"I really do want to stay…"

"Next time," I reply, and he's gone before I could even flirt with him. As he walks away, he glances back over his shoulder at me.

I must have the worst luck of all time. Dancing with that guy would've been awesome. Because *damn*. Right when I decide to go check out the cupcakes at the dessert table, Jack appears outside the tent.

"Who was that guy?" he asks, furrowing his eyebrows.

"One of the eight thousand Whitfield cousins."

Jack laughs and drags a hand through his hair. "So…want to dance?"

My heart stops. "With me?"

"Yeah," he says with a smile. "We need to celebrate your work with Star today."

Is that what Mr. Serious told his parents or something?

I shrug and let him pull me into his arms. On the outskirts of the dance floor, he and I sway together with an ocean of space between us. This is the most. Chaste. Dance. Ever. He's not looking at me directly, but I can still feel his hands shaking on my waist. His labored breathing gives away how nervous and excited he is. Even if he's pretending to not be interested in me, I can tell he is.

"You look pretty tonight," he says quietly, moving a tiny bit closer to me. "I haven't been able to stop thinking about last Saturday, you know, at Miller's Hollow?"

I suck in a deep breath. This feels like a trap. A trap I kind of want to get caught in. *Two roads diverged in a yellow wood…*

Earlier today, our fathers didn't freak out when we were hugging after the race. Maybe us being together would just take some getting used to. But maybe it's not completely off the table…? I mean, nobody seems interested in the fact that we're dancing together now. Except for the eight thousand Whitfield cousins who want to talk to the *girl horse jockey*.

As I'm swaying in Jack's arms, there's only one road I want to take. The road with him standing at the end. And it's not the easy road. I decide to be bold, to take the curvy, pothole-filled path. "I heard the Whitfields have a new litter of puppies in Tanglewood barn. Want to go look?"

A smile leaps across his face. "Get a head start. I'll meet you there in a few."

Without another word, I hustle over to the Whitfields' barn, my heels getting stuck in muddy divots. I follow the sounds of crying and barking, which I can barely hear over the band's music ringing across the countryside.

I find the dogs in a nest behind a toolbox, and when I see them nursing from the mama dog, I let out a low squeal. "Oh my gosh, you're so cute."

Not even a minute later, Jack appears in the barn doorway. He stops to light a lantern and carries it toward me. I instinctively take a step back then stop.

I swallow. "You actually came."

"All you had to say was puppies," he replies with a soft smile, kneeling to the ground.

"They aren't even twenty-four hours old yet," I say, squatting next to Ash's little nest she dug out. A puppy chirps, and the mama dog moves to lick it. Seeing how much she loves her babies makes my chest hurt. Love is so simple, but so complicated sometimes.

I pet the brown and white dog's ears. "You did such a good job, Ash." The exhausted dog looks up into my eyes.

"She did, didn't she?" Jack says. "What are there? Twelve babies there?"

The nursing puppies are all tangled together, wriggling and whining. "I think so."

A slow rock song blares from the wedding tent. I must have a wistful look on my face when I gaze in the direction of the band, because Jack takes my elbow and gently lifts me to my feet.

"Dance with me." He pulls me up against his chest, close enough that I can hear the rapid beat of his heart through his cotton button-down shirt. This dance is decidedly not chaste. Burying his face in my neck, he runs fingertips up and down my arms, melting my skin, making my toes curl.

"The wedding was beautiful," I say. "I liked dancing in the tent with all the candles and sparkling lights."

"Oh yeah?" Jack murmurs, swaying slowly. "I prefer this. It's quiet and private. Not to mention puppies are present."

He lifts my chin with two fingers and softly presses a kiss to my lips, and it feels so right it's wrong, so wrong it's right. I pull back, touching my mouth.

"What if someone's watching?" I say, my eyes darting around.

"Who's gonna see us?" He looks around the barn. "Charlie the mule? George Washington the duck? Ash the dog? I doubt Ash will notice us. She's got twelve babies to deal with. And ducks and mules are generally stupid. But you're right, James the pig will probably say something."

That makes me laugh.

"I want to show you a secret," he murmurs, slipping a hand onto my lower back. The heat from his skin burns through my dress.

"Show me," I demand, and he grabs my hand and pulls me out of the barn toward Cedar Hill. We jog together under the moonlight, laughing. Well, it's not so much jogging as it is him pulling me across the grass. I stop for a sec to take my strappy heels off.

We end up about a hundred yards from the manor house where Jack approaches an ancient oak tree and shows me the trap door beside it. "Wait till you see where it goes."

He lifts opens the door, we descend a ladder, and soon I find myself in a long tunnel. Thank God Jack lights a lantern, because otherwise I'd be spooked the hell out.

"My ancestors used this as part of the Underground Railroad." The pride in his voice is sure.

"And now you're using it to sneak a girl into the house and into your room?"

"How do you know that's where I'm taking you?"

"Because if you aren't, I'll be really pissed." My voice comes out squeaky and excited. It's dark in the tunnel, but there's enough light that I can see Jack's lips part slightly. He sets a hand on my waist and yanks me to his chest.

"I wouldn't want to make you angry," he says quietly, giving me another kiss. And then another.

"Jack."

He slowly kisses my neck, teasing a gasp from my lips. "Hmm?"

"Get me out of this tunnel."

"Yes, ma'am." I can hear the grin in his voice.

We walk briskly and end up in a cellar with a door that leads to another cellar, which is full of rotting wooden crates. Jack takes my elbow and leads me to a narrow staircase. The paint is peeling off the walls and the stairs need polishing.

When we reach the third floor, a floor I've never been to, Jack pushes a door open and I find myself in his bedroom. Jack's three hounds hop to their feet when they see him, their claws scraping the hardwood floor, but when he snaps and points at their doggie beds along the far wall, they lie back down.

The bay window is wide open, letting fresh September air and moonlight into the spacious room. Jesus Lord, it's so big, you could probably fit, like, a bowling alley in here. His queen-sized bed is made—the plaid duvet is perfectly pressed. Little horse figurines sit on his shelves and his backpack is slung over the desk chair. A pair of dirty socks is strewn across the hardwood floor, but otherwise the room is spotless. Unlike any other boy's room *ever*. The maids do their jobs.

"Does Yvonne know you have dirty laundry on the floor?" I tease, gesturing at his socks.

"Shhh," he says, placing a finger over my lips. "She'll hear you and want to clean up. And I don't know about you, but I don't want to be disturbed right now."

A world map covered in red thumbtacks hangs on the wall. Most of the tacks are concentrated in Italy, Switzerland, and Germany. "What's this?"

His eyes light up when he looks at the map. "Just places I want to visit one day, you know, when I have time."

I've never thought much about traveling—he and I have such different dreams, but seeing the little red thumbtacks makes me want to travel someplace romantic with him.

A pair of glasses, a bottle of Tylenol, and a picture of him and his dad with a horse sit on his nightstand. I suddenly feel really close to him, seeing his personal things.

"You okay?" he asks quietly, as he takes off his watch and sets it on his dresser.

From his shelf I pick up a little black horse figurine. I run my forefinger over its mane, thinking of Moonshadow. "Jack, you're not gonna sell Star, right?"

He drops his chin onto my shoulder and wraps his arms around my stomach. "Not right now, no."

"But you do sell horses."

"All the time. It's part of the business."

"Do you check out who you sell them to?"

"Always." Jack turns me around and stares into my eyes intently. "We do background checks."

"After my mom died, I started taking care of this mare. Her name was Moonshadow." I sniffle, remembering how she used to prance when I entered her stall. "We took care of each other."

He listens as I tell him what awful Mr. Cates did, how he sold Moonshadow to a man who forced her to race, even though her racing days were long gone. At her second race, she stumbled on her way out the gate and broke two legs. They shot her behind the track and left her body, not caring a lick what happened to it. Dad helped me bury her in the woods behind our trailer park.

That's why I hated rich people so bad. All they cared about was making more money. At least that's what I thought. Until I met Jack, who cares about family and honor and history.

"I'm sorry about Moonshadow," Jack says, hugging me. "Sounds like you were a good friend to her. I'm glad Star has you now."

"Yeah?"

"I was torturing the poor fellow, making him spend time with boys when he hates them. I should've known he's into girls. Just like his owner."

I give Jack a playful punch on the shoulder, and he hugs me again.

"I can't thank you enough for helping me with Star. On the way home from Kentucky this afternoon, my father told me how proud he is that I stuck to my guns. Maybe I'll pass this test after all, thanks to you."

"We're a pretty good team, huh?" I reply.

"Yeah we are," he says in a thick voice, and kisses me deeply, pushing me against the wall. We slowly make out and it hits me how right this feels, how there's no place I'd rather be.

And suddenly things speed up in a very good way. He cups my face with both hands, watching me unbutton his shirt. He twirls me around and unzips my dress, letting it drop to the floor, leaving me in just a bra and panties. Thank God I wore my matching set today. He brushes my curls out of the way so he can kiss my neck from behind, and I wrap an arm around the back of his head, weaving my fingers in his long hair. His chest presses against my back, his heart pounding hard and wild. His hands are everywhere, softly stroking my stomach, my hips, my breasts.

He yanks his boots off, hopping on one foot to do so, then he's kissing me again. I pull him to the bed. He falls on top of me. Our lips find each other hungrily. He holds both of my hands above my head as we kiss, trapping me.

"How am I supposed to unbutton your pants if you won't let my hands go?" I ask with a tiny voice, shaking all over.

"Not until I'm finished with you." He kisses a trail from my neck down to my stomach. "So that's where it is," he says, kissing the horseshoe tattoo on my hip before smiling up at me.

"Are you wearing a belt buckle that says *cocky*?" I peer down at his waistband.

"Oh, um…"

I roll my eyes, smiling like crazy. "Would you get back to kissing me already?"

"Yes, ma'am," he says, diving back in. I kiss the sensitive hollow of his neck. His pulse races beneath my lips. I bite his ear and his neck, as we squirm under the covers, our legs twisting together.

"Not too hard." He pauses to smile at me. "My parents will kill me if I show up at breakfast with a hickey."

"Oh." My face flames devil red.

"I'll give you one instead," he says, nipping at my neck. I laugh and try to pull away, but he snuggles me closer beneath the blankets.

We make out for ages, as he presses against me and rocks his hips, slowly at first, then faster and faster, and then he finally pushes past the elastic of my panties, to touch me for real. I love it, and can't stop murmuring his name over and over. I reach between us and unbutton his pants and tug his boxers down, exploring where he's hard and silky.

"I think you like me," he says, grinning.

"You're okay," I tease.

"Just okay?" he murmurs, tickling me, making me squirm and laugh. "Just *okay*?"

"Fine." I touch his cheek and return his gaze, feeling so many feelings. "I like you so much," I say quietly, and he reaches over to his nightstand, opens the top drawer, and pulls out a condom.

I'm out of breath, panting—about to tell him I don't want to do this yet, as he begins to slip my underwear down, when I hear a noise.

This house is so old you can hear every creak and groan, especially from the hardwood floors. The boards squeak—someone is coming up the stairs.

"Hide!" Jack whispers, throwing the bedcovers back, jumping off me, and fastening his pants. He rushes to his dresser and fishes out a T-shirt.

I grab my dress and shoes and catapult myself into the closet. It's bigger than my goddamned bedroom. I hide behind one of Jack's suits and try to listen to what's happening out in the room. Nothing yet. I take the arm of Jack's suit jacket and bring it to my nose, loving its guy smell. God, I've become a complete psycho.

I clench up when the knock sounds on the door.

"Come in," Jack says.

"Just came to say good night," his mother says. "You left the wedding early."

"Are you alone?" Mr. Goodwin asks.

A heartbeat. "Yeah, just tired. Gotta get up early."

After a long, heart attack-inducing silence, Mr. Goodwin says, "All right. Sleep well."

"I love you," Mrs. Goodwin adds.

"Love you too," Jack says, and a second later I hear the door click shut. I hide beside Jack's cowboy boot collection for several minutes, until the closet door finally swings open.

"Sorry about that," he whispers, reaching a hand out. I grab it and pull him to the floor. He laughs as he crawls up between my legs. From his pocket he whips out a red lollipop—one of the fancy ones you can only get at the Cracker Barrel. I hold it against my chest. I'll save it for a special occasion.

"You'd better get down to Hillcrest," he says quietly, helping me to my feet.

"Jack?"

"Hmm?" He doesn't return my stare. He's too busy running a thumb along the underside of my bra.

"All I want is to get back in bed with you."

He pushes me against the closet wall and our mouths meet again for another passionate kiss. "I've never—" he starts. "You and me—I've never felt like—" He doesn't finish his thought. He slams his lips against mine. When he pulls away, I feel his absence, like when I eat toast without butter.

"Jack? You're not dating anybody, right? Not Abby or Kelsey or some famous person's daughter, right?"

He chuckles. "Naw. I had a girlfriend…Jenna Lukens…we broke up."

"Why?" I whisper.

"My mom introduced us. And I liked her a lot at first…But

Jenna went to this private school up on Monteagle Mountain and we didn't do the long-distance thing so well, and she ended up cheating on me." His face turns a rosy pink. "And she was all sorts of drama. Always wanted me to buy her gifts and stuff."

"So you want somebody low-key?"

"I do." Jack nudges my nose with his. "Listen, if my dad catches you here, he'll roast me like a shish kabob."

"Mmm, I love shish kabob."

"I'll grill for you sometime."

"As if you know how to use a grill. You're a kept guy."

He grins mischievously. "I'll prove you wrong."

He picks my dress up off the floor, dusts it off, and holds it out so I can put it back on. I pull my hair to the side, and he kisses my back as he zips my dress.

He turns me around and we kiss again until he murmurs breathlessly, "God, you're beautiful."

I didn't know how bad I needed to hear that until he said it. He already had me in his bed wearing only my underwear. He didn't have to say I'm beautiful.

But he did.

The Walk of Shame

"I knew I was in trouble when I woke up and Luke Skywalker was staring back at me."

I'm sitting with Vanessa at Foothills Diner, sharing a slice of rhubarb pie with her. She said she desperately needed to talk to me, so here I am.

I pound a fist on the table. "I told Rory to get rid of those sheets! I knew something like this might happen…So you saw the sheets? Does that mean…?"

"It means that I accidentally fell asleep in his bed last night and his parents found us this morning and they called my papa and my brother! It was mortifying!"

I sit back and cover my mouth. "And, uh, what happened…?"

"Yeah, I wasn't, um, clothed." Her hand shakes as she sips her coffee. "Remind me never to drink champagne again, okay?"

"Oh man, I'm sorry. Did you get in trouble with your grandfather and brother?"

"Ty wanted to fly home from Arizona to 'kill Rory' but

then Papa reminded him he had a game today and it wouldn't be a good thing if the backup quarterback disappeared just to go kill somebody."

"Were Mr. and Mrs. Whitfield pissed?"

Vanessa taps her fork on her plate. "His dad made jokes, but like, his mom? She seemed really disappointed in me. I overheard her telling Rory that girls like me aren't 'girlfriend material.'"

"What the hell does that mean? Girlfriend material?"

"I've only had one serious boyfriend my entire life. But Mrs. Whitfield seemed to be under the impression I sleep around all the time. I've only slept with one guy!"

I clear my throat. "Well, now you've slept with two, right?"

Her face goes red. She shovels another bite of pie in her mouth and yells for the waitress. "We're gonna need more pie over here. ASAP! So…what happened to you last night?" she asks. "You ran off pretty quick."

"Well, umm…"

"Spill." Vanessa lifts her coffee mug to her mouth, giving me a look that says, *I just told you I woke up in a boy's bed and* Star Wars *sheets were involved.*

"Jack and I fooled around," I say softly, making Vanessa squeal. Other Foothills patrons glare at us, including a couple of trucker guys. But after they get a good look at Vanessa and her Amazon bod, they smile and sit up straighter.

"And?" she says.

"It was great," I whisper back. "But Mr. and Mrs. Goodwin stopped by and I had to hide in the closet."

"The closet."

"Yeah, and Jack has tons of cowboy boots. And then we made out some more in the closet."

Her mouth drops open and then she smiles. "So, are you guys, like, gonna hook up again…or get together…?"

"No idea," I say. "I don't even know what Jack wants yet. His dad would be pissed. My dad would be horrified."

She pops another bite of pie into her mouth. "Do you want something with him?"

I find myself slowly nodding. I want, I want, I want.

"Be careful…Jack rarely has serious girlfriends," Vanessa says slowly, cradling her cup. "Although you did make out with him two weekends in a row. That's a record for Jack."

I change the subject. "What about you and Rory?"

"I'm so embarrassed," Vanessa says quietly. "I'm afraid Mrs. Whitfield's never gonna let me come back over to her house. You know what she said to me? 'I wish Rory's younger brothers hadn't seen you here. What kind of example does that set?'"

"Did Rory get the same lecture?" I ask.

"No, his Dad just sent him outside to clean something called a manure collector before church."

I cringe and take a drink of coffee. "I'm sure Mrs. Whitfield was just shocked," I say. "I mean, all moms are protective, I imagine."

Not that Vanessa or I would know anything about that. Several years ago her parents were in a car crash: her father died on the scene and her mom died a while later from her injuries.

"It's just 'cause I look like this," she mumbles. "It's like, nobody ever bothers to get to know me. It's all about my looks. They think I must be evil because I'm pretty. Or they think I have the perfect life—when really I just miss my parents..."

I'm about to tell her that no one thinks that her life is perfect, but hell, I've thought it myself. We don't know what other people are thinking. We never will unless we ask.

"I'm your friend," I tell her. "And if Mrs. Whitfield doesn't see how great you are, then screw her."

Vanessa looks up and gives me a small smile. "I just hope Rory doesn't want to end stuff...you know? I haven't heard from him since this morning...I thought he would've found a way to call."

"Don't worry. He really likes you..."

She grins, looking into her coffee cup. "So how'd you end up in bed with Jack Goodwin last night?"

"How'd you end up in bed with Rory and Darth Vader?" I fire back.

"And Chewbacca."

I groan, laughing.

We finish off two more pieces of rhubarb pie and dish up all our gossip, and the pie tastes a little sweeter than usual.

• • •

Vanessa has this prehistoric plaid couch the color of Halloween.

Orange, red, gold, and more orange.

She invited me over to her house after we gorged ourselves on pie, and now here I am, gazing around at a tiny house with brown shag carpet and frayed curtains. Family pictures cover the walls and end tables.

"This is cozy."

Vanessa sprawls out on the Halloween couch. "My brother, Ty, keeps trying to buy Papa this house that looks like a castle, but we like it here. But Papa did agree to that TV." She points at a flat screen. "Ty always thinks we should have the best, no matter if it's practical or not."

"Do you miss Ty?"

Vanessa nods slowly. "He wanted me to move out to Arizona with him, but I didn't want to change schools senior year. And I can't leave Papa. I'd miss him too much…he's like, my best friend." She glances away, embarrassed. I've never heard somebody call a grandparent a best friend. Awesome.

"Couldn't your grandfather go with you?"

"He loves it here. He likes his job at the pajama factory. And besides, I'm going to college at Middle Tennessee state."

The house smells a little musty because it's old, but it's full of warmth, and it amazes me that a guy who came from this life went on to play for the Arizona Cardinals. He took his talents and ran. And now Vanessa is seeing the benefits and doesn't have to worry about money anymore. I don't want to worry about money anymore. But the NFL is on an entirely different echelon than horse jockeying.

College could give me new opportunities like Ty had. Maybe I should consider going to talk to the guidance counselor.

Vanessa and I sit down to watch a movie and she tells me how glad she is I moved here and that it's easy to talk for real with me. She admits that she and Kelsey have more of a surface-level friendship because Kelsey never lets people get close, which sort of shocks me. That girl is such a mystery.

Vanessa and I are still talking when the doorbell rings. She stands to answer the door, revealing Rory. They look at each other for a long moment before he launches himself into her arms, kissing her cheeks and lips and holding her tight. She wraps her arms around his neck and presses her forehead to his.

Jesus, it's like they're already in love.

"Are you in big trouble with your mom?" Vanessa asks. "Does she hate me?"

"If she does, it doesn't matter," Rory says. "I want you. Like, I want to date only you and I just…" He pauses to take a deep breath, looking into her eyes. "I like you so much."

"I'm really sorry I fell asleep last night."

"I'm sorry I let us drink so much champagne," Rory says with a nervous laugh.

"Never again."

"Agreed."

I'm getting a warm feeling watching them. He doesn't care whether his parents like Vanessa or not. They want each other, so they're going to be together. I love that.

What would happen if I told Dad and Cindy that I want to be with Jack? Would Jack make sure his father doesn't fire my family? Would Jack tell his father about us?

I love Jack's confidence, his smirk, his sense of humor, the way he cares for his little sister, the way he loves his animals, he edits his mom's cookbook, he helped me pour water at dinner that night. I just like him.

I want Jack, and I shouldn't let anybody—not even myself—get in the way of it.

• • •

When I get home, I find Dad and Cindy sitting on the couch, looking at a baby name book she borrowed from Mrs. Goodwin.

"Shortcake, what do you think of Arya?" Cindy asks.

"I like it, but it sounds too medieval," I say, squeezing onto the couch on the other side of Dad. I lean against his arm, rest my chin on his shoulder, and look down at the book with him.

"What about something modern?" I ask. "How about Marriott?"

Cindy laughs. "We are not naming the baby after a hotel chain."

We flip through the book for a while longer, checking out names like Crimson (love it!), Katherine (Cindy's choice), and Nina (Dad thinks it's sweet).

I sigh, snuggling closer to Dad, resting my head on his shoulder. "Can I talk to you about something?"

"Of course," Cindy says, snapping the book shut.

"You have to promise you won't get mad or jump to conclusions or anything."

"We promise," Dad says, taking my hand. "But you'd better not be pregnant."

"Jesus Lord, Dad! You need to get a filter."

"That's true." Cindy gently taps his arm. "So what's going on?"

I look around to make sure nobody else is nearby listening in. "Um…here's the thing. I've been spending a lot of time with Jack…and I want to try dating him—"

"No," Dad says, shaking his head fast.

"But I really like him."

"I told you not to start anything with him."

How do you tell your dad it's too late? It's not like I'd tell him Jack and I have already been to third base together.

"How could you disobey me?" His voice is angry and full of hurt. "You know the Goodwins don't want us interfering with their lives. They don't even want us in their house!"

Cindy pats his knee. "Shhh." She gives me a disappointed-mom face, even though she's not my stepmother yet. "After what happened with Moonshadow, I don't want to see you hurt again. Being with Jack might seem good today, but that could change."

Memories of kissing Jack one night and then having him back off the next day fill my mind. He played Abby Winchester. He probably wrote Kelsey Painter off too. But I could be different, right?

"But it's my decision," I say. Breakups are always a possibility, but without him, life will feel like riding a super slow mule. "I want this."

Dad and Cindy exchange a long look. Finally he lets out a long sigh. "We can't afford for you to a make a decision that'll mess up our jobs right now, understand?" He sets his jaw. "Ever since we moved here, every decision you've made has been selfish or dangerous—with your jockeying and exercise riding and looking at colleges on the computer or dating my boss's son. You know I can't afford to send you to college—" Dad's voice breaks. "Rory Whitfield is a nice guy. Why don't you date him?"

"I'm never gonna like Rory like that—"

"Our lives," Dad starts, blowing into his cupped hands. "We're never gonna have lives like the Goodwins. I don't know what ideas this place is putting into your head but it needs to stop before you get hurt and Cindy and your little sister get hurt too, got it?" His tone is fiercely mean and serious.

My hands and lips are trembling. I feel queasy. A stabbing pain rushes up my arm and into my chest. I start shaking all over.

Dad has never spoken to me like this. Ever.

Growing up, Dad told me stories about how his father, my papa, never could keep a steady job as a groom and they bought all their groceries with food stamps. Didn't Dad start working at Cedar Hill because he wanted a better life? What's so wrong with me going after something better?

"Can I still be a jockey?" I ask through clenched teeth, curling my hands into fists.

"I said you could until something else bad happens, didn't I?" Dad runs a hand through his hair, grasping it tightly.

Cindy says, "We just worry about you, Shortcake—"

"Stop calling me Shortcake!" I burst. "Only Mom and Dad are allowed to call me that!"

Cindy looks down at her stomach and starts crying. Dad's face immediately softens and he tells her he loves her and the baby.

Yvonne appears in the doorway with wide eyes, holding her needlework, looking at the three of us. She gives me a wink and a nod before disappearing back toward her room.

I stand up on shaky knees. "I'm going for a walk."

"Stay away from Jack Goodwin," Dad calls out.

I jet out the door, ignoring Dad, pulling a sucker from my pocket and jabbing it into my mouth.

• • •

I make it all the way to Greenbriar pasture before I start sobbing.

It's late on Sunday afternoon, and everyone's enjoying post-church supper with their families so the racetracks are deserted. Only a few farmhands are around, monitoring the grazing horses. I open the gate, and Star immediately jogs over to me, whinnying softly. He doesn't stop to show me respect; he buries his nose in my neck and sighs.

"I love you too," I whisper into his mane.

How could Dad yell at me like that? Doesn't he care what I feel for Jack? It's not like I ever yelled at him when he got Cindy pregnant when there's no way in hell he could afford another kid. And I haven't been selfish at all. Of course, Dad doesn't know I asked Mr. Goodwin to supplement Cindy's paychecks with my own…

Jack's three dogs bound up, panting and slobbering all over the place, chasing each other around the cedar trees. I turn to find Jack looking over his shoulder toward the manor house.

"I was hoping I'd find you here," he says, the corner of his mouth lifting into a subtle grin. "This is becoming our spot." He gestures at the pasture.

I nod, giving him a little smile.

"What's wrong?" he whispers.

I shake my head, not ready to talk yet.

"Let's walk," he says. I follow him out the gate and toward the lake. Star snorts, upset that I'm leaving him behind.

Jack leads me down to the lake with his hounds in tow. There, he wipes the tears out from under my eyes and I curl up against his chest. That gives him the opening he needs, I guess, because soon we're kissing and his hands are in my hair and I'm running my hands under his T-shirt, dragging my fingertips over his abs.

It's a warm September evening and the stars are just beginning to peek out. Twilight.

"If I take your clothes off, Jasper will steal them," Jack murmurs between kisses, as he unsnaps my bra, leaving my shirt on.

"Wouldn't want that," I say softly, laughing.

We lie down together in the grass, him straddling my hips, reenacting what we did last night. He unbuttons my jeans and slides them down until they're hooked around one of my ankles, and he kisses and touches me until I'm tingling all over. But we go a step further, doing something I've never done.

"Are you sure?" he whispers, threading his fingers through my hair, and I nod. I take him in my hand and go down on him—because I want to. It's awkward and I'm scared I'm doing something wrong, but I love feeling close to him. He seems to like what I'm doing...

When we're both finished, he presses his cheek to mine and whispers, "Are you feeling better?"

I nod, snuggling against his chest.

"I'm sorry we got interrupted last night," he says softly. "I'll have to take you up to our weekend cabin in Kentucky sometime soon, so we can have privacy..."

I love the idea of being his houseguest at their cabin. I've never been there, but I heard Jodi telling Cindy about it. Jodi said it was about the prettiest place she'd ever seen, covered in ivy like straight out of a fairy tale.

I smile into Jack's shoulder, close my eyes, and enjoy the sounds of water lapping gently against the banks. "Jack?"

"Hmm?" he mumbles, playing with my hair.

"If I were to, like, go see the guidance counselor tomorrow at school…would you, um, come with me?"

"What are you going to talk to her about?"

"I was looking at some colleges online but I don't know if any of them will work for me…because Dad can't pay for any of it." I suck in a deep breath, embarrassed out of my mind. "And if the guidance counselor says something I don't understand I thought maybe you could help me?"

Jack kisses my head. "Sure. I can do that. But don't you think you should bring your dad, not me?"

I grasp his T-shirt and twist it, holding on tight. "I talked to him and Cindy a little while ago, and my dad brought up college when I was telling them about me and you and how we might be together and I don't think he wants me to apply—"

"You told your dad and Cindy about us?" He sits up straight, knocking me off his chest. I bring myself to a sitting position and start to resnap my bra. Why's he acting so skittish? "Why did you do that?"

"I like talking to my dad," I say quietly.

"You told him what we did last night?" he exclaims.

"No, no," I say, waving my hands. I swallow hard, feeling tears burn my eyes again. "I just told Dad and Cindy that I like you and I'm not gonna stay away from you like they want me to."

"I wish you would've talked to me before just announcing we're, like, a couple or whatever," Jack says, dragging a hand through his hair. He looks seriously pissed.

"I didn't tell him that!" I nervously pick blades of grass. "I told them I like you...and wanted to be with you, that's all."

Jack lets out a long breath. "Look, I'm glad you feel that way, but we can't have a real relationship."

"We can't?" I whisper.

"You know we can't. I thought you wanted to be together... like, in secret. As friends with benefits."

Did he really just say friends with benefits?

"Like, we'd hook up, but we'd never go out on dates and stuff?"

"Yeah. We'd be together on the down low."

Did he really just say down low?

"Why can't we just try it for real? See what people say?"

Jack won't stop clutching his hair. "Is your father gonna tell my dad? You can't let him tell my father! I have to show him I'm a good owner who respects his staff."

Tears have already begun to drip down my cheeks. I wipe them away as quickly as I can. If he didn't hold all the power before, he does now. I gave it to him.

"I'll make sure my dad doesn't say anything," I say quietly.

"Good, because my dad hasn't finished the Paradise Park deal yet. If the Winchesters think I'm dating somebody else, it'll ruin everything for Dad." Jack shakes his head. He looks pissed.

This is one of those bad memories that's going to play on repeat over and over in my head. Like the memories of Moonshadow. I can't believe I shared her story with Jack. Maybe I was right before. Rich people are all alike. Only care about their goddamned money. Only care about what's best for them.

I dig my fingernails into my palm, trying to decide the best thing to say. Something I won't regret when I look back on this moment.

It's weird. I've never felt so many things at once. Anger. Shame. Sadness.

More humiliation than I've ever experienced.

But mostly pride for what I'm about to do.

"I won't do this in secret," I say. "It's terrible that a business deal is dependent on you playing Abby Winchester. I hate that a deal is more important than my feelings. Do you have any idea how shitty it's gonna feel to tell Dad and Cindy that they were right about you?"

"What about me?" he mumbles, his nostrils flaring.

I laugh harshly. "They said you lose interest in girls after a couple days and that I wasn't anything special. They're right. If I were special, you wouldn't want to keep me a secret."

"It's not that, Sava—"

"Save it," I reply, crossing my arms across my stomach. I feel sick. I can't believe what I just did with him…and then this happens. "You may not respect me, but I respect myself enough to not do this with you. I hope your dad gets his racetrack and I hope it's worth what it's costing you: me."

Dead Last

"Do you want me to kick his ass?"

I try to focus on my geometry homework through my anger.

"Because I can kick his ass," Rory goes on.

Vanessa nods. "And if you won't let Rory kick his ass, I'll do it."

"Guys, I can kick his ass myself," I say, sniffling and wiping my nose.

During study hall, I've just finished telling my friends about what happened with Jack. I left out the part about how I went down on him. Can you say Big Mistake? Vanessa and Rory warned me about Jack. I feel ashamed that they know I'm nothing special to him.

He didn't join me for lunch or study hall today, instead choosing to sit with Kelsey Painter and Colton Bradford. She's chattering to Jack nonstop and Colton's resting his head on the table. On the one hand, I'm glad Jack didn't sit with me, because I don't want to smell his cologne and risk burying my face in his neck. At the same time, the hurt and embarrassment are pumping through my veins.

"It's fine," I say quietly, chewing my eraser. "I mean, I could still be with him if I want."

"But you'd have to keep him a secret," Vanessa says. "That is such a dick move."

"I'd never ask a girl to be secret friends with benefits or whatever," Rory says, stretching an arm around Vanessa.

"You'd better not. You have a girlfriend now, remember?" she says.

They grin at each other lovingly and my insides curl up and die.

"My cousin, Alex, texted me yesterday." Rory gives me a sly smile. "He asked about you. Who you are and stuff."

"Really?" I ask. I haven't even thought about Alex since Saturday night.

"He's single now. We should all do something together soon," Rory says, and Vanessa nods. I don't need a guy to feel happy, but I like the idea of meeting more Tennessee people.

"Yeah, that might be good," I say softly, sneaking a peek at Jack. Even though lunch ended an hour ago and we're in the library, he's digging around in the cooler Yvonne packed for him.

"Don't look at him!" Vanessa blurts.

"I can't help it," I say. I hate that I feel weak.

"That's it," Vanessa says, throwing her pencil down. "Next weekend, you and I are going to the Infinity club in Nashville. The one that lets people under eighteen in."

"Sounds fun," Rory says.

"You're not invited. It's girls only," Vanessa says.

"But I have some new dance moves to share." Rory pouts.

"You can show me in private," Vanessa says, and I nearly barf.

I stuff my worksheet into my math book and stand. Vanessa and Rory are already too busy kissing to notice me taking off, but Jack follows me with his eyes as I leave the library. He seems sad—he doesn't even notice that Kelsey is stealing a Capri Sun from his cooler. When she sees him staring at me, she taps his hand.

He quickly shakes his head and turns his focus to her, listening to whatever she's saying.

And that's just fine.

• • •

When Rory drops me off at Cedar Hill after school, I go to Hillcrest to ditch my backpack before my training session with Gael.

Dad and Cindy look up when I enter the common room, but Dad doesn't meet my eyes. "Savannah," he starts. "I need to take Cindy to the doctor this afternoon. She's tired and couldn't hold any food down this weekend. I'm worried."

"Didn't you just see the doctor a couple of weeks ago?"

"I'm not taking chances," Dad says, touching her stomach.

I suddenly feel choked up. Not only because I'm worried about the baby, but because yesterday's argument with Dad is still hanging in the air. If Mom were here, would she know what to say to make me feel better?

"Savannah," Cindy says, rubbing her eyes. I go kneel in front of her chair. "Can you help me again? I'm so sorry to ask but I haven't finished something for Mrs. Goodwin and she's having a charity meeting in the morning—"

"What is it?"

Cindy pauses for a sec. "I had started to wax the parlor floor but the smell was making me feel sick—"

"I'll take care of it." I charge to my room to change into grungy clothes.

"Savannah," Dad calls, but I shut my bedroom door before I can hear what he wants. He doesn't care what I want anyway. Why should I bother with him? Especially after I've been trying to help our family.

When I come back out into the common room, it's empty. Dad and Cindy have left for the doctor without saying goodbye. Whatever.

Up at the manor house, Paula shows me where to find the wax for the floor and gives me a quick tutorial. I dip an old T-shirt in the wax and wring it out so the shirt won't absorb too much wax and kneel, massaging the wax into the wood floor. Paula said that when the wax begins to look cloudy, I should use a clean towel to buff the wood. Damn, being a maid is harder than riding a horse. Waxing is killing both my arms.

I hear laughter and footsteps coming through the foyer toward the steps. I look up to find Kelsey and Jack standing in the doorway to the parlor.

Hell. Could my life become any more embarrassing? Before you know it, I'll be cleaning toilets like Marcus Winchester's servants.

Kelsey focuses on me for a sec, looking confused, then goes back to typing on her cell and begins to climb the stairs. "Come on, Jack." Is she going to his room? Are they going to hook up?

He ignores her and steps into the room, his nose crinkling. "What are you doing?"

"What does it look like I'm doing?" I snap.

"Waxing the floor. Why isn't Paula or Cindy doing it? Or even Yvonne?"

"Because it's Cindy's job and she had to go to the doctor. And we can't afford to lose her hours. Somebody has to work." I bend back over and wax harder.

"What a good idea," a voice says. I glance up to find Gael standing there. Can this day get any goddamned worse? "I should have all my jockeys and exercise boys wax floors. It's great for upper body strength. Savannah, can you wax my truck before our training session?"

I glare at both of them.

"Gael, can you give us a minute, please?" Jack says in a soft voice.

Gael raises his eyebrows and vamooses quicker than you can say *on your mark*.

Jack squats next to me, picks up the old T-shirt, and sniffs it, getting a grossed out look on his face. I snatch it out of his hand and rub the floor, trying to ignore the fresh smell of his laundered clothes and cologne.

"I miss you," he murmurs.

I nod toward the staircase. "What about Kelsey?"

"Nothing's going on with her. We're just friends."

"Does she know that?"

"I've told her I don't want anything serious with her. But she's my friend and she's been ditched by friends before, and I won't do that to her. But about you and me, can we talk privately? I want to find a way for you and me to be together…"

"Well, I don't want to be waxing the damned floor, but we don't always get what we wish for."

Jack stands and takes a step back, glaring down at me. "Fine." He marches out of the room, his boots crashing down on the floor.

I wipe the sweat off my forehead and get back to work.

• • •

Later that evening, someone raps on my door while I'm reading the *Daily Racing Form*. "Come in."

Rory opens the door and sits down on my bed with me, pulling me into a hug. "I want to kill that bastard for making you feel so bad."

I laugh softly, clutching his T-shirt.

"You didn't sleep with him, did you?" he asks.

I shake my head. "I thought you like it when girls sleep with guys after two minutes?"

"Not you," he says. "Not you. I think Jack's a dumbass. He obviously wants you..."

I know.

"Come eat dinner with me," he says. "We can go to Tennessee Ballers."

"I'm not hungry."

"Will you run over my lines with me later? I'm auditioning for the school play."

I love that he's trying to distract me. "Are they doing the play you wrote? *Call Me When Your Mom Is Back in Town*?"

"No," Rory says, sighing deeply. "Mrs. Towne said my play was too risqué for high school. We're doing *Peter Pan*."

"Oh, I hope you get the role of Peter! You'll get to fly around the stage hanging from those cord thingies."

He winks. "You just want to see me in green tights."

"Ugh." I laugh, and then Rory goes to find dinner, because when you're a seventeen-year-old boy, food outweighs all else.

An hour later, Cindy shows up carrying a tray with a piece of chicken, some cooked carrots, and a small glass of milk. She brings it to my bed and sits down beside me, patting my leg. Just like Dad this afternoon, she can't seem to meet my gaze, and her face is red.

"How's the baby?" I ask.

"The doctor says she's fine," Cindy replies, sniffling. She pinches her nose. "I guess some women have more difficult pregnancies than others. He said I shouldn't be doing so much physical labor."

"Are you going to tell the Goodwins?"

"In the morning," she replies, wringing her fingers. "I'm afraid they'll let me go…I'm afraid I'll have to move away from you and your dad."

"Don't think that." I give her a hug. "It'll be okay."

That's when Dad appears in the doorway.

"I don't really want to talk to you right now," I say, making him wince.

"I wanted to say thanks for helping with the floors today."

"I didn't do it for you. I did it for my little sister."

Dad comes in and shuts the door. There's hardly room for him to stand in here.

"We need to talk about what happened yesterday," Dad says. "You need to underst—"

"I've been working hard on the track!" I interrupt. "I've been giving Mr. Goodwin money I make so that Cindy can take time off. So you'll have more money to spend on the baby. And then you yell at me and call me selfish and say I'm doing reckless things. And Jack has been so nice to me—I thought he wanted me—"

It all comes pouring out. Who is this weak girl speaking with my mouth?

My hands are shaking and my heart is thumping against my chest. A cool, slimy feeling flows through my body, as if somebody's dipping me in a vat of ice water.

"I didn't ask you to help with our bills," Dad says quietly. He moves toward me, as if he's going to hug me, but I hold up a hand.

"Don't," I cry, putting my face in my hands. "Just leave me alone."

"Shortcake," Dad says, but I shake my head.

"Please go away."

He sniffles and rubs his eyes, and Cindy's tearing up. I can't bear to hear them say *I told you so.* I just can't. Not after he yelled at me and wouldn't listen yesterday. I can't bear to tell them they were right about Jack.

I clutch my pillow and stare out the tiny rectangular window near the ceiling. Life is so damned unfair. When I looked out Jack's large bay window, I could see a million stars. My window is so small, I can only see a handful. If I had been born to a richer family, I'd have so many more stars to wish upon.

"I'm sorry I got upset," Dad says softly. His eyes glisten. "I'm so, so proud of you. For getting a jockey position at a top farm. For even thinking about college."

I nod and let him hug me and rub my back. Cindy holds my hand and combs my hair with her fingers. "You're the strongest girl I know," she says quietly. "I wish I were more like you."

I smile at her through my tears, and she takes my hand and

places it on her stomach, so I can feel a kick. I suddenly can't wait to meet my baby sister.

"I didn't mean to yell," Dad says. "It's just, you're growing up, and I can't protect you from everything."

I haven't cried like this since the day I found Moonshadow's body. I let them hug me, wishing I could forget how I hooked up with Jack and shared a part of myself with him. I gave him something I've never given anyone else.

The honest to God truth is that I'm mad at myself. I should've known better.

• • •

It's Thursday evening, and Vanessa, Rory, and I are meeting his cousin Alex at the county fair. A double date. I'm pretty excited about it, but I'm trying not to get my hopes up.

I love fairs. Something about the idea of walking around holding hands with a guy under the night sky makes me feel like I'll find my one true love here. The fair is full of hope.

We hop out of Rory's truck into muddy divots and begin making our way up to the ticket booth covered with flashing lights. The night is crisp and cool and smells of popcorn and cow poop. I wipe my sweaty palms on my jeans and anxiously scan the crowd for Alex.

"Calm down," Rory says with a smirk.

"Quiet, you," Vanessa says to Rory. She flashes me an excited glance.

A couple minutes later, I see Alex coming our way. I fight the urge to bounce on my tiptoes. He's dressed very comfortably—jeans and flip-flops, and his T-shirt and over shirt are untucked and a bit wrinkled. I love how Jack always looks so put-together, but I like Alex's look too. And of course I adore his floppy Whitfield hair.

He gives Rory a pat on the back then hugs Vanessa, and finally turns his focus to me.

"Hey," he says.

I stick out my hand to shake his and he takes it, smiling into my eyes. His fingers are warm, and I'm excited about what might happen tonight. I hope whatever happens makes me forget how much I miss Jack. I force his face and smile out of my thoughts.

We each get $5 worth of tickets—enough to ride the Ferris wheel, slam each other in bumper cars, and get queasy on the Tilt-a-Whirl. The smell of funnel cakes and fries wafts under my nose, mesmerizing me just as much as the flashing lights and bells dinging when kids win prizes.

Our first stop is the Tilt-a-Whirl, where Vanessa and I scream our heads off and get sufficiently nauseous, while Rory and Alex have a grand ole time. Then Rory and Vanessa want to ride the Ferris wheel, so we head that way. Alex and I watch them climb into a bucket seat and grab the handlebar as it settles in their laps.

"Riding the Ferris wheel must be code for making out," Alex says, as Vanessa and Rory start pawing at each other.

"Yup."

"Want to?" he asks, pointing at the ride.

"Make out?" I tease.

He pauses for a sec, looking freaked out. "I meant ride the Ferris wheel."

"I was joking." My face feels a million degrees.

Alex walks up to the ticket taker guy and when I try to pass over tickets of my own, he waves my hand away. "I got it."

"Thanks," I say.

"But wait. Are you tall enough to ride the ride?" Alex asks, pointing to the ruler.

I give him a faux evil look and go grab a seat. We grasp the bar, looking straight ahead as the wheel moves backward in a lurch, lifting us up into the black sky. From way up here, you can see all of downtown. The Franklin Theater marquee burns red and gold. A blue light flashes on top of the water tower.

Alex looks at me sideways. "In full disclosure, I haven't been on a first date in a while."

"I'll have mercy on you," I say with a laugh. He doesn't date often? That's hard to believe. Wind rushes against my face as the Ferris wheel reaches for the stars again.

"So you're a horse jockey?" he asks, lifting an eyebrow. "That's pretty sexy."

I give him a friendly shove and launch into telling him about last week's race and my hopes for this weekend at Keeneland and the upcoming Dixiana Derby. Alex watches my face and asks questions about jockeying and soon I'm quizzing him.

"I'm a biology major at Middle Tennessee State," he says. It turns out he likes rock climbing and spends most weekends in the woods.

When we get off the Ferris wheel, Vanessa and Rory say they want to ride it again—which is code for wanting to make out some more, so Alex buys us a funnel cake and we walk around, chatting and licking powdered sugar off our fingers.

I see lots of people from school. Colton Bradford and Kelsey Painter are hanging out with the cheerleading squad and guys from the football team. They're taking turns going down the Megaslide, squealing and banging against each other as they land on the cushioned bottom. Colton and Kelsey wave at me, and it doesn't escape my notice when they check out Alex.

Colton mouths at me, "He's hot!" and makes inappropriate gestures with his hips, and I grin back at him. What a perv. It surprises me that Jack isn't with them tonight. And it surprises me even more that Kelsey waved at me.

"How about the Fun House?" Alex asks, and we spend a few minutes giggling into a mirror that makes us look about a thousand pounds apiece.

"You need to go on a diet," I tease.

"On second thought, you're not my type." Alex chuckles as I shake my hips, making my thousand-pound self dance in the mirror.

His phone rings, he fishes it out of his pocket, and stares at the screen. "I need to take this. C'mon."

We leave the Fun House, and while he chats on the phone, I go over to the dime toss game where I pay three tickets to throw five dimes into little glass bowls filled with water. I miss all five times.

That's when I see them.

Jack and Shelby Goodwin. He has one hand protectively curled over her shoulder as they're coming out of the art pavilion.

Of course Alex is still pacing and talking on the phone. Did he forget he was on a date with me? Embarrassing.

I pay another three tickets and focus on the game. I miss all five times again.

"Wow, you are awful at this."

I turn to face Jack.

Shelby elbows her brother's ribs. "With that mouth it's no wonder you can't keep a girlfriend. Hi, Savannah."

"Hi," I say, and pass three more tickets over to play again.

"You here alone?" Jack asks, glancing around.

"No. I'm on a date." I point at Alex, who has a finger stuffed in his ear so he can better hear the person on the other end of the line. This had better be important because he's been on the phone at least five minutes now.

"Oh," Jack replies, furrowing his brow.

"Win me something," Shelby demands to Jack, so he pays

three tickets to play the dime game. He tosses four times before nailing a shot and winning Shelby a brown stuffed horse.

"I'll play again," Jack says, passing over tickets. As Shelby starts talking to a friend, gossiping about some boy in the eighth grade, Jack nails a shot on the second try, winning another stuffed animal.

"I'll take that one," he says. He points toward a small pink unicorn. The worker plucks it off the prize wall and Jack hands it to me. "For your room. It'll match your Strawberry Shortcake bedspread."

I scowl at him then take the stuffed animal, slipping it under my arm. "I'm naming him Seabiscuit."

Jack gives me a withering look. "Really? Seabiscuit? You know the best horses at our farm come from Nasrullah and Secretariat."

"Fine. I'll name him War Horse."

"Oh Lord." Jack laughs and shakes his head.

"I'm predictable, eh?"

"Not in my mind, no," he says quietly, rubbing the back of his neck. He glances over at Alex. "What's your favorite part of the fair?"

"The mule races."

"Oh yeah? Mine's going to the dog show."

I laugh, and we look into each other's eyes. He's quiet for a long, still moment. "I'm looking forward to Saturday. I think you and Star can win this one."

We're racing at Keeneland in Kentucky this weekend. Jack entered Star in a handicap with a $150,000 purse.

"I'm excited for Saturday too," I say, not able to keep the excitement out of my voice. "I know we'll win this one."

Jack grins. Then shakes his head and focuses on the Ferris wheel. It loops around twice as we stand in silence. When I was a little girl and watched older girls walk around with their boyfriends at the fair, I couldn't wait for the day I'd do it myself. And now here I am: practically alone since my date ditched me for a phone call. Alone, when I have the guy I truly want right next to me.

"Savannah," Jack says, glancing at his sister, who's still preoccupied with her friend. "I know I haven't been good to you, but I want to find a way—"

That's when Alex walks back over and drops a hand on my shoulder. "Sorry about that. A friend was having trouble sorting something out."

"I'm Jack." He stretches a hand out to shake Alex's. Alex introduces himself then asks if I want to ride the teacups. I nod.

"Bye, Jack," I say, and a panicked look rushes onto his face as I turn away with Alex. But I leave him behind.

"Who was that guy?" Alex asks.

"My boss."

"Huh. He's kinda young."

I glance back to see Jack putting an arm around his little sister's shoulders and guiding her toward the Ferris wheel.

Alex and I board the teacups and he cozies up next to me—it's getting cold out here. The rest of the night goes smoothly—no more Goodwins show up, and Alex doesn't get any more phone calls, and when we're leaving the fair, he gives me a quick peck on the cheek and asks if he can call me Saturday, so maybe we can grab a bite to eat or something that evening.

"Yeah, that'd be great." I smile. The night wasn't a complete win, but I had a nice time and I'd like to see him again. He's nice and he kissed my cheek and he treated me well. What more can I ask for?

But later that night, against my better judgment, I curl up with the pink unicorn and stare out my little rectangular window at the stars, imagining Jack's arms around me.

• • •

Thanks to a bad rain on Friday, the track at Keeneland is a big mud pit. The horses have to work double time just to make it around during practice. It's like when humans try to run on the beach. During practice, I take Star out for a warm-up, and on the backstretch, Star pulls up hard and I fall. I shoulder roll into a big puddle. The mud cushions the fall, but I'm covered in muck.

Star doesn't take off like he normally does when he bucks his riders. He pushes my head with his nose, as if he's telling me to get up. He snorts and digs a hoof into the mud.

As I'm standing up, wiping the mud off my gloves on my pants,

Jack, Gael, Dad, and Mr. Goodwin come slopping through the mud toward me. Gael grabs Star's bridle.

"Are you okay?" Dad asks.

"Fine," I say, keeping my voice steady. My butt doesn't even hurt.

"Let's get you off the track," Gael says, leading us back to the stalls. Rory comes to give Star a bath and get him fed.

"Son," Mr. Goodwin says to Jack, "I think you should either pull Star from the race or put Townsend on as jockey instead of Savannah. She just doesn't have the experience racing in muddy conditions. I don't want her to fall during the real thing."

"But—" I start.

"Mr. Goodwin's right," Dad says, scanning my filthy clothes.

"You don't know that," I say. "So I fell one time—"

"You've fallen during practice too," Mr. Goodwin says.

"She's gotta get experience sometime," Gael says, and I flash him a smile.

"I don't want a Cedar Hill rider falling in a race," Mr. Goodwin says. "It wouldn't look good for me and my farm."

"Are you really gonna let this happen?" I ask Jack.

He doesn't meet my eyes.

"I thought you made the decisions," I say. "You're supposedly acting owner of the farm."

"I am!"

"Just not when it's important, I guess."

Jack opens his mouth to speak then shuts it again. His forehead crinkles and he looks down before glancing up at his dad again.

"Use Townsend as your jockey," Mr. Goodwin says. "This is important."

"I'm sorry," Jack says quietly. "Dad's right—I don't want you to get hurt. I'm racing Townsend." He jets out of the stall, leaving me leaning over onto my knees, gasping for breath.

They know Star doesn't like boys. It pisses me off that they're willing to risk Star being uncomfortable. Besides, I came in third last time! That's a gazillion times better than Townsend ever managed on Star. I yank my gloves off, throw them on the floor, stomp out of the stall, and slam the door shut. Minerva sticks her head out of her stall, looking me in the eye, alarmed.

"Shit," I say, charging out of the barn. Rory sees me and chases after me, trying to talk.

"What's wrong?" Rory asks, grabbing my elbow.

"Just leave me alone!" I yell, storming toward the grandstands.

I find a place far away from the paddock to stand and watch Star's race. Jack already told me he can't date me because of who I am. And now he's taking this away from me? Asshole.

Before the race starts, Jack comes to join me in the grandstands. He brings me a hot cocoa from the concession stand because it's so chilly.

"I'm really sorry," Jack says, passing me the Styrofoam cup. I don't want to accept his peace offering, but only an idiot would turn down a free hot chocolate on a day like this. Stupid rainstorm.

"I'm sorry too," I say. "Are you gonna take orders from your dad for the rest of your life? When are you gonna actually stand up and act like an owner? Or is that just a title for you?"

Jack furrows his eyebrows, looking hurt and pissed, and I know I've dealt a low blow, but I need to put shields up around myself.

"I didn't do it only because Dad told me to," Jack says. He musses his wet hair, and rain drips down his face.

"Then why did you do it?" I snap.

"Because I care about you!" he roars. People in the grandstands stare at us. "I care about you so much and I don't want to see you get hurt." He drags a hand through his hair again. Everything goes so quiet I can hear my heart pounding inside my chest. "Drink your cocoa. It's cold and I don't want you to get sick."

"You don't need to take care of me, Jack."

"I want to take ca—" He hesitates and breathes deeply.

I sip the cocoa, shaking my head at the racetrack. "I'm really pissed at you right now. First you got my hopes up about being a jockey and being able to do something different with my life. And then you got me excited about us. That maybe we could be something special, because I really *feel* something when I'm with you. And I mean *really* feel..." I grind my teeth together.

Jack is staring at his boots now. "I told you I want you."

"And I told you that I won't settle for being your secret."

"But you will settle for that guy you were with the other night. Rory Whitfield's cousin."

"That's not settling! It was a real date!"

"Oh please. A real date with no chemistry. Of course you were settling." He steps closer, getting in my face space. "Be with me. Please don't date him."

"Oh, so you'll stoop to date me now that I could be interested in another guy? That sucks."

"I care about you!"

"Then prove it."

I face the racetrack, not meeting his gaze again. After several seconds of stewing in silence, Jack finally leaves me standing there alone. I take my hot cocoa and find a dry place to sit.

During the race, Townsend rides the rail and never gets Star out in front of the pack. The horse whips his head from side to side at one point, and I think Townsend will lose control, but he hangs on somehow.

They come in fourth place.

If Circumstances Were Different

Jack is giving Star a weekend off from racing because the Dixiana Derby is next Saturday.

Out in Greenbriar, I'm all alone as I give Star a bath. After I brush his teeth, he reaches out as if he's gonna bite my hand, but then he slowly nuzzles it. I look into his eyes and he nickers.

"Hello," I reply. "Are you glad you have a day off?"

Star snuggles against my shoulder.

"No wonder you haven't been winning races," I whisper. "You've become a big ole pansy. Racehorses are supposed to be aggressive." I pump my fist and try to show him I mean business, but he goes back to eating his grain. What a pig.

I hang out with Star the rest of the day, cleaning up his manure and letting him graze in the pasture. Last Saturday night, I went to dinner with Alex at the Cracker Barrel, and we had a good time, but nothing much happened between us. When he drove me home, he gave me a quick peck on the lips. Later tonight we're going to a movie and I hope this'll be the night we kiss for real. I don't mind that we're taking it slow, but I'm kind of aching for some passion.

Leaning over the fence, I watch Star chase a filly, teasing her, and then he gets ornery and squeals when a yearling colt tries to play with him. I laugh, and Star rewards me by nuzzling my face and hands.

Watching the horses run into the orangey-pink sunset, I totally lose track of time—I need to take a shower soon to get ready for my date, and that's when I hear footsteps behind me. I look over my shoulder to find Jack dressed in his comfy clothes—sweatpants and a long-sleeved tee.

"It's late. We should put Star and the others back in their stalls."

"Am I gonna get to ride Star in the Dixiana Derby next week?" I ask.

Jack sniffles, watching Star roll around in the grass grunting. "We'll have to see what conditions are like that day."

What he means is he has to see what his father says. How ridiculous.

"Why are you home?" My eyes trail over his sweats. "It's Saturday night."

He folds his hands together on top of the fence and studies the horses. "There's nobody I want to go out with."

"Not even Colton or Vanessa or Kelsey?"

"Don't feel like it." He looks at me sideways, giving me a sad smile.

That's when Star jogs back over to me. He makes a deep snorting sound and pauses a few feet away. I cluck my tongue. The horse turns his focus from me to Jack then slowly walks forward, squeezing between us. Star nuzzles against Jack's cheek and nips at his hair.

Jack scratches the colt's face. "Aw, thanks, buddy."

Bright stars poke through the lovely pink-orange sunset as Jack and I stand together, petting the horse. I wish he could show the same courage that Star just did. Will Jack ever shove aside the things that scare him?

After we lead Star to his stall, passing farmhands along the way, Jack walks me back to Hillcrest.

"Can we talk later?" he asks quietly. "We could meet out by the lake?"

I shake my head. "I can't." *I won't.* I won't get into another situation where we might hook up, no matter how much I want it.

"Please?" he asks softly. "Just as friends?"

"Jack," I say in a tiny voice. "Don't...I told you, I can't. I have plans."

"I need to talk to you about something...I need you, as a friend, you know?"

How could this end well?

"I got you something." He reaches into his pocket, pulls out a weathered, tiny box, and hands it to me. I don't want gifts. I want to race his horse, I want him to support me in front of his father, I want him to man up.

He nods at the white box. With shaky hands, I carefully open it to discover a silver chain with two charms: a horse and a horseshoe. The chain is kind of rusted, but it's delicate and pretty. No guy has ever given me jewelry before. I look up into his eyes, searching.

"It belonged to my great-grandmother," Jack says quietly. "She had red hair and loved horses. Just like you."

My lips tremble as I stare at the bracelet. "I can't take this."

Jack frees it from the box and loops it around my wrist, fastening it. "But it's perfect for you…and it matches the necklace your mom gave you. Please keep it."

Mom told me to study history so I could learn from it. Well, everything in my history says that Jack is a player, that he only wants me in secret, that he never actually dates girls, but now he goes and gives me something that belonged to his great-grandmother? It's like he's linking our histories together.

I could see a guy giving an expensive, new piece of jewelry to a girl he wants to entice into bed, but not a family heirloom.

"It's beautiful…"

"You know how important family is to me, right?" he asks. I nod, wiping my nose. "Then you understand what this bracelet means to me."

I brush a tear out of my eye, not knowing what to say.

He peeks up at me under his eyelashes. "I miss you."

"I miss you too," I admit, touching the bracelet. "But I need more..."

"I'm working on it."

• • •

On Sunday evening, Rory asks me to dinner at Tennessee Ballers.

As soon as we sit down at our table, he pushes his new scene under my nose. This screenplay is about CIA agents—a guy and girl—who are partners fighting for the same promotion, but they're also secretly in love with each other.

"Will you read my query letter again too?" Rory asks, shuffling through his papers. He's looking for an agent to sell his screenplays to Hollywood. "I want to send it out tonight."

"Yeah, after I finish reading this scene."

"So I take it you like it then?"

"It's full of gratuitous sex," I say. "I hate it but I can't look away."

Rory laughs softly and pushes the rice around on his plate. Strange. He usually inhales his food.

"How was the date with my cousin last night?" Rory asks.

"Great," I say, smiling. We ended up parking after the movie and we made out for a little while. He's a good kisser. "I like him."

"I'm glad," Rory says. "I'm not as close with him as my brother is, but Will said it's a good thing he's getting out. He had a bad breakup a couple months ago."

"Oh really? He didn't mention it..." I worry on my lip. Last night was great. He paid for the tickets and we shared popcorn and laughed at the same parts in the movie. But it's not like we're close yet. I haven't told Alex about any of my hopes and fears or how scared I am for my family now that a little sister is on the way.

"What happens if you never sell a screenplay?" I ask Rory, thinking of my future as a horse jockey.

"I'll keep trying. I hope I will anyway."

He wraps straw paper around his finger, peeking up at me. It's easy to tell when something's nagging him.

"Okay, what's going on?" I ask.

"Um, my father has to declare bankruptcy."

I cover my mouth with my hand. The farm's financial problems are that shitty?

Rory rips the straw paper in two. "And we have to move. I guess Dad is gonna try to sell our animals. He hopes the Goodwins will buy our land." Rory swipes at his eyes and pinches his nose.

"What is your dad gonna do?" I ask with a wobbly voice.

"Mom can get a job as a teacher, we hope, and Dad is gonna try to get on down at the co-op. He knows people there. But it's like, most of the jobs don't pay well."

"It's a good thing Will went to college instead of staying home to take over the farm," I whisper, and Rory nods.

"This is all the more reason for me to go," Rory says. "My dad doesn't have a degree, so he doesn't have many job opportunities, not like my mom does. I mean, Mr. Goodwin would probably hire my dad but it would embarrass him bad..."

I grasp his hand. "I'm here for you. It'll be okay."

He nods with a sad smile.

"Now let me see that query letter."

• • •

Later that night, I'm still thinking about what would happen if someone else in my family got sick and I had no money to help them to get better. Before Mom was diagnosed with breast cancer, we didn't have health insurance.

I've been basing everything on working as an exercise rider or a jockey. I thought this was the ticket to finding a better life. But what if the opportunity to be one dries up? I fell off Star after he got spooked by those raccoons, even though I was being safe as can be. The Goodwins wouldn't let me race at Keeneland. I love riding horses, but even horsemen don't bet all their money on one race.

I find that out firsthand when I eavesdrop on Cindy telling Dad, Paula, and Yvonne what she overheard while serving dinner to the Goodwins.

"Mr. Goodwin told the family that Mr. Winchester didn't accept his initial bid on Paradise Park, and if he wants to stay in the running, he's gonna have to come up with another million dollars."

A million dollars!

"Was it because of Master Jack not liking George Winchester's daughter?" Yvonne asks.

"No," Cindy replies. "Someone else bid more money apparently."

Then why did Mr. Winchester blabber on and on about honor and family? It all came down to money?

I wrap my arms around myself, hating that Jack gave up what we had to help his father. Hearing that the Paradise Park deal is all about cold, hard cash makes me feel cold and hard all over. Mr. Whitfield thought he didn't have to go to college because his farm had existed for over a hundred years. What if, in forty years, I'm dirt poor and living in a shack because I put all my chips in horseracing?

• • •

Monday morning, Jack isn't in first period Life Lessons—he must've decided to skip, but I see him in the hallway after. He's standing with Kelsey Painter, talking quietly to her. She's rubbing his elbow and he seems upset. When he glances up and sees me, he turns and goes the other way. Kelsey gives me a questioning look, as if she's trying to figure me out. That's when she walks up.

"Is he okay?" I ask, staring past her.

She clutches her books against her chest. "You really care about him, huh?"

"I did." I still do, but I'm not gonna admit that to her.

"That sucks," she says. She doesn't sound bitchy or anything; she sounds sad. Is she in Rory's drama class or something? Because she's a good actress.

"He really likes you," Kelsey says.

"Did he tell you that?"

"No…he's my friend…I can just tell. You should give him another chance." She looks down the hallway toward where Jack just disappeared. "If I could go back in time, I'd fight harder to keep someone who was important to me—"

She suddenly turns and walks down the hall, meeting up with Colton and Vanessa before heading into English class. What was that all about? Am I supposed to feel sorry for the most popular girl at school? It's crazy that she feels insecure at her level.

I decide to skip second period and go to the guidance counselor's office. I swallow as I push open the door, walk up to the assistant, and ask to see Miss Brady about college options. I take a seat and doodle pictures of horses and horseshoes in my notebook as I wait.

Twenty minutes later, she invites me into her office. Along with the inspirational posters, she has loads of pictures of cats wearing clothes…?

I shudder, not sure what freaks me out more: CONFIDENCE or a kitten wearing a plaid beret and matching vest.

"Savannah Barrow?" she says, opening a file folder as she sits down behind her desk. I take the seat in front of her and grasp my knees.

"Why are you interested in college?" she asks, chewing on a pen.

For a lot of reasons, I think. To have lots of paths to choose from. To have the ability to back out of something if it's not quite what I want. *Two roads diverged in a yellow wood*...and I want to take the one less traveled by.

But what I tell her is: "It's something I have to do."

She looks at my file, twisting a lock of her hair. "Your grades aren't bad, but I'm not sure if you'll have much of an opportunity for scholarships...maybe we could look into some grants and federal aid. And you need to take the SAT or the ACT."

Miss Brady passes me a pamphlet and I open it.

"These tests cost money," I say slowly.

"Everything costs money."

I clear my throat, thumbing through the pamphlet.

"Depending on your family's income, we could apply for a fee waiver so you could take the ACT for free."

"Okay," I reply quietly, and we go silent for several moments.

"I encourage all kids to go to college, but if you wanted to take a year off or go to community college, you could do that too. Although one time, I read a statistic that said 80 percent of people who don't go to college right after high school never go. They never find the time."

I glance down at the Coca Cola T-shirt I bought at a yard sale. Think about my background. All of it is part of me that has led me to now, to this point. Miss Brady is right. If I don't go now, I'll never go.

I pull a deep breath. "I want to try," I say, making the guidance counselor smile.

"Great! What do you want to study?"

The creeptastic motivational posters intimidate me. "I have no idea."

"And that's totally okay."

She spends ten minutes loading me up with more pamphlets and handouts so I can learn about the different state and community colleges in Tennessee.

"Come back and see me next week," Miss Brady says.

If I want anything in life, I need to take it one step at a time. And if I want to pay for these college application fees or tuition, then I need to do something for me. It might hurt what I can give my baby sister in the near term, but it could help us all in the future.

I walk out into the hallway where I find Jack sipping from the water fountain. He wipes the water from his lips and faces me. Looks down at the papers in my hand. A smile begins to stretch across his face. I return the smile and walk toward the gym.

Before PE, I meet up with Vanessa at her locker, and right then, Rory approaches us.

"Vanessa," he says breathlessly. "I have an important question for you."

But before she can react, music rings out in the hallway and random kids start dancing to Lady Gaga's "Telephone." It's all choreographed. Wait. Are these kids from Rory's drama class? Is this a flash mob?

Vanessa and I burst out giggling as the students keep dancing and then Rory joins in, holding up a sign asking Vanessa if she wants to go to Homecoming.

"Yes!" she says, and they start kissing, and the flash mob keeps grinding away around us. Colton whistles and Kelsey cheers, looking happy. Jack gazes over at me and grins, and I can't help but smile back.

"Woooo!" I yell, cupping my mouth, my voice ringing out through the corridor.

After school, Vanessa gives me a lift home from school, and we totally take over the Hillcrest common room to eat candy, read magazines, and gossip. Ethan—Jodi's son—has a friend over, and they keep peeking around the corner at us. Preteen pervs.

Vanessa bites into a Twizzler and turns the page in her magazine. "I was thinking a dress like this one." She points at a short blue wispy thing.

"I love that! For Homecoming?"

"Yeah." She flips the page and points at a white dress. "You should get something like this."

"I like it..."

"Are you going with Alex? Did you invite him yet?"

I shake my head. "I might…there's a big race that day in New Orleans at Fair Grounds. Gael has been saying that Jack might enter Star…but I'm not even sure if I'll get to ride him."

Vanessa pats my hand. "Don't give up, okay? You know you can ride—it was just muddy before that race and Jack wanted to keep you safe. He told me so himself."

I nod slowly, feeling heat spread across my cheeks. I'm kind of embarrassed how bratty I acted that day. I must've been channeling Star.

"If you decide to go to Homecoming, you and Alex should ride with me and Rory," Vanessa says, and we dive into a discussion about the guys, talking about how far we've gone with them. "I only slept with Rory that one time after his brother's wedding. We want to take things slower, you know?"

"I get that."

"Have you done anything with Alex yet?"

"We've kissed…" The big difference between our situations is that I can tell how much she loves Rory already, and I haven't felt that way about Alex yet. Maybe it just takes time?

Vanessa talks about how she and Rory were fooling around in his truck in the Whitfields' garage, and his father caught them and made Rory go clean the manure collector again. "I think Rory thought it was worth it though." She laughs, and Ethan and his friend gasp from the hallway.

"Get out of here, you little perverts!" I yell, throwing a couch pillow at the boys. Vanessa and I collapse onto the floor in a fit of giggles.

"You silly girls." We peek up to find Cindy smiling down at us, one hand on her stomach. "Savannah, do you want to come out to eat with me and your dad? He got a bonus for some races and wants to treat us."

I glance at Vanessa. "We're hanging out right now."

"Vanessa can come too if she wants."

Vanessa nods, and I shrug okay. We've never had the money to invite a friend of mine out to eat. I'm really proud of my father—for taking a risk and moving us to Cedar Hill and trying to do something good for his family.

The next thing I know, we're at the Roadhouse, one of the best restaurants in Franklin. Old street signs and highway markers cover the wooden walls and rock music blares. People love coming here because you get to eat peanuts and throw shells on the floor. And don't even get me started on how good those breadbaskets smell.

We're seated at a table, and a girl from school is our server. I've never talked to Annie Winters before, but she seems nice and smiles as she takes our drink order. Vanessa leans over and whispers that she and Kelsey used to hang out with Annie freshman year, but after Annie started dating this guy, they grew apart and Kelsey is still upset about it. Still, Vanessa is friendly enough with her. Annie brings us a free appetizer of cheese fries and an extra breadbasket.

"Shortcake, if you don't stop eating that bread, you're gonna gain too much weight to be a jockey," Dad says with a grin, and I smile through a mouthful, glad he still thinks I've got what it takes to race.

Vanessa keeps asking Cindy a bazillion questions about the baby. "Like, do you know what the baby is thinking?"

"I think I know when she's mad—she kicks up a storm. She's doing it right now."

I reach over and touch her stomach. The baby's feet feel like drumbeats. "Porsche is gonna be a drummer."

Cindy gives me a wry smile. "We are not naming the baby after a car."

• • •

When Rory drops me off at Cedar Hill after school the next day, I find a Facebook message from Alex asking me to call him. Sometimes it really sucks not having a cell.

I use the house cordless to call him and he picks up on the second ring. "Hey, you," I say, unable to keep the smile off my face.

"Hey." I can hear his grin through the phone.

"What are you doing?" I lie down on the couch and point my toes toward the ceiling, excited that I'm talking to a cute boy on the phone. The gardener, Mr. Wallace, looks up from his newspaper and shakes his head at me.

"I wanted to talk to you about something...We've been having fun the past few weeks, right?"

"Yeah."

I hear him take a deep breath. I slowly lower my legs to the couch.

"My ex and I…well, we dated since high school up until a couple of months ago, and I wanted to let you know that we still talk—"

"And?" I say, suddenly out of breath.

"I'm not saying she and I are serious again or anything."

"What?" I'm so confused. It's not like Alex and I are exclusive, but we did make out.

"It's not fair to you if I'm starting to talk to my ex again."

"Yeah, it's not…" I say with a wobbly voice. "Do you love her?"

"I'll always love her…but just because you love somebody doesn't mean you should be with them. It's harder than that."

It sure is.

"I want to keep spending time with you," Alex says.

"So you're telling me that we can keep seeing each other, but you might work things out with your ex?"

"Yeah, kinda," he says quietly. "God, that makes me sound like a complete asshole."

"Yeah, kinda." Believe it or not, hearing that he loves someone brings a small smile to my face. I don't want to lose him, because I've enjoyed kissing him and hanging out, but I want to be with a guy who's 100 percent there. I want a guy who's all mine. And considering how often I think of Jack, I never would have been 100 percent there for Alex. And that's just not right.

"It might be good if you focus on her, all right?"

Our conversation doesn't last much longer—it's just Alex apologizing over and over, and I tell him it's okay, even though I don't really feel okay.

We hang up and I set the cordless back in the docking station. Well. That sucks. I stick my thumbs in my eyes to keep the tears at bay. I want someone I can laugh, cuddle, and talk with anytime I want, someone who truly wants me. Loves me.

At least I've got other things to do this afternoon. After blowing my nose, I go to my room, put on my nicest outfit—black pants and a white shirt that belonged to Mom—and charge up to the manor house. I know I'm not allowed inside unless I'm working, but I'm not gonna sit around waiting for Mr. Goodwin to cross my path.

I sneak in the back kitchen door and head through the dining room to the main staircase that leads up to the suite of offices. I spot Paula spraying Windex on a mirror. I sneak down a different hallway and go up another set of stairs.

When I reach Mr. Goodwin's assistant's desk, she sets down her letter opener and the envelope she's holding. "Can I help you?"

"I'd like to make an appointment," I say, holding my chin high.

Jack appears in the doorway of his office. "Are you here to see me?" he asks, looking hopeful.

I summon my strongest voice. "No. I need to discuss something with your father."

"Can I help you with it instead?" Jack asks, sticking his thumbs in his belt loops. "Dad's a busy guy."

I shake my head. "Only your dad."

"Janet, tell my father Savannah needs to see him."

The assistant presses the intercom button and speaks into it. Then Jack goes and opens the double doors to Mr. Goodwin's office, jerking his head, indicating I should walk on in.

I bite the inside of my cheek as I pass by Jack. The door clicks shut behind me and I find myself in a room lit with floor-to-ceiling windows and softened with sheer, wispy curtains. The sofas and chairs are covered with a creamy fabric and fancy rugs cover the hardwood floor. Unlike Jack's office, there are no TVs or computers. Am I in an Elven palace from *The Lord of the Rings* or something?

Mr. Goodwin glances up with a brief smile. "What can I do for you?"

He doesn't invite me to sit, so I stand in front of his desk where he's sorting through yellow message slips and writing in a leather-bound journal.

"Sir, I know I asked you to keep the money I make exercising your horses and racing in case Cindy and my dad need it, but I'd like to change that arrangement."

That gets his attention. He sets his pen down, crosses his hands, and looks up at me. "Oh? How do you wish to change it?"

"I want to keep the money I make from now on for myself."

A tiny smile flits across his face. "What are your plans for the money? If you don't mind me asking."

I look out the window, at the rows of huge barns and the racetrack and all the workers, amazed that one person owns all this. Mr. Goodwin didn't build it, but his family did.

And now I want to start building something for me. For my family. For the future.

"I want to use it for college applications," I say. "And to take the ACT."

Mr. Goodwin nods and smiles. "Good. I'll make sure you start getting regular paychecks."

"Thank you, sir. Hope you have a nice day." I turn to leave but Mr. Goodwin calls my name. I swivel around to face him.

"Savannah, I didn't take any of the money you've made so far."

"What?" I say, leaning forward.

"I saved it all." He pushes an intercom button and asks his assistant to send Mr. Blakely in. "You've worked hard for that money and you need to spend it on you. A man should settle his own debts."

A minute later, a tall man dressed in a suit appears in the office.

"This is Mr. Blakely, one of my stall managers," he says. "Michael, how much money has Savannah made so far? Including the race where she placed third?"

The man opens a black portfolio and shuffles through the papers, dragging his finger down a ledger. "About $1,750."

I sit down on the couch, unable to stand. I cover my face. I've never seen that much money in my whole life.

"Before you send out your college applications," Mr. Goodwin says, "make sure you have my assistant and Jack look over them, understand?"

I taste salty tears at the back of my throat. "I will."

"Blakely," Mr. Goodwin says. "Give us a minute." After the man leaves, Mr. Goodwin raps his pen on his desk. "Savannah, your father came to see me the other day. He wasn't aware you'd asked to help with Cindy's paychecks."

I nod.

"Your father wanted to make sure I hadn't done what you asked…and he asked me for help with college advice."

My head pops up. "He did?"

"I ordered him some books and catalogs on student loans and scholarships to look at. We were going to meet about it next week."

"You were?" I exclaim. Dad didn't tell me anything. Maybe he didn't want me to get my hopes up? "But why?" Mr. Cates's uncaring expression flashes in my mind. "Why do you care if I go to college? Wouldn't it be better for you if I just stay here and exercise horses and wax the floors or whatever?"

Mr. Goodwin smiles and slips his pen behind his ear. "When I was about your age, my father taught me something. He said that my staff is everything.

"I don't do any of the important work like training a yearling.

Keeping a mare calm as she delivers a foal. Making sure the horses are clean. I don't even feed my own kids. Jodi cooks them healthy meals. My staff takes care of me and my family."

I nod slowly.

"I've always tried to take good care of my staff. I'm going to make sure Cindy has some time off before and after the baby comes. I won't let anything happen to your family, understand? You all have been good to us. My staff is too important."

I wipe the corner of my eye, smiling as I nod.

The intercom buzzes. "Mr. Goodwin, your four p.m. appointment is here," the assistant says.

"Thank you, sir," I say. He gives me a friendly nod and goes back to studying his notebook.

I open the heavy wooden doors to let myself out. "Oh, and, sir?" I say loud enough for both Jack and his father to hear me. "I want to race Star in the Dixiana Derby at Paradise Park."

"We'll see."

"Yes, sir," I reply in a low voice, stepping out of his office and shutting the doors behind me. I'm proud of myself for trying at least.

Jack gives me a quizzical look when I march past him. "What's going on?"

"I was just getting something I want," I say with a smile, and race down the stairs, feeling Jack's eyes on my back.

I head for the stables—I want to take Star out for a while. And hopefully Dad is in Greenbriar and can help me saddle him up.

Show Time

The Winchesters' racetrack, Paradise Park, is located between Lexington and Louisville on the greenest patch of land you've ever seen. Any time now, I'm expecting the Lucky Charms leprechaun to pop up and tell me I'm in Ireland or something. It's times like this when I don't believe karma is real; it's unfair that douches like the Winchesters get to own such beautiful land.

As Dad pulls the truck into the parking lot beside the barns, I feel a slight pang of guilt for Mr. Goodwin because he'll never own this beautiful place if he doesn't pony up at least another million bucks. At the same time, I'm pissed because Jack hasn't said a thing about me riding Star in today's race, even though I brought my silks to wear. Is he waiting to make sure we have good weather before getting my hopes up?

Dad works with Minerva, Echoes of Summer, and Lucky Strikes while Rory and I are having a hell of a time with Star. He won't stop rolling on the floor, scattering his hay bed, and snorting. He hops to his feet and jogs around his stall, making grunting noises. He is one unhappy horse.

"Get out of here," I finally tell Rory, and my friend eagerly leaves the stall, latching it behind him. Mr. Goodwin and Jack need to hire more girls, I swear.

I take a deep breath through my nose and step forward, getting in Star's face.

"Stop it, boy," I say in a strong voice. "You're such a big baby. You just want attention, right?" The horse stops snorting and moving around like he's on drugs. His ears twitch and he stomps the ground with his front right hoof.

I stroke his face, inhaling his muskiness. "Ror?" I call out. "Would you bring Echoes of Summer in here?"

A minute later, Echoes of Summer has joined me and Star, and the mare calms him down even more. I stay with the horses, feeding them grain and brushing their hair, singing to Star to keep him calm.

Before the race, Jack and his father appear, along with Gael. Jack is wearing an elegant suit and tie, and his hair is slicked with gel.

"Get him ready to go, Whitfield," Mr. Goodwin says. Did he forget Star hates boys or something? The minute Rory comes in the stall, Star gets agitated again. He slaps his head from side to side.

"Get out," I say to Rory, putting up a hand. "I'll get him ready. He's comfortable with me," I say to Mr. Goodwin. I want to do right by the horse. "I'll walk him to the paddock."

"Wait," Jack says, standing up straight. He's nearly taller than his father. "I want Savannah to ride him."

"I think it's best if you race Townsend," Mr. Goodwin says. "He's got more experience on this track and the purse is half a mil. You need to make the money back for the stud fee and I don't want to see your reputation go to hell. I don't think you can afford to lose."

"I know I can't," Jack says. "That's why Savannah's gonna race Star. I'll go tell the officials myself."

"I'll come with you," Gael says.

Mr. Goodwin grabs Jack by the shoulder and stares him down. "Son—"

"I want your support on this, Dad," Jack interrupts. "I've supported you in everything. I used Townsend as a jockey in the last race. I came on to Abby Winchester when I didn't have any feelings for her. And because of you, I lost something important to me." He finds my eyes.

Mr. Goodwin slaps his notebook against his palm and glances around the park, looking partially pissed but mostly wistful. He blows out air, sighing.

"I'm the owner of Cedar Hill and it's my decision," Jack says, and a chill shoots through me. "Go big or go home."

"You'd better go get dressed," Mr. Goodwin says to me. "Nobody's riding a Cedar Hill horse unless they're wearing the family silks."

"Thank you!" I say, grinning.

I haul ass to the truck to change clothes, to get ready for the biggest race of my life. I reach into the cab for my backpack that contains the silks I'll wear during the race. Glancing around at the other trailers, I make sure I'm alone and shielded by the truck door before pulling my T-shirt off over my head. I'm about to slip my Slytherin Cedar Hill shirt over my bra when a voice behind me says, "Hey."

I cover my breasts and duck behind the door.

Marcus Winchester slowly walks up, and even though he can clearly see I'm changing, he doesn't vamoose. He stares at me like he did that night in the Goodwins' dining room. What. A. Perv.

"Go away," I say, trying to cover my breasts with the shirt. "I'm changing."

He reeks of alcohol and it's not even noon. "You work for the Goodwins, right?" he asks.

"Yeah…?"

"Wouldn't it be a shame if my dad raised the cost of our track even more? You know, because of you? Because you haven't been respectful of me?"

I pause for several heartbeats. "What's wrong with you?"

"What's wrong with *you*? Servants *want* to sleep with me."

Does he have a sick desire to dominate people or something?

"Get lost," I say when he grabs my arm. My teeth are chattering as I scramble toward the next trailer. He latches on like a leech and I'm dragging him behind me.

"I tried to give you something special. You should be grateful," Marcus blurts. I shove him in the gut and rush toward the barns. Seconds later, Marcus overtakes me.

"I'll make sure the Goodwins can never buy our track and it'll be your fault," Marcus says, grabbing me from behind. "I'll make sure you lose your job and can't get hired anywhere else."

Mr. Goodwin still wants to buy this place, but I believed him when he said he'll take care of my family. Of me.

"I don't have to do anything I don't want to do, you crazy asshole," I say, stomping on his foot. Marcus groans and hops up and down.

Right then, Jack comes barreling up. He slams his right fist into Marcus's jaw, smashing him to the ground. Marcus trips Jack, and Jack takes a punch to the chin. Then Jack leaps onto Marcus and smashes his knuckles into his nose three times. Jack pins him to the dirt.

"Jack, I already got him!" I say, like we're hunting and Jack stole my kill.

Marcus wipes blood off his nose. "Fuck you, Goodwin."

"Go ahead, Savannah," Jack says, holding him down. "Do your worst."

I kind of want to kick him where it counts, but I don't care enough to waste any more time on this dickwad. I thrust out a hand and pull Jack up from the ground then hug him. He rubs his hands up and down my back.

Yeah, I stomped on Marcus's foot and gave him a piece of my mind, but I can't stop shuddering and gasping for breath.

"Shhh," Jack whispers, gently rubbing the back of my neck. He takes the green shirt from my hand and helps me slip it over my head. I touch the bruise forming on his chin.

Marcus fumbles his way to his feet. "I'm going to tell my father."

Just because he's rich and powerful doesn't mean he can do whatever he wants and get away with it.

"I'm calling the police to report you," I say.

"Who'd believe your story over mine?" Marcus snorts.

"Me," Jack says calmly.

"I hope you enjoy telling your family you lost Paradise Park for them."

"Who gives a shit?" Jack says. "You tried to assault my jockey."

"So what?" Marcus replies.

"So Savannah's gonna call the cops, and I'll make sure your mom and sister don't get invited to the Governor's Christmas Ball this year. You don't want to disappoint your mother, do you?"

Marcus's eyes balloon and he actually looks freaked out. I stare up at Jack through misty eyes and wrap my arms around his waist.

"Hell, if you ever come near my girlfriend again, I'll kill you," Jack adds, making my shoulders tense up. Wait. Did he say girlfriend?

"Now get the hell out of here," Jack says, and as Marcus

scrambles away, Jack turns to me and lifts my wrist to touch the bracelet he gave me.

"Girlfriend?" I whisper. "That's pretty presumptuous of you."

"Are you still dating Alex? Whitfield's cousin?" I slowly shake my head and he gently kisses my wrist. "Did Marcus hurt you?"

I know my place, but I stood up for myself anyway and didn't think about anything except for what's right. And even though we come from completely different stock, Jack did the right thing too.

"I'm fine...actually, I'm great."

• • •

Jack holds my hand the entire way back to the barn, and when we see our dads, I expect him to drop it. But he keeps holding on tight.

"Is this for real?" I mumble. "What you said about me being your girlfriend?"

"I'm serious," he whispers, holding our hands up where anyone can see them. "I've never cared about anyone else like this."

"And we're exclusive?"

"Yup," he says.

"But what about Paradise Park? Mr. Winchester'll never sell it to your father now."

He rubs his thumb across the back of my hand. "I'll tell Dad there are other racetracks. And besides, Paradise Park has crappy plumbing."

"Crappy plumbing."

"That's right."

I grin and he grins back. As we walk up, Mr. Goodwin looks from his son to our hands and shakes his head.

"Savannah and I are going out now," Jack announces to our fathers and Rory.

Rory drops the brush he is holding and his mouth falls open. He digs in his pocket, yanks out his cell, and starts texting. Such a gossip that boy is.

Dad rubs his eyes.

"What happened to your face?" Mr. Goodwin asks Jack.

"Marcus Winchester looks a lot worse, I promise."

Mr. Goodwin looks freaked out for a second, but then he grins. "That's my boy."

"I'll tell you what happened in private," Jack says to his father, pulling me up next to him. "It's time to get Star and Savannah ready for the race."

Mr. Goodwin says, "Your mother will be angry with me for allowing you to date one of our staff. It won't look right, and there could be issues if you don't work out."

"You sneak hot dogs behind Mom's back all the time! I'm responsible for the farm, and I can make my own decisions."

"A man stands by his decisions," Mr. Goodwin says.

"Yes, sir, he does," Jack replies.

"We'll talk more about this later, understand?"

"Yes, sir," Jack replies in a strong voice.

"I don't agree with this any more than Jack's father does," Dad says to me slowly. "But I want you to be happy, whatever that means for you. I know how much you care about your family and want to do the right thing by us. And I want to do the right thing by you." Dad wraps me in his arms, hugging me hard.

Jack faces our fathers. "After the race, can Savannah stay the night at our house in Kentucky with us?"

"I'd love to," I say, and I catch Mr. Goodwin and Dad exchanging a freaked-out look.

"I want to cook you dinner," Jack says to me, ignoring our gaping fathers. Dad wipes sweat off his forehead. "She thinks I can't grill, but I can." He squeezes my hand. "Wait...I'll be back in a few. I've gotta do something. Whitfield—come help me."

He sprints out of the barn with Rory at his ankles. Jesus Lord, where's he going now?

"Jack!" Mr. Goodwin calls, following his son.

The other men clear out of the barn, leaving me to collect Star's tack and get him in the zone for the race. I pat his nose and look him in the eye. We have a staring contest that goes on for at least a minute, but then a mare passing by our stall distracts him.

"I win!" I hug his neck. "I love you."

He nips at my hair, saying he loves me too.

• • •

Jack meets up with me at the paddock after Shelby helped me get Star saddled up and ready to go.

"How you doing?" Jack whispers in my ear.

"Good," I say. I don't want to jinx myself by saying that I've never been on such a high, that I have a feeling Star and I are in good shape for today. "Thank you for this."

"Thank *you*," Jack replies, smiling at me before turning his focus back to his horse. He walks around Star one last time, inspecting him, before wishing me luck and pecking my cheek.

Dad mounts a pony and leads us out onto the track. He leans over and pats Star's head as we begin to warm up. Star barely pays attention to the pony. He must know this race is important.

When we get to the starting gate, I take a deep breath and Dad pats my back. "I'm proud of you, and your mom would be too."

I smile as Star enters the gate and the gates close behind me. I'm in the fourth position, the best place to be. For the first time ever, the horse doesn't go crazy when we're inside the gate.

"You got this, Star," I say, breathing calmly.

The bell rings loud and clear. The gates bang open.

"And they're off!" the announcer says, and everything goes silent except for the sound of hooves slamming the ground.

Star breaks well. I settle behind Dancing Delight and That's My Boy. Everybody eases up around the first turn. I grab a good position on the rail. Dancing Delight leads the way to the backstretch. I'm two off the lead when the pack moves together on the far turn.

I own the rail and we pick up speed as we make our way past That's My Boy.

I yell, "Move your ass, Star!"

That's My Boy challenges us, making me settle back into third. At the home stretch, I'm two lengths off the lead. On the final furlong, I use the whip and yell Star's name. I make up the distance. Overtake Dancing Delight on the final furlong. But he grabs it back.

My heart pounds and I'm biting down hard on my lip as we cross the finish line.

We lose by a length!

Second place. Damn.

As Star begins to relax, I pull my goggles off and set them on top of my helmet with a sigh. Is he ever gonna win one? I lean down and hug Star long and hard. We circle back around, and the only person I want to see must be swallowed up in that sea of reporters, because I can't find him anywhere.

I ride up to the paddock. Reporters are all over me. Cameras are flashing. People are hollering. Second place with a half a mil purse is nothing to cry home about. Star just won $125K for Cedar Hill.

"Jack!" I peer through the crowd to find him wedging his way between people. He breaks free and darts up to slap Star's side and rub his ears.

"Good boy," Jack says, rubbing the horse's muzzle and smiling up at me.

"I'm sorry," I say with a sob.

"You'll win next time. I know it." He holds my gaze, grinning, and I squeeze his hand. "Come down here," Jack says, and I let him pull me off the horse. Gael grabs the reins. And when a photographer gets in my face to snap a picture, Jack pulls me into a long kiss, wrapping his arms around me, cocooning me like he'll never let go. And I kinda hope he doesn't.

"I swear," I hear Mr. Goodwin say. "Do you have to kiss her in front of everybody?"

"Yes," Jack replies, then dives right back in, kissing me again.

"I thought Jack had a girlfriend—that Winchester girl," Mrs. Goodwin says, sounding confused and pissed. "John, why is our son kissing Danny's daughter? John, what's going on?"

"How romantic," Shelby sighs.

"I'm going to kill him," Dad says.

"This would be a great climactic scene," Rory adds, and out of the corner of my eye, I catch him jotting down notes.

Star sniffs my hair and nuzzles his neck between our heads. Jack and I break apart.

"Is my horse trying to cock block me?" he whispers in my ear.

"Appears so."

"If he hadn't done so well, I'd send him to New York to drag a tourist carriage. For real this time."

Jack and I smile, continuing to kiss, and even though we're not in the winner's circle, I feel like I won.

Laughter and hooting and hollering distract me, and when I pull away from his lips, he turns me to face the scoreboard. It reads:

Sav-Will you go to homecoming with me?-Jack

I laugh. "That's so much better than a skywriter!"

• • •

After the press has melted away and while Jack is attempting to smooth things over with his mother, who is super agitated that her son was making out in front of a crowd, Mr. Goodwin walks up to me and Dad with a gentleman I don't recognize.

"Danny and Savannah, meet Thomas Alexander. He runs the Kentucky Thoroughbred Village in Lexington."

Mr. Alexander shakes Dad's hand first and then mine. "You're quite talented, Savannah."

"Thank you."

He hands me his card. "We have a jockey-training program at the Village you might be interested in. We offer college credit that's accepted at the University of Kentucky. You'd have to spend several hours a week exercising the horses, and you'd work as a sort of apprentice instructor, teaching younger kids how to be a jockey. If you're interested, I can have my assistant get in touch with you to discuss the details."

Mr. Goodwin smiles down at me. I peek up at Dad, who's picking at the inside of his eye with his thumb, trying to act manly by pretending he's not tearing up.

"I'm very interested, thank you." I bounce on my toes.

I give Mr. Alexander my phone number and email address, and after he's gone, Mr. Goodwin pats my shoulder.

"Thank you for doing that for me," I tell Mr. Goodwin, cradling the man's card in my hands.

"Don't thank me. Jack asked me to make the introduction. It was all his idea."

• • •

I lounge in a cushy chair on the patio, watching Jack work the grill. Wearing an apron, he whistles as he flips the burgers. The smell of cooking meat wafts over along with the sound of the radio. He likes listening to college football games. I never knew that about him until tonight. What else don't I know?

"What are you smiling at?" he asks.

"Wondering if you have any secrets."

The edge of his mouth lifts into a smirk. "I won't keep any secrets from you…except…"

"Except what?"

His grin is full of mischief as he abandons the grill to come give me a kiss. "I can't tell you what I want to do to you later in private. It's a secret."

Stomach butterflies flutter up into my chest and heart,

leaving me breathless. Smiling, he returns to his position at the grill, and I pull my knees to my chest, incredibly content. It's a chilly autumn night, and I'm cozy in one of Jack's extra large sweatshirts. He gave me a guest bedroom with a queen-size bed, with a fluffy white duvet and pillows made of lace. When I sleep there tonight, I'll feel like a princess…who's also a horse jockey. Bad. Ass.

"I told you I could grill," he murmurs, smiling as he serves me a cheeseburger.

After dinner, and after a crazy make-out session in the hot tub where he let me in on the secret things he wanted to do to me, we curl up in the hammock together. His parents won't be home from some fancy dinner for a while, and his sister and the housekeeper are inside, so it's almost like we're in our own little world. Except for Jack's hounds resting on the ground below us. Thor is a big snorer.

"This is my favorite place," Jack says, wrapping his hands behind his head, staring at the stars.

"It could easily become mine too." I love the soft sounds of the crisp night. Crickets. A stream babbling in the distance. My boyfriend's steady breathing.

"Thank you for supporting me today," I say, curling up against his chest.

He kisses the top of my head. "Thank you for believing in me."

Future Plans

The little bell on the door jingles as we walk into Tennessee Ballers.

Jack and Rory head straight for the counter but Vanessa grabs my elbow. She loops her arm through mine.

"Tell me everything," she whispers.

Jack took me on a day date to Fall Creek Falls today, where we went horseback riding around the waterfalls and did some hiking that involved lunch in a deserted meadow. And lunch led to dessert which led to more. Red and gold leaves fell around us as we stretched out on the picnic blanket, taking our time.

"We did it," I whisper back, and Vanessa squeals.

"Details!"

"It was great…well, until Jasper—Jack's dog—stole my shirt," I say, laughing. "But I do have some questions…"

She pats my arm. "Let's talk more later."

I don't regret giving myself to him, not one bit, but there's stuff I need to know, and I'd rather sing a solo in the school musical than ask Rory stuff about sex. Like, what in the world are you supposed to do with your hands? And am I supposed to help him put the condom on?

"What do you want to eat?" Jack asks me.

"Cheese quesadillas and tortilla chips."

He grins. "Stake out a seat for us."

I weave around the tables, saying hi to kids from school, then grab the corner booth. While Jack collects our food and brings it to the table, Rory pushes Vanessa up against the counter and kisses her so passionately I have to look away.

"Whitfield! I'm sure that's a health-code violation. Stop!"

My head pops up to find a humongous guy pointing at Rory, who keeps on kissing Vanessa like he can't hear a thing.

"Who's that?" I ask Jack.

"Joe Carter. He used to play football for Hundred Oaks and now he owns Tennessee Ballers."

"I'll kick you out of here, I swear, Whitfield, and you'll never eat my tacos again," Joe Carter says. "No tacos for you!"

Rory grins as he kisses Vanessa.

"That's it," Joe says, clearly exasperated. "If you don't stop right now, I'm calling Vanessa's brother—"

"No!" Rory roars, ripping away from Vanessa. He picks up their tray and yells over his shoulder, "You're evil, Carter."

Vanessa and Rory slide into the booth with us. "If he calls your brother, I'm dead," Rory says.

"If my brother kills you, can I have your *Star Wars* sheets?" Vanessa asks, smiling at him sideways as she bites into a chip.

"And I want your truck," I say.

"I'm glad my friends care about my welfare," Rory says.

"Can I have your dog, Ava?" Jack asks, wiping his mouth.

"I hate you all," Rory replies.

Across the room, now Joe Carter is raising his voice to Sam Henry, the hot usher from the wedding, and his blond girlfriend. "Get out if you don't like it!"

"What is this?" Sam Henry says, looking disgusted. "I've had better tacos at Taco Bell!"

"Oh, you did not," Joe Carter replies.

"Did."

"Out!" Joe roars, pointing at the door, but Sam Henry just waves a hand at him and goes right back to shoveling chips into his mouth.

"Jordan, you really gotta try these," Sam says to the blond girl, talking through a mouthful of chips.

Joe steals the chip basket away from Sam and speeds into the kitchen as if he's carrying a football. Sam leaps to his feet and chases after Joe, and then I hear raucous yelling and the sound of silverware and pans crashing to the floor.

"Morons." Jordan shakes her head and starts playing with the salt and pepper shakers. She stacks the pepper on the top of the salt and yanks the salt out from under the pepper.

I smile.

"What are you thinking about?" Jack murmurs in my ear.

"I hope that we're all still friends when we grow up."

He softly kisses the skin under my earlobe. "My mom told me that Jordan Woods got a job at the school. She's gonna help coach football."

"Really?" I ask. "A girl coaching football?"

"It's true," Vanessa says. "She told my brother that she's starting in the spring."

That's when Colton comes jogging up to our table. He squeezes in beside Rory and Vanessa. Kelsey pours in behind him and pulls a chair up to the table. She starts texting on her phone but Colton steals it from her, pocketing it. She gives him a look before digging into the tortilla chips.

"You're late," Vanessa says, throwing a chip at Colton.

He picks it off his shirt and eats it, shrugging. "I was watching this new show called *I'll Eat Anything*. It's disgusting! But I couldn't look away. People win money based on how much weird shit they eat. Like, today, this one lady had to eat a coconut shell full of frog fallopian tubes!"

Vanessa chokes on her food and gives Colton the look of death, but he doesn't notice because he's eyeing Kelsey.

"Annnnywayyyy," Rory says, talking with his mouth full. "I've been thinking. Do y'all want to go to that Halloween Haunted

Forest thing up in Cookeville next weekend after the homecoming dance?"

"I'm in," Jack says, squeezing my hand under the table. "As long as we take some fireworks with us."

"And set them off in the Haunted Forest?" Rory asks.

Vanessa says, "That should definitely get us kicked out."

"My thoughts exactly," Jack says with a laugh. He faces Rory. "You'll bring the fireworks?"

Rory grins. "Sure thing."

Epilogue

June, eight months later

"What's wrong with you?"

At dusk, I'm standing in Greenbriar pasture, lecturing the young filly that's causing me all sorts of trouble. Cherry Lollipop, who Jack named after me, is a descendent of Secretariat. Lollipop should be faster than a bullet, but she's too easily distracted. She loves chasing birds and butterflies and other fillies. One second she'll be cantering along and the next she's streaking off the track and into the gardens to chase a bunny rabbit. She's also been known to terrorize a colt or two.

"You have to do better, young lady, understand?" I smooth the chestnut hair on the filly's face. Jack plans to enter her in races starting next year, and I think she'll be a winner. If I can get her trained up good, that is.

"What are you doing out here?"

I whip around to find Jack leaning against the white fence, wearing a tuxedo. His hair is slicked back with gel and he's grinning. His smile speeds away with my heart.

"Just checking on Lollipop," I say.

He opens the gate and walks over to us, scanning my dress appreciatively. I found this beautiful black gown at a thrift store in Nashville. It hugs me just right.

"My mother asked where you are," Jack says, wrapping his hands around my waist. Our parents have sort of gotten used to the idea of us dating—they know our relationship isn't a passing thing.

"Mom wants to introduce you to the governor's daughters," Jack goes on. "They want to meet the *famous* girl horse jockey, Savannah Barrow."

"Oh hush." I gaze at the white tent set up on the Goodwins' lawn. Classical music rings across the countryside. Today is the 215th anniversary of Tennessee becoming a state, so the Goodwins are having a party. "Do we have to? I mean, we're finally alone."

My little sister Nina wails every time I leave her. She's addicted to me like I'm addicted to candy. And even worse, even though she's three months old, she likes grabbing at Jack's cell phone. She cries every time he pockets it. I love her, but I love alone time with my boyfriend too.

His mouth lifts into a smirk. "You know the deal. I let you ride my horses, and in return you accompany me to all my boring social events."

"No one will notice we're gone for a few minutes," I say, getting up on tiptoes and kissing his nose.

"May I have this dance?" Jack pulls me against his chest, right in the middle of the pasture.

Ever since I told Jack I wanted to learn to dance fancy, he loves sweeping me into his arms all over the place: between classes, at the mall, in the middle of graduation. One time at the grocery store, he twirled me into a waltz in the produce section. We glided past the lemons, people rolled their eyes at us, and he murmured in my ear, "It doesn't matter where you dance. It's only who you're with."

Laughing, we spin around in circles beneath the stars, barely avoiding a patch of manure.

Jack sweeps me into an elegant dip. "You like me."

"You're okay," I tease.

"Just *okay*?"

I whisper how much I love him.

He weaves his hands in my curls, capturing my lips with his. "I love you too."

Acknowledgments

Growing up, my family didn't have much money. I felt bad about myself for not having brand name clothes and sneakers, and I thought that wealth equaled self-worth. By the time I entered high school, things hadn't changed much for me. My clothes still weren't cool. I still had low self-esteem. But I wanted more for myself—I wanted other people to respect me. I didn't understand that people would respect me if I respected myself.

With this book, *Racing Savannah*, I wanted to show readers that no matter who you are, where you come from, what you look like, how much money you have—you have the right to go after whatever you want. You have the right to make your dreams come true. Of course, you have to work hard too. Please don't ever put yourself down. Figure out what you like about yourself and keep learning and going after what you want like Savannah does. You rock!

I had a lot of fun writing this book, but it sure was hard to write. I knew nothing about horses or horse racing going in, so it became a team effort.

I am most grateful to the wonderful people at Charles Town Races in Charles Town, West Virginia, Kentucky Downs in Franklin, Kentucky, and The Thoroughbred Center in Lexington, Kentucky, for answering my many questions, taking me on tours, and letting me snap picture after picture. Mike Cameron, a horse owner I met at The Thoroughbred Center, gave me so many great details and even let me hang out with his beautiful mare, Tellalittlesecret. C.J. Johnsen, the son of the owner of Kentucky Downs, gave me a tour of the racetrack in a golf cart, which was fun.

Thank you to book bloggers Maggie Desmond-O'Brien and Lisa Lueddecke. Maggie grew up on a farm in Minnesota and Lisa rescues abused racehorses. You both were such a help to me in learning horse lingo.

Many thanks to my Washington, D.C., writer friends, who spent hours discussing the plot and characters over cheese and wine: Jessica Spotswood, Robin Talley, Andrea Coulter, and Caroline Richmond.

As always, I couldn't do this without insightful readers: Allison Bridgewater, Julie Romeis, Sarah Cloots, Tamson Weston, Tiffany Schmidt, Tiffany Smith, Kari Olson, Natalie Bahm, Jen Fisher, Shanyn Day, and Jessica Wallace. Thank you to Trish Doller for keeping me sane. Christy Maier—thank you for taking the time to read this book and give such helpful feedback.

I'm also grateful to Marguerite Coffey and Michele Truitt

for their friendship and many thoughts on the culture of horse racing! To Susan Curley, thank you for being such a good friend and supporter of my work. Thanks to Leslie Moeller for sending me articles about horse racing.

Thank you to everyone at Nelson Literary Agency: Sara Megibow, Kristin Nelson, Anita Mumm, and Angie Hodapp. Sara—you are the best literary agent ever! I love how when I ask if there's anything I could be doing to promote my books, you always say, "Just get back to writing and let us do the work!" I love your editorial eye and I'm grateful that you keep pushing me to get better and better.

I am so thankful for the team at Sourcebooks and all the wonderful support they give me. Leah Hultenschmidt, you are such a great editor and advocate for my books. Derry Wilkens, thanks for all the great publicity work you do. To Jillian Bergsma, my production editor, I appreciate your keen attention to detail and the guidance you have given me. Thank you to Todd Stocke and Sean Murray for your tireless efforts to promote my books and for the fabulous distribution.

Thanks to my family for supporting me, especially my parents, brother, and sister. Also, Bob and Jackie Kenneally, Pam and Bob Beggan, and my husband, Don. Dad, I think you should write *Tattoos of the Clinically Depressed*. For real.

Finally, thank you to my readers. I love your reviews, your comments online, and your emails. You make it all worth it.

About the Author

Miranda Kenneally grew up in Manchester, Tennessee, a quaint little town where nothing cool ever happened until after she left. Now Manchester is the home of Bonnaroo. Growing up, Miranda wanted to become an author, a major league baseball player, a country music singer, or an interpreter for the United Nations. Instead, she became an author who also works for the U.S. Department of State in Washington, D.C., planning major events and doing special projects, and once acted as George W. Bush's armrest during a meeting. She enjoys reading and writing young adult literature and loves *Star Trek*, music, sports, Mexican food, Twitter, coffee, and her husband. Visit www.mirandakenneally.com.

If you liked *Racing Savannah*, check out these other great titles from Sourcebooks Fire.

How I Lost You

Janet Gurtler

Grace and Kya do everything together, and nothing can get in the way of their friendship. Only Grace knows what Kya's been through, or how much she needs someone to stick by her. Kya keeps life exciting—pulling Grace into things she'd never dare to do on her own. But inch by inch, daring is starting to turn dangerous. And Grace will have to decide how far she can go to save their friendship…before she ends up losing everything else

If He Had Been with Me

Laura Nowlin

"If he had been with me, everything would be different."

Finn and Autumn used to be inseparable, but middle school puts them on separate paths going into high school. Yet no matter how distant they become, or who they're dating, Autumn continues to be haunted by the past and what might have been. While their paths continue to cross, and opportunities continue to be missed, little do they know that the future might separate them forever.

Blaze

Laurie Boyle Crompton

Blaze is tired of spending life on the sidelines. All she wants is for Mark the Soccer Stud to notice her. When her BFF texts Mark a photo of Blaze in sexy lingerie, it definitely gets his attention. After a few hot dates Blaze is contemplating her imminent girlfriend status when Mark dumps her.

Blaze gets her revenge by posting a comic strip featuring uber-villain Mark the Shark. Mark then retaliates by posting her "sext" photo, and suddenly Blaze is in an epic online battle to the (social) death.

The Summer of Skinny Dipping

Amanda Howells

After getting dumped by her boyfriend, sixteen-year-old Mia Gordon is looking forward to spending the summer in the Hamptons with her glamorous cousins. But when she arrives, her cousins are distant, moody, and caught up with a fast crowd.

That's when she meets Simon Ross. Simon isn't like the snobby party boys her cousins seem obsessed with; he's funny, artistic, and utterly adventurous. And from the very first time he encourages Mia to go skinny-dipping, she's caught up in a current that's impossible to resist.